STAR VIRUS

MICHAEL COLE

SEVERED PRESS
HOBART TASMANIA

STAR VIRUS

CHAPTER 1

Glorric was a dark planet. Its skies were dominated by enormous dark blue clouds that blanketed the sphere from the black vastness of space. High winds in the stratosphere always had a rolling effect on the clouds, causing the sky to resemble an ocean in the middle of a storm.

Down below, Private Buck Gaden stared at the phenomenon from the prop of his mounted heavy-blaster turret. The humidity weighed down on him, as well as his sand dollar tan uniform.

There wasn't much else to do out at Post 13. Nor any of the guard stations for that matter. Glorric was on the outer rim of Tarkadon territory. The United Galactic Systems Navy would have to punch through a vast armada of Tarkadon Defense ships to get out this far. There was a specific reason the High Command wanted the Top Secret experiments conducted out here. Gaden understood this, but it didn't change the fact that this post was excruciatingly uneventful.

He heard the front door open.

"You trying to guess shapes in the sky?" Private Vergo asked. Gaden looked back at him. They were about the same height, though Vergo was already getting increasingly stocky in shape. It was a consequence of constantly being placed on a static post. Sooner or later, Major Liskai would return and be very displeased with his security staff and their failure to comply with physical fitness standards.

Gaden cleared his throat.

"It's either the clouds or the damn swamp." He lowered his gaze to the surrounding jungle. Glorric was an odd planet. The ground was practically rock. However, it contained a large variety of green and red colored plants, some of which stood up to twelve feet in height. Their leaves were wide to collect the neon colored sunrays that successfully broke through the atmosphere. The terrain wasn't excessively thick; one could easily walk between the plants without getting residue on their uniforms. "Is it time for our hourly check-in?" The words dragged out like a complaining child. The check-ins were the worst part of the job. It was the damn atmospheric interference. They usually got nothing but static. That wasn't the annoying part. The annoying part was that they would often be accused of failing to perform their annual check-ins. Of course, the Staff Sergeants were aware of the equipment problem. It was just an excuse for them to demonstrate authority.

"I...I don't know," Vergo said. Gaden looked back at him. He saw the flustered look on his comrade's face.

"What do you mean?"

"The radio's been going off and on for several minutes," Vergo said. "Seems like something's going on, but I'm not sure what it is."

Gaden stepped back into the small guard shack and sat at the desk. In front of him was standard radio equipment. He didn't even have time to reach for the frequency knob before more static came in through the receivers. He took notice of the amount of air-time for each transmission. Though he couldn't make out what was being said, there was definitely some back-and-forth going on between the other posts.

"What the hell's going on?" Vergo asked.

"How the hell should I know?" Gaden said.

"I was being rhetorical," Vergo said, annoyingly. "I wonder if something's going on at one of the lab facilities."

"I have no idea," Gaden said. If the Tarkadon military had done anything successful, it was maintaining absolute secrecy regarding the objective of Glorric's main facilities. All he knew was that there was some kind of testing, and they were bringing in human subjects to test the research, whatever it may be. Whatever it was, it was obvious that it was intended to be used in the galactic war against the U.G.S. Naval forces.

More static came through the receiver. Both men could feel a tinge of anxiety creeping up their spines.

"Don't tell me the bastard U.G.S. is attacking," Vergo said.

"No. I was just looking at the sky, remember? If it was the U.G.S., we'd know it already. Besides, there'd be signs of conflict out to the west. We'd see ships, blaster fire, explosions---"

A shockwave rippled beneath their feet, followed by the faint bellow of a distant blast. Both Troopers glanced at each other with wide-eyed alertness. All at once, they grabbed their blaster rifles and hurried out the back door. They ran twenty yards to the perimeter line, which overlooked the west valley. The orange-green glow of hyper-fuel flames was immediately evident.

"Maybe we *are* under attack!" Gaden said.

"But where are the ships? How did they get past the security satellites?" A thought came to Vergo's mind. "Oh...what if the prisoners escaped? Perhaps they've overpowered the guards and have taken over the research facility."

"Any trooper foolish enough to let measly peasants overpower them deserves what they get if that's the case," Gaden said. "Let's get back to the radio." They hurried back to the shack. Already, there was an onslaught of static. Gaden adjusted the frequency.

It was odd. Radio signals were bad on this planet, but not *this* bad. Usually, he was successful in receiving a signal by now. Unless...

"Which way's the radio tower?" he asked Vergo.

"South of us," Vergo answered. He glanced outside and scanned the horizon. "There's smoke. Buck, I think there was another crash."

After several more attempts at fixing the signal, a few discernable words broke through the electrical growling.

"Advance...Checkpoint C...Priority One...detect all..."

"Shit," Gaden said. He got on the transmitter. "This is Post 13 calling Command. Please give update on situation?" All that came through was static again. "Son of a bitch!"

"Let's get down there," Vergo said. Gaden thought for a moment. The general rule was to remain at your station at all times until instructed otherwise. However, it was evident that Command was trying to reach them. And there was no doubt a conflict of some kind was taking place.

Not doing any good sitting on my ass here.

"You drive," Gaden said. With blaster rifles loaded, they hurried outside and boarded the Roller. The vehicle was a primitive design, with four large wheels to carry it over the rocky terrain. But it was a design most suitable for this planet aside from aerial vehicles. On the rear was a D29 Turret, capable of firing over two-hundred blaster bolts a minute. Vergo stood at the mount and strapped himself to the rail. He rotated the turret in two complete spins while Gaden started the engine.

He pressed his boot to the accelerator.

Giant metal wheels crunched rock and flora as the roller raced down the small hill. He followed a paved pathway that led west until it hooked over to the south. Gaden wasn't concerned for adhering to basic rules of driving; they needed to arrive at the scene of that explosion and quick.

He kept straight at the bend, driving off the road and into an array of vegetation and rock. The roller rocked slightly side to side, but had no problem plowing through the rock swamp. Up ahead, Gaden could see the valley. The flame continued to burn, surrounded by a world of green and black terrain.

"Blaster fire," Vergo said. "I see blaster fire. Near the blast site." Gaden could see it. From this distance, the blaster bolts looked like tiny red sparks zipping through the landscape. There were hundreds of them, their resulting explosions invisible to his eyes due to distance and terrain. But there was one thing he did notice. Every gunshot went in the same direction. There was no return fire coming back at the shooters. It appeared only one side was engaging.

The route to the flames took over four minutes. By the time they reached it, many of the flames had died out, leaving a hunter-green glow on the ground where the burnt fuel had solidified. Trees and bushes continued to burn around it, lighting the area in a dull orange.

Gaden plowed through a wall of flame, then slowed after entering the clearing. He and Vergo gazed at the wreckage of a Tarkadon dropship. The fuselage had exploded into unrecognizable chunks of metal that had scattered about. The only fragment that was partially identifiable was the cockpit, barely. It had been split down the middle, exposing the pilot's seats and control instruments.

"What the hell happened?" Vergo said. Gaden carefully steered around the wreckage. A thousand feet beyond it was a guard post, similar to theirs.

"They had to have been making a pickup," Gaden said.

"And they just crashed? Where are the shooters? Where are the bodies?" Vergo said. Gaden stopped and looked around. Vergo had a point. Dropships usually had a minimum of three crew. The cockpit was empty by the looks of it, though he couldn't really tell as it was still smoldering. He continued on to the guard shack. The flora around it had been scorched with blaster fire. However, as Vergo had stated, there were no bodies.

He parked alongside the guard shack and disembarked. Vergo covered him with the turret as he entered the building. Less than five minutes later, Gaden stepped out.

"Nobody! There's nobody here," he said.

"What the hell's going on?" Vergo said.

"I have no idea. Can you see any more blaster fire?"

Vergo rotated the turret. "Southwest. There's much less of it now. Maybe the situation's…under control?"

"I don't know," Gaden said. He started walking back to the roller when he heard something behind him. It was a sickly sound; a moan, coming from somewhere behind the guard shack. "Hang on…" He shouldered his blaster rifle and slowly worked around the steel structure. He passed through a cloud mixture of fog and smoke on the other side. The machine gun barrels were still hot, indicating the weapon had been fired recently. On the ground was charred residue that appeared to have been from uniform clothing. There were other substances that had been burnt to ash. Gaden stood back up. It was burnt flesh and blood. He recognized it from his experiences from rifle practice in advanced training, in which they used live targets. Blaster bolts cut through clothing like butter and exploded the flesh it connected with. Someone had been shot here. Either they were carried off or it was a flesh wound.

He heard the moan again.

Gaden quickened his pace and cleared the side of the building. He peeked around the corner and scanned the area, looking down the iron-sights. Up ahead, he saw the greyish-tan uniform of a Tarkadon trooper. He was on his knees, reaching to the ground. That's when Gaden realized that there were TWO troopers. The second appeared to be on his back. He could barely see either of them in the blasted fog, but the situation was clear; the trooper was wounded and the other one was rendering first aid to his injuries.

Gaden looked over his shoulder and shouted, "Vergo! We got survivors over here!" He started for the troopers. "Hey Trooper! Private Buck Gaden from Post 13! We have a roller handy. Let's load up the wounded and haul ass to the infirmary in Site A."

There was no response from the trooper. There was another moaning sound, though this one sounded more like a growl. In addition, there was the grinding of teeth, followed by a wet sticky sound of tearing fabric.

Gaden approached.

"Medic? Trooper? You hear me? What's going on—"

A gust of wind had stirred the fog, giving him a clear view of the carnage in front of him. The fallen trooper stared skyward with dull lifeless eyes. His lower jaw and throat had been ripped away entirely, exposing soft red meat surrounding the bone. A pool of blood had formed at the medic's knees, soaking his trousers and boots.

It was then that Gaden realized that the medic was not applying bandages or pressure…he had lowered his whole face into the exposed belly of the dead trooper, burying his mouth inside a huge gorge. He pulled back, his teeth clamped down on intestines. In a single swift motion, he spun toward Gaden. His face and uniform were covered in blood. For a brief instance, he looked at his 'rescue' with discolored eyes.

Gaden stepped back in shock, staring at the grotesque sight. He pointed his weapon, but the delay had cost him. The blood-covered trooper lashed out with hooked fingers. One hand struck his rifle barrel with superhuman strength, knocking it free of his grasp. Gaden yelled in horror as the trooper lunged. Those hands were like lion claws. They pressed through his uniform and into his skin like daggers, pulling him closer to that widening jaw. The ghoul's mouth hyperextended, splitting the cheeks.

Gaden struggled and screamed, but could not outmuscle the demon-like creature that had once been his brother-in-arms. His scream lowered into a wet gurgle as the teeth closed down on his larynx. Blood spurted from his throat into the attacker's mouth. Eyes wide, Gaden convulsed until the strength left his body. He fell to the ground, the ghoul coming down on top of him, snarling like a rabid dog as its teeth ripped through his flesh.

It heard another sound approaching; the sound of running feet getting increasingly nearer. Then it heard a voice.

"Hey Gaden, where are you? I got the med kit and…" Vergo turned the corner and saw the ghoul on top of his partner. It raised its head to look at him, trailing strands of flesh from its jaws. Vergo froze, questioning his faculties. The trooper was…EATING…his friend.

It stood up, blood pouring in rivers from its open jaws. Vergo staggered back, dropping the supplies and grabbing for his blaster pistol. The demonic trooper took a step forward, its foot coming down on Gaden's still-twitching body.

"Stay back!" Vergo warned. The words were uselessly spoken. It was clear that he was no longer talking to a human. The thing took a forward leaning stance, like that of a carnivorous prehistoric reptile, and sprang at him.

He fired the pistol. Hot blaster bolts whipped from the muzzle, striking the crazed ghoul in the chest. Hot flesh blew off its body like tiny meteors, burning to grey ash. Vergo fired repeatedly, burning several holes in the beast's torso until finally it fell on its back.

Vergo ejected the spent ammo battery and slammed a fresh one into his pistol. He watched the fiend for several seconds. It appeared to be dead…as a matter of speaking. He looked down at Gaden. The twitching had stopped. He was dead, staring aimlessly at the sky. He coughed near to the point of vomiting after seeing the mangled corpse of the other trooper slain by the fiend. Intestines lay uncoiled around his body, the rips pulled apart like gutting a turkey.

A series of questions raced through his mind: *What could've happened? Had the trooper gone mad? How many others had he killed? Who else knows about this?*

Like worms in dirt, those intestines started to move. Vergo stood frozen. Once again, he wondered if he was going insane. The ravaged body lifted its torso off the ground. It stared ahead into nothingness with its one remaining eye. Blood continued spilling from its many wounds. Finally, it stood up, its entrails falling completely from its belly into a pile on the ground.

Vergo was getting light-headed. The trooper was dead, yet it was still coming. When it saw him, it quickened its pace from a couple of weak steps to a staggering walk. He raised the pistol and took aim. His finger rested on the trigger and began to squeeze.

Movement on the ground caught his attention.

In less than a second, his vision was obscured by thrashing hands and biting jaws. The trooper he had shot sprang back to its feet like a bolt of lightning. Hands lashed at him with hooked fingers, tearing his uniform.

He had shot it repeatedly in the chest. Its heart, lungs, and stomach should be jelly by now! Yet, it came at him with the strength of a Rothine Wildebeest. Vergo yelled, thrusting the pistol into its face. He fired, catching it in the cheek. The thing arched backward, still clinging to his uniform. Its head turned back to face him, the cheek and ear dangling in hot, meaty shreds.

Its jaw stretched obscenely, the tongue flapping freely over the enormous gap. A hand squeezed over his wrist, the nails digging into his skin. Vergo yelled with desperation and terror, unable to angle the muzzle to the thing's face. He pushed his other hand against its throat, keeping it away as it leaned in to bite. The two stood locked in a horrid embrace. The thing now had Vergo's gun-arm locked in both its hands. Its brain, lost in a primitive state of basic function, never registered the subsequent blaster shots that entered its abdomen.

Another snarl permeated the air as the gutless ghoul entered the fray. Vergo yelled as its body slammed him and the other, sending all three of them falling to the ground. His head connected with the rocky ground beneath him, his vision spiraling into a hazy mess. Then, there was pain. Lots of pain. Piercing. Pulling. Tearing.

Vergo's vision cleared just in time for him to see both of the reanimated corpses pulling his stomach apart as though it was warm bread. Blood gushed in fountains as the meat separated. Hands tug into the breach, pulling entrails free from his gut and lifted them to their mouths. Jaws clamped down and shook, tearing the meat further. They munched, then bit again.

Vergo groaned, unable to muster the strength to fight back. He raised his arm weakly, only to realize he had dropped the pistol.

Shadows encompassed him, as a horde of other ghouls emerged from the rock swamp. Drawn by the sounds of struggle, they converged on the fallen trooper and helped themselves to his flesh. The feeding frenzy had commenced, filling the air with hungry snarls and moans. A series of bloody, infected hands grabbed at his body. Bones snapped as arms were wrenched from their sockets. Ribs snapped one after another, unable to sustain the weight of the many creatures that piled on him like ants.

The last thing Vergo felt was a clawed hand reaching under his exposed ribcage and seizing his still beating heart, before ripping it free to feast on it.

CHAPTER 2

Dawn had arrived on the woodland planet of Boracan. The rising sun's golden rays touched down on the autumn-colored leaves of the forest that covered the western side of the planet. The morning air warmed, bringing out the many critters that began another day's struggle of life and death.

Two feet in length, the spike-tailed rat emerged from the cover of its den. Brushing the canopy of twigs and leaves out of the way, it searched the surrounding area for snakes and other carnivorous reptilians. With no sign of immediate danger, it scurried from its hiding place and darted into the forest in search of food. An omnivorous creature, it had plenty of options to scavenge food. There was almost no shortage of half-eaten critters that it could rummage meat from, while additionally it could dig up vegetable roots from carrot plants.

It scurried for a hundred yards, passing under thick bushes and between trees when its nostrils finally found the scent of a starch plant. The creature darted for the scent, increasing speed until finally locating the familiar green stem, containing three arrow-shaped leaves. Immediately, the creature started digging. Dirt flew in tiny fountains until finally the creature exposed the spherical shape of the potato. It was small, but nutritious all the same. The creature dug it out, gave one more cautionary look around, then continued digging for the plant's roots.

It only took another split-second for the creature to detect the faint vibrations under its feet. Something was coming; something of greater mass. And it was approaching fast.

Survival instincts sparked in the rat's brain. It turned and began darting back, abandoning its loot. Now, it could hear the pounding footsteps. There were many of them, from several biped creatures that dominated this area. The rat had waited too long to flee, as it was caught in the path of the human stampede.

The prisoner felt the thud against the toe of his boot as his running foot kicked the unsuspecting critter out of the way. It was just the next of many things he collided with in his desperate escape from the evil that pursued him. Branches tore at his already ragged clothing as he darted between the trees. Behind him, two of his friends kept pace. They were spaced out by a half-dozen yards. None of them were sure of where they were going. The air behind him was sizzling hot from blaster fire. Red bolts of hot energy whizzed past them, exploding against trees and scrubs.

The sand dollar uniforms of the Tarkadon troopers stood out against the autumn colors of the forest. There were six troopers chasing the prisoners, and the odds were in their favor. They were well fed, well-conditioned, and well trained compared to the meager standards of living for the prisoners they kept. This was evident in the fact that they were quickly closing in on the group of three…the last of an initial group of twelve.

The Tarkadon squad leader took point. He wanted to get at least one more kill in this training exercise. It was the most action he'd get out here in the outer rim, where there was no United Galactic Systems military to shoot at. Six more months in this boring hole to go, after which he'd finally get his wish out in the star system of Ormsby, where much of the heaviest fighting was currently taking place. Hopefully, there'd be some action left by the time he got there.

For now, he'd have to settle for these live target training exercises. At least it was entertaining.

Sweat glistened at his brow as he led his five troopers to the remaining targets. He pointed a finger and waved it in a circle, ordering the men to branch out. They did as ordered, forming a crescent line which closed in like a pincer on the prisoners. As they closed in, they created a crossfire.

Small red explosions popped everywhere as blaster bolts cut into the small group. Through the barrage of gunshots came a pained scream as several of those shots found one of the prisoners. What came next was the thumping sound of his body hitting the ground and the smell of charred flesh.

The squad leader smiled as he leaped over the smoking corpse. Less than a hundred feet ahead were the other two prisoners.

"Left flank, take out the fella with the bad haircut," he said into the commlink in his helmet.

A volley of blaster bolts punched through the jungle. The squad leader watched the second prisoner's back explode into a charred pink mist. The last remaining prisoner glanced back long enough to see his friend hit the dirt, and the squad closing in quickly.

"Slow it down, everyone," the squad leader said. "This one's mine." He shouldered his rifle and took aim. The prisoner took a sudden turn to the right, narrowly avoiding his blasts. The squad leader cursed under his breath and resumed the chase. The target was heading for a thick grouping of trees with intent to lose him.

Two of his squad joined him in the chase, while the other three remained to police the bodies. They ran in a wide arc to the left, lining up for a shot. This last target was fast and somewhat cunning, which made for a more interesting kill. The chase went on for over another hundred yards, at the end of which, the prisoner had neared the cluster of corkscrew-shaped trees.

The two troopers fired off several rounds. The prisoner ducked and zigzagged, desperately trying to evade the blasts. The maneuver ended up lining him up with a tree, which he collided into face-first. The following moment, he was dazed and struggling to remain on his feet. He stumbled backward, his world spinning, providing the perfect opportunity for the squad leader to take his shot.

He took aim and squeezed the trigger, sending a single blaster bolt streaking through the woodland. It found its place in the prisoner's abdomen, erupting in a brief red explosion that spilled blood and tissue. The prisoner folded over, both hands covering his injury. He dropped to his knees, mouth gaping from extreme pain, then fell to his side.

"Nice shot, sir," one of the troopers said.

"Hey, look at that! He's still kicking!" the other said.

"I can see his forehead from here. You can take another practice shot!"

"Don't get too excited," the squad leader said. He lowered the rifle and drew a knife from his belt. Its blade was curved backward, like a miniature version of ancient swords. He had killed many targets with a blaster rifle, but he never experienced the sensation of slicing a blade across the throat of a live target. So far, in close-quarters combat, he had only stabbed artificial figures made of thick gelatin to resemble human anatomy. Now, he had an opportunity to experience the real thing.

The three troopers approached the fallen prisoner. Blood soaked the grass beneath him. He was in a fetal position, with both arms wrapped around his ruptured abdomen. The squad leader kicked his heel into his shoulder, rolling him onto his back. He then stomped on his chest, pinning him down, then knelt with the knife raised.

The prisoner sucked in a breath. He couldn't manage a scream; he was in too much pain. He clenched his teeth together and waited for the blade to end his suffering.

In his peripheral vision was the red flash of a blaster bolt. The squad leader jerked back and looked at his men in anger.

"What the hell are you shooting at—" his voice trailed off as he saw the smoldering hole that encompassed the face of one of his troopers. As the trooper fell, the leader saw the silvery sparkle of a knife spiraling past him. The blade plunged into the throat of the second trooper. Caught off guard, the trooper fell backward and clutched the blade handle, instinctively pulling it out of his neck. That was his undoing, as blood spilled freely from his severed arteries.

The squad leader grabbed his rifle and turned around to fire into the woods. In front of him was an armored figure whose face was concealed by a steel commander's helmet. There were no visible eyes through the black slit visor that cut across the face. By the time the trooper recognized the camouflaged combat fatigues of U.G.S special forces, the weapon had been kicked from his hands.

The warrior drew his own knife and descended on the trooper. He threw an elbow into his nose, knocking him down, then descended the blade. The trooper let out a brief yell as the blade plunged through his heart.

"That's what it feels like," Captain Trent Livingston said. Four of his men emerged from the thick tree line and surrounded the dead troopers, confirming each one had been neutralized.

There was Corporal Victoria Jackman, the combat medic; Adam Weatherford, the demolitions specialist; and John Neill, the heavy weapons specialist. Standing at six-foot-seven, the giant carried a Viper-HG180 minigun. Typically mounted on dropships, it was an enormous weapon which weighed nearly a hundred pounds. But the muscular giant held it as though holding a briefcase. A big briefcase, that could fire three-thousand blaster bolts per minute.

The only one taller than Neill was Luke. Luke stood over seven feet, which would stretch nearly to eight if he straightened his long neck to the sky. Luke, whose name was unpronounceable in the human tongue, was a member of the reptilian species of Vickel. They were biped creatures, but aside from having two arms and two legs, and a similar colored uniform, they bore no resemblance to their human allies. His skin was covered in seaweed colored scales. His pupils were slit like a cat's, his jaw segmented into a single upper jaw and two lower jaws that opened diagonally, each lined with a row of jagged teeth.

Despite his pain, the prisoner cracked a smile. There was a sense of satisfaction in knowing he outlived these fascist foot soldiers. The U.G.S. soldiers quickly approached. Only the Captain wore a face helmet, which was a chrome design he had seen in the Quarterfar System. They were used in medical facilities, particularly with patients with extreme facial injuries. The fact that a Special Forces Commander was wearing it was indicative of horrific war experiences. It served many purposes, one of which was filtering air into his lungs. The metal was so solid that it could protect his skull from blaster fire.

"Corporal Jackman. See to the wounded," Livingston said, the voice module giving his voice a mechanical sound.

"Yes, Captain," Jackman said. She knelt by the prisoner and opened her med-kit. "Stay with me," she told him. The prisoner was shaking.

Blood loss had paled his skin. All he could do to stay awake was to focus on her. He stared at the medic, studying her features. Years of combat had added a few wrinkles to the twenty-eight year-old's face, giving her a hardened look. Her black hair was already showing slight shades of grey.

"Three…" he whispered. "Three more."

"We're already on it," Livingston said. He turned away and spoke into his commlink, "Sergeant Park. You're clear to eliminate the next group."

"*Yes, Captain,*" Park replied.

****

Sergeant Zachary Park watched the three Tarkadon troopers like a lion stalking a herd of antelope. The moment he received the go-ahead, he didn't bother alerting his team members. He wanted these troopers to himself.

The troopers conversed among themselves, wondering why their companions hadn't yet returned. Their small talk came to an abrupt end as Park sprang from cover. They all turned, seeing his scarred face bursting through a flurry of falling leaves. Red blaster bolts spat from his blaster rifle, striking the nearest trooper in the chest. A slight turn to the left centered the next trooper in his sights. Red energy shredded his midsection, nearly splitting him in half.

The third trooper made a mad dash to the left, fleeing into the woods. Sergeant Park watched him through the iron sights, calculating his speed and distance, then fired a volley of blasts.

Blaster bolts cut through both of the trooper's legs, sending him tumbling into the ground. Park loaded a fresh battery clip into the rifle and advanced. Behind him, his four squad members emerged from cover.

"Zach," Dawn Ramos called to him. Park didn't answer as he marched toward the fallen trooper. "Za—Sergeant!"

"Stand fast," Park replied. "Secure the area. I'll take care of this one." Ramos sucked in a breath, then looked away. Her two companions approached, their uniforms covered in soot. Douglas Soto was the youngest of the bunch. He remained silent as Ramos passed him. It was clear she didn't want to witness the upcoming carnage that was about to happen.

"Should we stop him?" Maurice Webb, the team's computer engineering expert asked.

"Yes," Soto replied.

"Are we going to?"

"His orders are to stay put," Soto whispered, shaking his head. "Doesn't mean we can't say something to the Captain." Both men winced as they watched the Sergeant stand over the injured trooper. The trooper rolled onto his back and raised his hands in surrender. Sergeant Park grimaced his hatred for the Tarkadon soldier, then raised his rifle like a sledgehammer. He cracked the butt of the weapon on the trooper's right forearm, cracking the bones. The trooper screamed in pain, which intensified after the Sergeant brutally smashed his other arm.

"We don't take in filth. We dispose of it," Park growled. He struck down on his forehead, breaking the skin. A second strike cracked his skull. Park sneered, then proceeded to bludgeon the trooper's head, smashing his face into the grass.

Both Soto and Webb turned away at the sound of breaking bone. Both of them carried the same disgusted expression on their faces. They had seen plenty of war and death. But this? This was something different altogether. And the worst part was they had to serve under this madman.

"Definitely saying something," Soto reiterated.

"Shh," Ramos hissed. "If they tortured your father like they did his, you'd act the same."

"Losing a loved one doesn't give the right to murder unarmed prisoners," Soto replied. Ramos ripped off her helmet in frustration, exposing her neck-length brown hair.

"What about people who capture innocent civilians and murder them for sport?" She pointed at the dead prisoners.

"Listen, just because you're sleeping with him doesn't mean you have to defend his every action," Soto said. Ramos squared up, only to be stopped by Webb.

"He wasn't insulting you," he said. "Believe me, if he wanted to piss you off, he would've reported you two long ago." Ramos glanced at him, then at Soto.

"Sorry." She placed her helmet back on. "Maybe we've all been out here way too long." Webb and Soto nodded. It was true. Getting out into the outer rim undetected was a daunting task in itself. Now they had to conduct their missions without the Tarkadon High Command being alerted of their presence. With each engagement, that probability grew less and less likely.

Park marched back to the group, stopping by one of the dead troopers and wiping the blood off the rifle stock with their fatigues.

"Team Two to Team One, hostiles are neutralized," he radioed Livingston.

"*Regroup with us immediately*," Livingston replied.

"Yes, Captain," Park said. He looked to his three subordinates. "What are you staring at me for? You heard the Captain. Move out." Soto and Webb hustled off, while Dawn Ramos remained. As much as she didn't want to admit it, Zachary Park was not the same man she fell in love with three years ago. He was a Corporal at that time. She was fresh out of Basic and sent directly into his unit for advanced combat training in preparation to engage the enemy at the Woldmire Rings. They hadn't begun their romance until after his promotion. At that time, sexual relationships were forbidden between squad members. If one had a rank over one level higher than the other, the penalty could result in court martial.

"Private, I said move out," Park snapped.

"Yes, Sergeant," she replied. She followed her teammates over to the corkscrew trees. Park gave one last look to the dead troopers. He snorted, gurgled, then spat on their faces, then proceeded to regroup with the others.

****

Corporal Victoria Jackman looked up to the Captain and shook her head, mouthing the words, "he won't make it."

"It's okay…" the prisoner said, spitting blood. The Captain knelt down beside him.

"I'm sorry we didn't get here in time," he said.

"Don't be," the prisoner said.

"How many more prisoners are there?" Livingston asked.

"Not…ugh!" the prisoner jolted from abdominal pain. Jackman looked back at Livingston. He saw the look in her eyes; she wanted to give additional pain medication, which would be fatal due to the fact he was already maxed out. Livingston nodded. It would take a few minutes for the meds to shut down his brain, which was probably all he had anyway. At least it would be more comfortable.

The prisoner relaxed, then continued speaking.

"Not many. Fifteen others. The Tarkadons have a base. Two miles from here. There are at least thirty troops guarding the base. Eight guard towers, always manned with a sniper."

"Only thirty?" Weatherford said. "Damn! I was hoping for a challenge!" The prisoner groaned and coughed. His breathing shallowed.

"Fences. They have electric energy fences on perimeter. To keep prisoners in."

"Those things will fry anyone who touches them. We won't be able to blast through those," Neill said.

"There's always a way in," Livingston said.

"East side. Main entrance," the prisoner gasped. "Prisoner holding is directly in front of main building." He leaned back and groaned.

"That's good enough. Thank you," Livingston said. He looked back and saw Soto and Webb approach. Behind them was Dawn Ramos. All three of them failed to hide their forlorn expressions. It all made sense when he saw the bit of blood and dirt sticking to Sergeant Park's rifle stock.

Sergeant Zachary Park had been a good soldier up to this point, but the execution of his father had taken a toll on his mind. A year ago, he was a soldier fighting for galactic freedom. Now, he was just a stone-blooded killer. More than once, he had seen Park standing over the bodies of Tarkadon troops. Interestingly enough, many of those men were either unarmed, or even in restraints. The injuries suffered from flamethrowers clearly didn't help his state of mind. Though nothing compared to the injuries that scarred Livingston's face, it still was enough to require skin grafts, which left permanent scars over his brow and right eye, giving the Sergeant a near-demonic appearance.

Now wasn't the time to deal with the situation. The priority was overwhelming the base, rescuing any remaining hostages, and determining where the secret bio-weapons site was located.

He looked down at the prisoner. He had died without speaking another word.

A brave man, Livingston thought.

"Thirty troops. Should be a breeze," John Neill said. He sported a grin and stroked the top barrel of his minigun.

"Quit jerking your gun off," Weatherford quipped.

"Mind having a little compassion here," Jackman said, annoyed. A growl reverberated from Luke's reptilian throat. It was his way of agreeing with the medic. Not even the brute Neill was going to argue with a Vickel.

All eyes went to the Captain.

"Webb, is your computer prepped?"

"Yes, Captain."

"Good. Be ready to hack into their security systems once we get near," Livingston said. "Let's go. We have work to do."

"What? We just gonna walk in through the front door?" Weatherford asked.

"Yes, actually. At least, you and Webb will," Livingston said.

"Oh, *thanks*," Webb griped.

"This group should have a roller somewhere. We'll find it, and you will take it and use a key card from one of these troopers to get in. Shield walls are powered by a generator. You will go in and shut it down. As you do that, you will also hack into their comm links to prevent them from alerting the Tarkadon High Command. Once the shields are down, we'll hit the guard towers and move in. Any questions? Good. Move out."

"Don't hog 'em up, sir," Neill quipped. The team hustled northwest, with Ramos taking point to track down the Roller. Corporal Jackman hesitated long enough to close the dead prisoner's eyes, then replaced her helmet and followed her team.

She noticed a slight sluggishness in Livingston's movements.

"Sir?" she said, catching up with him. That expressionless facemask turned toward her. Hidden behind it was a man in agony, who in her opinion, was not medically fit to be leading an operation of this caliber.

"What is it, Corporal?"

She made sure none of the others were paying attention to them, then leaned in. "Do you need something for the pain?" There was a moment of silence before he answered.

"No."

She knew he was lying. She had seen his files. The chemical burns had destroyed much of the muscular tissue in his face. Part of the side effect of the burns was that the nerves were constantly shooting pain signals to the brain.

"I can give you something—"

"Negative, Corporal. Get a move on." The mechanical voice was stern.

"Yes, Captain," Jackman said. She continued on. Livingston waited for her to get far enough away before drawing a deep breath through his mechanical apparatus; his own way of managing the pain through focus.

CHAPTER 3

It was five miles of trekking before they spotted the south guard towers. Made from black Elisian steel, the towers looked out into the surrounding forest. The trees had been thinned around the facility, giving the lookouts better view of anyone approaching.

Captain Livingston and Dawn Ramos army-crawled toward a patch of red bushes located near the trunks of two large trees facing the south side. It was one of the few areas that provided cover, while providing a decent view of the base. Livingston extended a foot-long scope and studied the base with a magnified view.

The fortress was roughly two-thousand feet long from its main entry on the east to where the west guard towers overlooked the barracks. The plasma walls were a thin blue light. To a layman, they didn't look like much. But Livingston and his team knew the truth. Those energy walls could deflect an anti-tank missile. The only section of the perimeter that didn't contain the light was the entry port between two pillars.

There were two towers at each of the four sides. Livingston checked the nearest guard towers. The thermal imaging in the scope displayed the human figure inside each one. He could tell by the relaxed posture of each sniper that they were bored. This planet was on the outer rim, meaning they had no reason to suspect outside intrusion. The most they usually had to worry about was a prisoner attempting to escape. They occasionally glanced out beyond the perimeter, but it was the bare minimum at best. The other six appeared to have the same laid-back attitude.

Poor discipline would be these snipers' downfall.

Livingston zoomed in through the wall of light. In the center of the fortress was the main building. It had two floors, and knowing how the Tarkadons built their structures, there was likely a lower level as well. On top of the building was an enormous satellite dish for long-range communication. These Tarkadon bases always had a radioman on duty at all times. Before launching the attack, Webb would have to hack the comms to prevent the base from alerting reinforcements.

To the west of the main building were the prisoner holding cells. They were black buildings, cylinder in shape. Tarkadon troopers moved between various guard posts, and to the barracks on the west side. Up on the north side was a rectangular building for storing rollers and aerial ships. And near that was the power generator for the energy barrier.

Guards were stationed all about, each looking as bored as the snipers. This facility had likely been here for years. With no security risks and being so many lightyears away from the heavy fighting, these troopers had no reason to suspect intrusion.

"Regroup," Livingston whispered to Ramos. The two U.G.S. soldiers crawled backwards and slipped into a small incline where the team waited. The team huddled close and awaited instructions. "Webb. Weatherford. Get back to the roller. Check in at the main gate and take the fork to the right. You'll see the generator. It's near Vehicle Storage, so they won't suspect you right away. Jam the radio signal first, then lower the barriers. Weatherford, be ready to provide cover for him in case you're spotted."

"You got it, sir," Adam Weatherford said. He pumped his HIVE-12 Blaster Spread-shot and hustled with Webb back to the roller. Both men wore Tarkadon jackets pulled off the bodies. Hopefully, the blood stains would go unnoticed until the shooting began.

"Park," Livingston continued. "You and Neill circle around to the north side. Luke, Soto, Jackman, you guys hit the west. Ramos and I will approach from the south. As soon as those barriers go down, hit the guard towers."

"Aye-aye, Captain," the team replied unanimously. They dispersed and hustled to their designated attack areas. Livingston and Ramos returned to the bushes at the top of the small mound. The Private First Class checked the cylinder of her grenade launcher.

"It's been a while since I've gotten to use one of these," she said.

"It's been a while since you've killed anything with it too," Livingston retorted.

"I resent that, Captain. Besides, how was I supposed to know you had already sniped those Gretic Sandtroopers?"

"The fact that they were dead should've given it away," Livingston said. Ramos knew he was grinning under that mask, despite the dry tone in his voice. She repressed her own smile and focused on the mission at hand. Fortunately, Webb had the hardest part of this ordeal. The specialist was a master hacker, who could make a planetary defense system re-aim their defense lasers onto the planet they were defending. Hacking a comm system was not the concern; it was being spotted.

Webb and Weatherford boarded the roller, the former taking the driver's seat. He twisted uncomfortably; the damn jacket was too small, and worse, he was wearing it over his own uniform.

"Let's make this quick," he said. Webb opened his small computer. It was a small device, but in the right hands, it could prove to be deadlier than a planetary purge ray.

Weatherford drove the roller from its hiding spot and found the trail. He took a right and followed the bend, which circled around to the main gates. He reminded himself to look casual as he approached the entry port. He looked ahead at the two pillars. Two red lasers stretched between them, ready to melt through any unauthorized vehicle foolish enough to plow through. Directly behind the energy barrier were the two guard towers. Both snipers glanced through their loopholes, then resumed their casual waiting out of their shift after realizing it was their fellow troopers returning from their training exercise.

Weatherford tucked his cap low and approached the pillars. There were two guards on the other side, each carrying blaster rifles at the hip. On the side of the left pillar was a scanner pad. He took the tag taken from one of the dead troopers and held it out. The red light flashed green and the lasers disappeared.

The guards spaced out, allowing passage. Weatherford slowly entered the facility. As soon as he cleared the pillars, the laser barriers returned.

"This better work, or else getting out is gonna be a bitch," he said. He drove slowly while watching his surroundings. Armed troopers patrolled the barrier walls while others moved between the interior guard posts. Beyond the rumble of their engine, he could hear the heavy thumping of nine-foot-tall exo-suits walking around the main building. These nine-foot-high maintenance machines were piloted by a single maintenance technician who would inspect the buildings and equipment and conduct any necessary repairs to keep everything up to spec. The pilots would change the gadgets in the maintenance shed using automated droids to install whatever power tool that was needed onto the arms.

Weatherford could see Vehicle Storage over to the right of the main building, and in front of it was the power generator.

Webb activated his computer and hit a series of buttons. He extended a small antenna and punched in a code. A digital frequency line appeared on the screen.

"Is that the radio signal?" Weatherford asked.

"Will you shut up and let me concentrate?" Webb replied.

"Concentrate faster, because we've got *seconds* before these jackasses realize we came from a different kind of target-practice."

A whirring sound came out of the device. The frequency line erupted into a series of chaotic loops like a heart monitor going haywire.

"Signal's blocked," Webb said. He looked up from the screen and gazed at the numerous troops posted throughout the compound. To the left, he saw the Confinement facility. Two Tarkadon guards escorted a prisoner to the front doors, zapping him with batons the whole way in. He bit his lip as he watched them disappear through the entrance. Several troopers laughed as they watched the abuse. Years of indoctrination had poisoned their minds as well as their souls.

Weatherford pulled up next to the generator and hit the brakes. Webb immediately bolted out the door and knelt by the generator's main console.

"Can't we just blast it with my shotgun?" Weatherford whispered, looking around cautiously. Already, a few guards started glancing in their direction.

"It'd be a waste of a shot," Webb said. "These things are designed to withstand plasma caster rounds. You'd be shooting at this thing till tomorrow before you made a dent in it."

Weatherford remained in the vehicle, shotgun on his lap. He pulled an impact grenade from his belt and pressed his thumb to the activator. All he would have to do is throw it, and watch whatever it touched get blown to chunks. He watched his mirrors and gazed all around. His gaze moved up to the towers. He could see one of the snipers pacing about in the confined space. The sniper gazed out the loophole, watching over the compound offhandedly.

Park took position at the north side and took cover behind a tree. He extended the stock on his rifle and pressed it to his shoulder. Several meters to his right, Neill knelt with his Viper Minigun.

The Sergeant used binoculars to search for their men.

"Any minute now," he said. He put the glasses away and gripped his rifle and leaned forward, ready to charge.

"Don't get too excited, Sarge," Neill joked.

"Fuck excitement," Park growled. "I won't sleep until all of these Tarkadon assholes are buried in shallow graves. Every one of them, on every bastard planet they inhabit."

Jackman and Luke readied themselves three hundred feet from the west barrier. She could smell the stale breath from the huge Vickel warrior.

"You really need to brush those teeth," she remarked. Luke looked down at her, then spoke in a growly dialect that she didn't understand. "You're saying something mean, aren't you?"

Luke's head reared back. He cleared his throat, then slowly worked out the English words.

"Oh! How would you like it if I leaned…closer?!" Luke leaned in, jaw agape. Jackman jabbed him in one of the lower jaws, causing him to bite down accidentally on his tongue. "What? So, you can insult me, but I can't retaliate?"

"You make it so much fun," Jackman said. They could hear Soto groaning several feet behind them.

"Hey, why don't you two flirt somewhere else? Christ! Make out for all I care, just do it where you won't give away our position," he hissed. Jackman winced in disgust, then noticed a crude alien smirk forming on Luke's tripod jaw.

"God, you're sick. BOTH of you. I swear, all around the galaxy, men are pigs. Don't care what species you are." She sighed, shook her head, then readied herself to charge the compound. "Just be ready to blast those guard towers. Think you can handle that, you oversized iguana?" Luke let out another growly sentence, then tapped her ass with his claw. Jackman directed her cold stare at the Tarkadon fort. "Don't know what the Vickel ladies see in you."

"On my planet, my reproductive organs are far larger and far more pleasurable than—"

"Holy fuck, I was not asking!" Jackman said. She shook her head in an attempt to get the image out of her brain. "Okay, I'm ordering you to keep that jaw clamped shut. Only open it if…you're gonna bite the head off an enemy combatant."

"As you wish, Corporal," Luke growled. He proceeded to snicker as they waited for the tech expert to complete his task. She didn't say he couldn't do that.

Big gecko!

Weatherford grew impatient in his seat as he waited for Webb to finish up. He watched the energy barriers, expecting them to vanish at any moment. He glanced up again at the guard towers. The guard that had been gazing out had resumed pacing about. He couldn't see the other one.

"Let's see what's going on over there."

The chatter came from several yards behind them. Weatherford checked the mirror. Three troopers were coming their way. Two of them were human. The third, to his dismay, was a Crikken. It stood twice as tall as its human companions, its eyes as large as their heads. Its jaw resembled that of a piranha's, except that it was large enough to bite Webb in half.

"Webb," Weatherford whispered. "You almost done?"

"Working on it. Going as fast as I can."

"Make it faster."

"I'm trying. If you'd shut up a minute, I might be able to—" As Webb turned to look back at Weatherford, he saw the Tarkadon group approaching. "Going faster!" He punched in the codes as best he could to hack into the system. Weatherford waited and kept an eye on the troopers.

"Hey!" one of them said. "What's going on over here?"

"He's just patching up the internal fusion system," Weatherford replied. He watched one of the Troopers step alongside the vehicle. By the looks of the insignia on his jacket, he was a Sergeant.

"Why is Infantry doing work designated for Maintenance?" the Sergeant said. "Step out of the vehicle. You! Back away from the generator! Now!" Webb glanced back, then proceeded with the hacking, using his body to block his computer from the Sergeant's view. "You two don't listen. Maybe your hearing will improve after a month in the hole. Step. OUT. Of. The. Roller!"

"You know," Weatherford cocked his head back, "you look like someone who likes to take it in the mouth. Am I right, Sarge?" If the Sergeant's temper had gotten any hotter, there'd be smoke coming from his ears. He drew his pistol and yanked the door open.

"Alright, you smartass prick! You wanna play it rough? I—"

Weatherford lunged with the shotgun, plowing the barrel into the Sergeant's open mouth. A squeeze of the trigger sent a twelve-shot blast exploding the Sergeant's head like a pinata.

Weatherford jumped from the seat and fired his shotgun at the next trooper, bursting a hole in his chest. The Crikken roared and raised its plasma blaster. Weatherford fired first, striking it repeatedly in the arm. Blaster bolts punched through its red skin, splattering thick green blood onto the grass. He continued the assault, blasting its face and neck. With a deathly scream, the beast fell on its back, blood gushing from its many wounds.

A blaster bolt streaked down by his face, passing within an inch of his nose. Weatherford rotated to his left and saw the sniper aiming down at him. Without hesitation, he hurled the impact grenade high. The tower erupted into chunks of smoldering metal that rained to the ground below. In the middle of that debris was fragments of a ravaged Tarkadon sniper.

Troopers converged from around the compound. Officers barked orders, directing their soldiers to the sound of the blasts. Alarms rang out. Radiomen tried to alert fleet admirals on the other side of the solar system, only for their signal to bounce back at them.

Weatherford reloaded his shotgun, then ducked behind the Roller. A sniper round from the second north guard tower struck the engine. Right then, two troopers burst from Vehicle Storage and aimed at Webb. Both Webb and Weatherford drew first, punching blaster bolts into the enemy troops. Weatherford rose from cover and fired a spread-shot up at the guard tower. His blaster bolts exploded around the loopholes, missing the sniper, but driving him back momentarily.

Several troopers converged on the east side of the compound and began closing in. Weatherford fired a series of blasts, causing them to break ranks.

"Webb! Anytime now!"

"I got it!" Webb shouted. With one final press of a button, the generator shut down. A high-pitched mechanical sound echoed across the compound, followed by the hum of the energy barriers disappearing.

The troopers closed in on the two soldiers. Weatherford and Webb sprinted west, avoiding several blaster rounds. They only made a dozen yards before encountering another group of Troopers.

A spiraling mechanical sound filled the air; a sound that both men recognized. They dove to the ground as Neill charged the north perimeter. Thousands of blaster bolts tore from the six barrels of his minigun, tearing through the cluster of troops. Panic struck the confused guards, causing some to pull back while others were cut to pieces.

Park advanced beside him. He armed an impact grenade and launched it up into the guard tower. It exploded with a deafening roar, sending chunks of the shack raining below on fleeing troopers.

Webb spat as he lifted himself off the ground. An enormous hand gripped his collar and yanked him the rest of the way up. Neill grinned and tapped him on the shoulder.

"Nice work, kid." Neill picked up his rifle and handed it to him. "Now go play!"

Another blast shook the compound. They looked to the east and saw green flashes from Luke's plasma cannon exploding one of the east towers. Two seconds later, another blast hit the second one, expanding in a yellow ball of plasma fire.

"Neill! Six o'clock! East towers!" Sergeant Park barked, pointing behind Neill. "Pick 'em off!"

Neill spun on his heel and aimed the minigun high. Hundreds of blaster bolts hit the guard tower on the left, flying so fast that they appeared to be one large stream of energy. The blasts punched through the metal siding and found the sniper, ripping him to pieces. With his finger still on the trigger, Neill panned the weapon to the right and ravaged the second east tower.

Weatherford hurled another grenade and watched as two Tarkadon bodies were sent airborne from the resulting explosion. He and Webb proceeded south toward the prisoner holding, only to be met with a dozen armed Tarkadons. Webb fired from the hip, punching a blaster bolt through the skull of the one unfortunate enough to be in the front. Spinning on their heels, they turned left and ran toward the now-burning main entry. Blaster fire zipped around them, turning the air scorching hot.

Behind the group of Tarkadons came another explosion. They each jolted from the resounding shockwave, then turned to see one of the south guard towers collapsing into a heap of metal.

"Yee-hah," Ramos yelled. She fired a second grenade and watched as the final guard tower erupted into chunks.

The pieces had barely touched down when Livingston charged the compound. Gathering near the debris were four Tarkadon troopers. They opened fire on the Captain, but not before he threw a hand grenade into the center of the group. Body parts went skyward, trailing smoke as they vaulted in different directions.

Livingston aimed the rifle and blasted a fifth, exploding the right side of his skull. Another explosion shook the earth several meters to his left. Half a moment later, he saw bodies hurling through the air like volcanic fireballs.

Ramos closed in on the perimeter, her grenade launcher smoking at the muzzle. She fired the last three grenades in rapid succession, striking the south entrance of the main building…right as a group of soldiers came spilling out. A massive cloud of smoke and dusk obscured the grisly sight of bodies breaking apart. The blast imploded the sliding doors and broke the outer frame into fragments, widening the entrance.

Livingston ran for Prisoner Confinement and took cover behind it. He emerged from around the corner and fired at the dozen troops that had Weatherford and Webb pinned. His spray caught two of them center mass while they scattered. He dipped behind the structure as they returned fire. Blaster bolts popped along the thick steel structure. He peeked around the corner. One tenacious trooper ran wide in an effort to flank him. A three-round burst from Livingston's rifle caught the soldier in the chest, killing him instantly.

Another took advantage of the distraction and charged the front of the building, but did not anticipate the Captain's lightning reflexes. Livingston swung the rifle to the right and fired another burst. The blaster bolts struck just below the collar bone. The trooper fell with the forward momentum, first falling to his knees then plowing headfirst into the building.

Ramos joined the fray, discarding the grenade launcher in favor of her blaster rifle. She fired a series of bursts, dropping one target, then a second. A volley of blaster fire streaked from behind the troopers as Weatherford and Webb closed in. Hot energy ripped through flesh and bone, finishing the remainder of the group.

Livingston hustled along the wall to the front of the building and attempted opening the sliding doors.

"Locked."

"I can get it open," Webb said.

"Not yet," Livingston said. "Let's clear the area first. Secure the main building and the barracks."

The group converged on the devastated entrance and took position along the outer wall. Livingston was the first to enter. The entrance led into a twenty-foot corridor which concluded at a guard post. So far, no troopers. Livingston pressed forward, while his squad trailed behind him.

He cleared the guard posts and entered the check-in lobby. Running feet at the back of the room caught his attention. Three troopers burst through a sliding door and took aim, only to be impaled by a spray of hot energy.

Livingston loaded a fresh battery into his weapon and moved further into the lobby.

"You're hogging 'em all, sir," Weatherford said. Livingston ignored the comment. Rarely did he express humor during a firefight.

"Ramos, Webb, secure the basement. Weatherford, you and I will take the stairs up to the radio room. Watch your corners. There might be troopers left on the lower level."

"Yes sir," Webb and Ramos said. Simultaneously, the group entered the stairway. Livingston aimed high. As he suspected, there was a trooper aiming down at him. He jumped back, and a split-second later, a blaster bolt struck in his place. He dipped under the entry frame, rifle pointed high. His shots struck under the trooper's crotch, causing him to fall. Subsequent shots punched through the platform and into his back.

"Clear," he said. He proceeded up the stairway with Weatherford, while Ramos and Webb descended the opposite direction.

Explosions rocked the west perimeter as Jackman's team entered the compound. Luke bellowed triumphantly, firing streams of plasma from his Vickelian heavy blaster rifle. The energy bolts were yellow in color and twice as large as the puny red ones of the human weapons. Enemy troops caught in their path exploded at the midsection, losing bone and entrails in a fiery display.

Soto trailed behind the big brute, providing support fire, while Jackman engaged a trio that took cover behind a roller. A puff of pink mist and smoke signaled a headshot, which was confirmed by sight of the body collapsing around the front of the engine.

"Luke, hit that vehicle," she ordered. Luke growled and shouldered his big gun. Balls of yellow energy hit the roller, gradually eroding the siding and roof. Realizing their cover was quickly disintegrating under the punishment, the two remaining troopers made a run, for it, only to be caught in Jackman's iron sights. She fired two bursts, cutting both of them down at the midsection.

A burst of blaster rounds came at them from behind. The first two missed, while the third struck Luke in the shoulder. The reptilian creature roared in pain, then spun back to face the threat. He fired a single shot, driving the trooper back behind the guard post where he had been hiding. Luke charged like a wild animal, holstering his weapon in favor of making his revenge all the more personal. He ripped the guard post from the ground with the ease of digging out a weed, then descended on the trooper. A swipe of his mighty claw knocked the blaster rifle from his grasp. Luke proceeded to impale the guard in the stomach and lift him over his head. Grabbing him by the shoulder with his other claw, Luke bent the trooper backward into a horseshoe, snapping his spine in the process.

"When you shoot a Vickel, you'd better kill him!" he roared in his growly native dialect. He reloaded his weapon and proceeded to advance on the barracks with Jackman and Soto.

Several troopers had set up defenses inside the building. They fired at the three from portholes in the side, forcing them to spread further out. Jackman returned fire, but could not land a shot through the narrow space. Soto threw a grenade, which exploded near the back entrance. He could see through the smoke the twisting body of a dying trooper. It was his seventh confirmed kill in ground combat; nothing compared to his record in space combat.

A stream of blaster fire pierced the back of the barracks. Several of the defenders switched position to engage the two soldiers that advanced from the north side.

Neill pressed the assault, ravaging the northeast corner of the building with his minigun. Metal panels succumbed to the punishment, falling off the building and creating a wide entrance. Troopers returned fire, only to be cut down by the relentless onslaught.

Sergeant Park assisted in the attack, then rotated left as he spotted a group of troopers running out from the main building with rocket grenades launchers. He squeezed the trigger, sending a dozen rounds cutting through all three of them. Fire and blood erupted from their torsos. As they collapsed, muscular reflex caused one of them to squeeze the trigger of their launcher, sending the explosive into the ground. The resulting explosion tossed them several yards apart, while fracturing the sliding doors of the northwest entrance.

Park approached the entrance to make sure no other troopers were coming out. After confirming so, he returned his attention to the barracks. Neill had stopped firing, as had Jackman's team. The Sergeant ran at a wide angle and approached the north doors to the barracks, which were open. Inside were four Tarkadon troopers, all of which had their hands raised high.

"Should've kept your guns," Park growled. He entered the building and started blasting, ending each of their screams with a shot to the head. Breathing intensely, he walked through the room, making sure every trooper was dead.

Up ahead, Jackman and Soto arrived at the opposite entrance. Park noticed them staring at him with questioning eyes. His temper stirred again.

"Secure the main building and assist Captain Livingston," he barked. Jackman felt herself starting to shake. She knew what he'd done; the bodies without weapons made that plain. Unfortunately, there was nothing she could do about it at the moment.

"Go," she said to Soto and Luke. They converged on the east entry port while Park and Neill took the north. They proceeded down separate corridors, quickly securing the first level of the building, then moved downstairs. She knew to avoid the elevators, as those proved to be death traps in a firefight. She led her team down a flight of stairs, which led them down to the armory.

The sound of blaster fire spurred her to double her speed. She hugged the wall and allowed Luke to blast the door off the frame with his weapon. The circular door flew into the room, hitting a Tarkadon trooper in the head. Across the room, his comrade hesitated with surprise, momentarily losing focus on the duo he was firing at on the east entrance.

Ramos took advantage and emerged from cover, planting a blaster bolt through his temple. They converged on the fallen trooper.

"Discard your rifle and place your hands on—"

The trooper shouted in alien language and pointed his weapon at Jackman, who proceeded to empty her battery charge into him.

She exhaled sharply and looked to Ramos and Webb.

"Lower level's secured, Corporal," Ramos said.

"Barracks and outside region secured," Jackman replied.

Livingston hugged the wall and counted the blaster bolts that zipped through the juncture. There were two troopers around the corner, each armed with standard rifles.

Fifty-eight, fifty-nine... "Go!" he ordered. He and Weatherford turned the corner. Livingston fired first, sending a three-round burst into the nearest trooper. Weatherford took the second, the force of his shotgun sending the target reeling backward several yards.

"Clear," Weatherford said.

"Not quite," Livingston said. "Move ahead. The radio room is just around the corner." The two men proceeded, stopping only to check another juncture. There was one soldier to the left, which Livingston quickly neutralized with a shot to the neck. After confirming no more enemy presence in the corridor, they converged on the radio room. A red light on the door panel indicated they had been locked from the inside. "Weatherford, use a charge and blast that door open."

"You got it, Captain," Weatherford said. He moved ahead and removed a disc-shaped charge from his pack. He placed it at the center of the door and armed it, then quickly backed away.

The charge completed its five-second countdown and discharged, ripping the door into the interior of the room. Inside were four Tarkadon troopers, all armed with rifles.

Livingston fired two bursts, killing two of them instantly. He breached the interior and fired another burst at one who stood on the right, exploding his head with a three-round burst. Weatherford killed the last one, the shotgun blast launching the trooper into a radio panel.

"Whew!" he said. He looked around, seeing the four bodies lying in the middle of the semi-circle row of computers. "Looks like we got 'em all, Captain. Time to break out the cigars and..." he looked down, seeing the fragmented piece of door wobbling on the floor. Suddenly, it flew upward, flipping over end and knocking the shotgun from his hand. Under it was a fifth trooper, who had been knocked down when the door was destroyed. He leapt to his feet and swung his damaged rifle like a club, striking Weatherford across the face.

He spun like a crazed maniac and swung the rifle at Livingston, knocking the gun from his hands. The trooper raised the rifle and closed in to bring it down on his skull. Livingston raised his arms in a cross-block, catching the trooper at the elbows, then used his momentum to flip him over his shoulder. The trooper crashed down hard, losing his grip on his club. He rolled to his feet and threw a haymaker at the Captain.

Livingston parried the blow with his left palm, causing his enemy to spin counterclockwise with his own momentum. With his back partially turned, Livingston kicked the back of the trooper's knee, dropping him to the floor. Before he could offer surrender, the trooper had already begun lifting himself back up. He was halfway to his feet when he felt the Captain's arms squeeze around his neck and head. A sudden twist resulted in a dull crack, and the trooper went limp. Livingston lowered the dead trooper to the floor, then found his rifle and looked at Weatherford. The demolitions specialist was back on his feet, rubbing his temple.

"Son of a bitch! He was dedicated!"

"They usually are," Livingston said. He activated his transmitter. "Park. Jackman. What's your status?"

"*All clear, Captain,*" Jackman replied.

"*First level secured, Captain,*" Park said.

"Second floor secured," Livingston said. "All units move to Prisoner Containment. Jackman, have your med kit ready. Weatherford got himself roughed up a bit."

"Oh, thanks, Cap. Broadcast it to the whole team, why don't ya?" Weatherford said. He could envision the Captain grinning under that stupid chrome helmet. "Oh, right. Battle's over, so you've got your sense of humor back."

"All units," Livingston said. "Let it be known, Weatherford got his ass kicked by a short little Tarkadon radioman."

"What?!"

The radio traffic exploded.

"*I always said Adam needed to learn how to fight!*"

"*No surprise. You know he got knocked down in basic...by a girl.*"

"That was a cheap shot, Dawn!"

"*Don't worry, Adam.*" It was Jackman's voice. "*I have band aids with cartoon illustrations just for YOU!*" A few of the other teammates broadcasted their laughter.

Weatherford's face scrunched as he absorbed the abuse, then glanced over at Livingston.

"Thanks, Cap."

"It was the least I could do," Livingston retorted.

"Your generosity is overwhelming," he said as they exited the radio room.

CHAPTER 4

The sky had turned grey from a continual dosage of smoke that billowed from the ravaged fortress. The air had a stale smell to it, the lush surrounding landscape now hellish. Some of the fire had spread to the surrounding trees, which Neill and Soto worked to extinguish with a portable Co2 unit from Vehicle Storage.

Livingston and Weatherford exited the main building and saw the team gathered by Prisoner Confinement. The building had been marked heavily by blaster fire, though the walls were durable enough to protect those inside.

Livingston immediately noticed Jackman's uneasy glare.

"What is it, Corporal?" he asked. She said nothing, but tilted her head to the right and nodded. Several meters behind her was Sergeant Park. He was checking the bodies and scavenging weapons.

"We have a problem, sir," she said. "A problem you'll have to address sooner rather than later."

"Quit the riddles. Speak plainly," Livingston replied, his mechanical voice sounding cold.

"The barracks," she said. She pulled a chip from her helmet and extended it to the Captain. "I encourage you to examine this when we get back on the ship." Livingston gazed at the chip. It recorded footage from the team's bodycams. The fact that she handed it to him without simply explaining the problem was enough for him to know there was a risk of retaliation.

Already, he suspected what the problem was.

"He's unstable," Jackman continued. "Sir, I don't think he's mentally fit to be in service, much less be in a special task force operation."

"Hey," Ramos butted in. "He's been through a lot. We all have. Cut him some slack."

"This doesn't concern you, Dawn," Jackman said.

"I know what you two are talking about," Ramos continued. "Park's been more dedicated to this mission than all of us combined."

"Private Ramos," Livingston said. Ramos registered the expressionless tone.

"Yes…Captain," she said, clearing her throat.

"Remove yourself from this conversation. Immediately."

"Sir…yes, sir," she said. She gave Jackman one final glare, then backed away. Livingston secured the clip.

"Corporal, tend to Weatherford," he said.

"Yes, Captain," she said softly. She moved to Weatherford and removed his helmet.

"I'm fine," he protested.

"Captain's orders. You gonna take off your helmet or am I gonna make you?"

"Don't test her!" Neill yelled out. "You already got your ass kicked once today!"

"Great. It'll probably end up in the Captain's report," Weatherford groaned.

"He's gotta include all casualties in the log," Jackman said, smiling. "Now, OFF with the helmet!" With one final protesting groan, Weatherford removed his helmet, then winced as she applied disinfectant over the small abrasion on his temple. "Don't be a baby!"

Livingston approached the doors. Webb wired his computer to the control console and began running a bypass. Ramos and Park exchanged some quiet words, then accompanied the Captain.

"No sound," Luke growled, pressing his tiny ear to the door.

"Will you get out of my light?!" Webb said, shooing the giant away with his hand as though scaring off a fly. He resumed the bypass. "He is right, though."

Silence in these Confinement stations was not common. Usually, when rescuing prisoners, they would hear ecstatic commotions. Instead, they heard nothing, which alarmed everyone.

"Just get the door open," Livingston said. Webb typed in a code and the panel turned green. He backed up with the others and readied his rifle. The doors hummed, then slid open.

"Oh...my God," Ramos said. The group fell into silence. They were staring at a massacre. The Confinement building was one large room, with a single partially obscured bathroom area. On the floor were over a dozen bodies, each laying in grotesque postures. Looks of terror were frozen on their faces, those that still had faces. The air stank of plasma burns.

Neill and Soto hurried over to the group and saw the carnage.

"Jesus, they murdered the prisoners," the pilot said.

"Look there," Neill said. He pointed a finger to the back corner. There lay the bodies of two uniformed Tarkadon officers. Both of them had been ravaged by plasma fire.

"Maybe a few of the prisoners were able to disarm the guards and give them a taste of their own medicine," Park said.

"Jackman. Luke. Ramos. Move inside and check to see if..."

"If any are still alive?" Ramos asked. She scoffed. "I think we know the answer. Problem is we got here too late and—"

"Ramos, I didn't ask for a commentary," Livingston said. "Do your job."

"Yes, sir," she said. The soldiers entered the building and examined the first row of bodies. There wasn't much to examine, as most of this group had suffered head and body shots from blaster fire. It seemed the guards had simply sprayed blaster bolts at the group.

Jackman moved ahead, while Luke began the process of loading bodies. Neill and Weatherford joined in to help.

"Sergeant Park. Take Corporal Webb to Operations and see what information you guys can get from the main computer," Livingston ordered.

"Yes, Captain," Park said. He and Webb re-entered the building and ascended to the top floor.

"You think they purged their files?" Soto asked. "They likely killed these people to prevent them from supplying information about prisoner trafficking."

"I don't waste time with speculation," Livingston said. "If there's something on those computers, Webb will find it."

"Sir, what should we do with these bodies?" Neill asked.

"Jackman will get a DNA sample of each one to confirm identification. Unfortunately, we can't take them home, nor can we bury them. Doing so will confirm our presence to the enemy. We'll log the DNA and transmit it on our secure frequency so the families will be notified."

"So, the bodies will just have to remain?" Soto asked.

"Yes, sadly," Livingston said. It was one of the pitfalls to this mission...and war itself. These people deserved more than to be incinerated in a large-scale blast. But doing anything else would be like leaving a footprint for the enemy to track.

Jackman moved to the back of the building. As she suspected, every prisoner so far was dead. She stepped near the two guards. One was bent back over a bunk with a plasma burn where his throat was. The other was on the floor. This guard's punishment had been more severe. The uniform was ragged and torn, probably from a scuffle. The body had two deep cavities in the chest, but that carnage was nothing compared to the face. There was nothing there to identify the person, as the face had been completely eaten away from energy burns.

At that moment, she realized the trooper didn't have a weapon near him. This guard must've been overpowered, his weapon used against him. Him, or her. There was no way to tell. The body looked more like a man's, but the uniform jacket appeared to have been built for someone smaller.

One of the bodies moved, causing Jackman to jump back. She pointed her rifle instinctively, then lowered it, as the 'corpse' lifted itself up.

"Got a live one!" she said with relief. The survivor was a woman with mid-length hair that was golden in color. Her face was bruised and covered in grit, as was the tan prisoner jumpsuit she wore. Her boots were cracked and worn through. In her hand was a Tarkadon blaster rifle. "It's okay!" Jackman announced. "We're U.G.S. We're here to help you."

The prisoner panted heavily, eyes wide with fright.

"Mind lowering the weapon?" the big man with the minigun asked. A few more moments of staring passed, and the prisoner finally held the weapon out by the barrel. Ramos secured it while Jackman escorted the prisoner outside.

"Can you tell me your name?" Jackman asked.

"Soviar. *Doctor* Anna Soviar, from the Ayres Star System," she replied. She stared in amazement at the surrounding devastation. "*You* did this? Just the seven of you?"

"Nine. Two are in the building," Livingston answered. Soviar studied the man with the steel mask. His suit was different than the others. It had reinforced plating, capable of protecting against numerous blaster shots. She saw the insignia on his shoulder.

"You are the Captain," she said.

"Affirmative," Livingston replied. "I'm sorry for the loss of your friends."

"Me too. Many of them went down fighting when the guards started shooting. I held back...I froze. Until one aimed at me. I reacted, grabbed the gun and redirected it at the other. I made the guard kill his friend. Then we fought. He hit me many times. But I didn't stop. I got the weapon away and I just--" She mimicked firing a rifle with her hands, then calmed herself. "I guess I blacked out afterwards. What of the ones they took outside the barriers?"

"They didn't make it," Weatherford said.

"Pity you didn't get here sooner," Soviar said.

"We tried," Livingston said.

"Not hard enough," Soviar muttered. It was moments like these that made Livingston grateful he had a mask. There was no use defending his team's actions to her. It would turn into an endless debate that would circle over the same topics over and over. She would accuse his actions of getting the prisoners killed, he would reply that the prisoners would likely be dead soon anyway had they done nothing.

"How long have you been here?" he asked.

"Not long. Last shipment was a month ago, I think. I don't even know where we are."

"You're on Boracan," Livingston said.

"*Boracan*?! That's on the Outer Rim! We're talking on the edge of explored space. How did you guys get here?"

"We've got a top-of-the-line stealth fighter," Soto said. "Advanced prototype. Capable of disguising the ion particles from the thrusters to appear that we're nothing more than an aimless meteor hurtling through space. So far, it has successfully fooled the scanners of enemy ships and defense satellites."

The news did not provide any comfort. Dr. Soviar fell to her knees. Not only was she overwhelmed by the massacre she had witnessed, but she realized she was deeper in Tarkadon space than anyone in the United Galactic Systems had ever been. Her mind could barely comprehend the distance between her and the nearest U.G.S. spaceport.

"You need medication?" Jackman asked.

"No…I'll be fine," Soviar said. She took in a few breaths. "How'd you guys know about this facility. What's your mission? A small group like you, this far from reinforcements…you're obviously not fighting a grand scale war." Her eyes went to the ravaged base around her. "Though you're probably capable of it."

"Coordination between the many intelligence agencies, coordinated between several planets, has uncovered reports of prisoner trafficking out in these far reaches," Livingston explained. "From what we can gather, Tarkadon forces are extracting civilians and shipping them out to this end of the quadrant. Some for target practice. Others, for something else."

Soviar stood up, intrigued. "Something else? What else?"

"Intelligence went over the identities of many individuals confirmed to have been taken by Tarkadon forces. We've noticed a number of people with advanced specialties in bio-engineering, chemistry, medicine, pharmacology… which brings me to ask you; you mentioned being a doctor. What is your specialty, exactly?"

"Uhh…" Soviar appeared put off by the question. "Biomolecular Engineering. I was at a research facility on Torrell. Before the Tarkadon Navy bombarded the planet."

Livingston nodded. "Something tells me you weren't brought here to be used as rifle practice."

"If not that, then what? What's the point of holding me here? What were they gonna do with me?"

"I suspect they were gonna take you somewhere else," Livingston answered. "This place is simply a holding area for prisoners. There's another facility out here in this system. Whatever this facility is, it contains the true purpose for harvesting prisoners. I think they were gonna use your friends here as test subjects."

"Test subjects?"

"For bio-weaponry," Livingston said. "More than likely, they needed a biomolecular engineer to craft whatever abomination they're creating. Our job is to find this facility and destroy it."

The radio buzzed.

"Park to Captain Livingston."

"Yes, Sergeant."

"Good news. Webb hacked into the computer. And sir...we've found it."

"I'm on my way now." Livingston turned to Weatherford. "Plant charges at the energy reactor. Make sure we get rid of all traces."

"You got it, Cap," Weatherford answered.

"You're gonna blow this place up?" Soviar asked.

"Better than that," Weatherford said. "We're gonna make it look like there's been a reactor explosion. The big bad Tarkadons will never know we were here." Soviar looked back at the bodies, her face displaying disgust that these people would never receive a proper burial. Jackman finished collecting DNA samples and stored them in her pack.

"Come here," Jackman said, getting her first aid supplies out. "Let's see if I can do anything about that swelling."

Corporal Maurice Webb scooted back and forth between computers, bringing several yottabytes of data. The files flashed on an enormous viewing screen at the front of the rectangular room.

"There it is," he said, freezing the screen at a page concerning the planet Glorric. Livingston stared robotically, reading the paragraphs of information outlining the structure.

"Well done, Corporal. You found the research lab."

"That I did, sir," Webb said, basking in his glory. "I'm already downloading all the files. So, if I may ask, what happens next?"

"We go there and blow it up," Park said.

"First, we must find out if there are any prisoners there," Livingston said. "We're not savages." There was emphasis in that final word, and Webb knew it was no coincidence that he looked the Sergeant in the eye at the same moment. "Besides, we need to understand exactly what it is they're making in that lab, and to know if there are other places like it. Whatever it is, it could be a population killer."

"Can't be worse than a Planetary Death Ray," Park muttered under his breath. Livingston heard him, but decided to do nothing. At least, not at the moment. He looked at the screen, which displayed a basic schematic of one of the facilities.

"If the mission is successful, can we finally get the hell out of here?" Webb asked.

"That's the plan," Livingston said.

"Good." Webb completed the download. The screen went blank as the entire memory was sucked into his device. He unhooked it and collected his gear. "Because I'm sick of this place."

They exited the building and regrouped with the others outside. Weatherford extended the antenna of a radio detonator and grabbed his shotgun.

"Explosives are in place, sir," he said. "At the touch of a button, this place will look like a bad day on a lake on Zerion." Only Jackman didn't get the reference, as she had never seen the volcanic planet.

"We have the data. Let's get back to the ship and finish our mission," Livingston said.

"Wait," Soviar spoke up. "What about me?"

"We're gonna put you on a Tarkadon shuttle and send you out toward the Jekai system. There, you'll be collected by U.G.S. ships," Livingston said.

"Sure. If I'm lucky enough to get past the ten thousand Tarkadon ships between here and there, that is," Soviar protested.

"We can't risk taking you with us," Park said. "We're going into hostile territory. There's no guarantee you'd make it out in one piece."

"It's more of a guarantee than tossing me into space at the mercy of an autopilot computer," Soviar said.

"That's the way it's gonna have to be," Livingston said.

"That's your plan? Save all the prisoners and toss us out into space? Hope we don't get caught in the *weeks* it would take to get to Jekai?"

"Correct," Livingston said bluntly.

"Umm...sir?" Neill raised his hand. "Forgive me for not saying something sooner, but we might have to take her with us."

"What do you mean, soldier?"

"Soto and I checked Vehicle Storage. The shuttles have been severely damaged."

"Damaged? How? From blaster fire?"

"Hard to say, sir," Neill said. "All I can say is that Park and I secured that building during the fight, and I don't recall shooting the shuttles."

"Soto, come with me into the hangar bay and examine the shuttles. I need to know their operational status," Livingston said. He immediately marched toward the hangar. Soto followed, along with Neill and Park.

They entered a facility marred beyond recognition by carbon scoring. It was evident that there was more damage done here than what could possibly be achieved with mere blaster bolts, even from Neill's heavy gun.

Upon first sight, it was obvious that a diagnostic would be a waste of time. The shuttles' engines had been completely destroyed, as though struck by artillery. The vessels were everywhere, billowing smoke from the breached hulls. Livingston approached the nearest one. The steel was still hot. The portside landing strut had broken off entirely, leaving the shuttle leaning forward on its nose.

The other shuttles were in even worse condition. The explosions to the ion engines had ruptured the hulls, breaking the bodies down the middle. Fragments of charred metal lay about the hangar deck.

Livingston walked to the northeast corner, where two Tarkadon troopers lay next to a crate, their bodies riddled with blaster burns. The top of the crate was still open.

Livingston peered inside, then sighed. "Looks like we found the culprit." He reached inside and pulled an object resembling a grenade.

"Ion over-loaders?" Soto exclaimed.

"Yep," Livingston said. "They're mainly used for sabotage missions. Place them on the engine, activate them, and the device will overcharge the ions inside, which'll essentially turn the engine into a bomb."

"I guess it happened during the firefight," Neill said.

"Maybe," Livingston said. "Though, why would they explode their own shuttles? In the heat of a firefight, of all times? Were they *that* certain that all was lost?"

"They're Tarkadons. If they had any sense, they knew they were fucked when they encountered *real* soldiers," Park said.

"Maybe they thought we would infiltrate through here," Soto suggested. "Plant the over-loaders on the shuttles, draw the enemy in, then detonate them with us inside. Then, when Neill tore them up, one of them activated the detonator." He shrugged. He was simply making suggestions on the fly.

"It doesn't matter," Livingston said. What good would fixating over it do? He had seen members of all galactic species do crazy things in the heat of battle. Hell, he once witnessed a soldier get turned around and blast over a dozen members of his own squad, thinking they were the enemy.

Livingston secured the over-loader and its detonator into a pouch on his belt, then glanced at the decimated shuttles. As far as he knew, there was no other means of transport. The reality was clear; they would *have* to take the civilian along.

The soldiers marched out of the hangar bay and joined the others. Judging by the sudden tranquility in Soviar's body language, she knew she had won the debate.

"Alright, you win. I can't risk abandoning our objective for the life of one hostage. Sorry if that sounds cold, but many more lives are at stake. So, hear this: you will follow every order I give WITHOUT question. You may not be a soldier, but you will act like one nonetheless. That's how you will stay alive. Are we clear?"

Soviar smirked. "Yes...sir."

"Good enough." Livingston glanced at his squad. "Move out."

The team boarded the roller and rode it seven miles to a rock bank. Weatherford was at the driver's seat, singing an alien folk song, butchering the language the entire time.

"Oh God. Make it stop," Neill complained.

"Have a problem there, tough guy?" Weatherford quipped.

"Yeah, only the fact that we're cramped back here in this very rusty Tarkadon transit vehicle listening to you sound like a chicken being choked to death."

"Well, *you* would know best about choking your chicken. You do it all the time," Weatherford replied. After several moments of dead silence, the group descended into laughter. Even the stone-faced Sergeant Park allowed a smile to slip through.

"Okay, behave now," Webb said. "There are ladies present."

"Wish Neill kept that in mind when he forgot to lock the bathroom stall," Ramos said. More laughter ensued.

"Oh, good lord," Soviar chuckled. "Maybe I *should've* taken the shuttle."

Luke growled a few Vickelian words. Neill glanced at him with a lighthearted scowl on his face.

"Go ahead. Spit it out, lizard-face."

Luke smiled. "What I saw was puny." The squad erupted into laughter. "You'd never make it on my planet."

Jackman was near the point of shedding tears. "I see you're now turning red, John Neill."

Neill tapped on the barrier between them and the driver.

"Weatherford, next time you get into a barfight with that radio technician from Scabbrati, I want to be there to cheer him on."

"I need to hear this story," Dr. Soviar said.

"You'll probably hear it so many times, you'll have it memorized by the time we get back," Weatherford said. He steered to the right and stopped the vehicle. "Everybody on the ship."

The team filed out of the back exit. Soviar looked around, seeing nothing but a large rock bank in the middle of a clearing in the forest. But there was no ship.

"I don't get it. What sh—" A glimmer of light answered her question as the ship decloaked. Panels of energy rippled across the hull, gradually bringing it into view. After a count of ten, she was looking at a Recon-Valley stealth ship. Two-hundred and thirty feet long and fifty-seven feet wide, it was armed with twin ion blasters and a rechargeable rector cannon.

"I call it the RV," Weatherford said.

"You're hilarious," Livingston deadpanned. "Get on board, everyone."

CHAPTER 5

Dr. Soviar inhaled slowly in an effort to overcome the nauseating sensation of adjusting to the artificial gravity. She was standing in the rec area, which was a small circular room near the crew quarters. On the starboard side was a viewing window, where she gazed down at Boracan, specifically at a bright red dot which had previously been the base. They were halfway out of the planet's atmosphere when Weatherford detonated the charge, rupturing the fusion reactor and causing it to explode.

She saw silver streaks of light stretch horizontally across the glass as Soto engaged the hyperdrive. An instant later, the planet was nowhere in sight.

Footsteps pounded the metal flooring behind her. Soviar turned around and saw Corporal Jackman clearing a small fleet of steps. In her hands was a pile of clothes.

"Hope you don't mind wearing U.G.S. military attire," she joked. Soviar forced a smile, then looked back to the window. Jackman gave up the attempt at humor and placed the uniform on a chair. At that moment, she remembered that the doctor had been in the middle of a massacre that nearly claimed her life. "Sorry. I guess I'm so used to seeing bullets fly and people killed, I forget it's actually an uncommon thing."

"Or maybe it's too common," Soviar said. She sat down and took off her boots. Jackman had to force herself from wincing as she watched the doctor pry the old boots free. They were meant for someone at least one size shorter. The bastard Tarkadons hadn't even bothered finding decent clothing.

"Well, if you want, I can give you a tour of the place when you're done," Jackman said. "But first, I have to get to the galley. The boss is about to hold a briefing."

Soviar paused. There was a brief look of apprehension in her eyes, which disappeared as she relaxed.

"Okay," she said. She stood up with the pile of clothes and walked toward the cargo hold where she could change.

"You sure you'll be alright?" Jackman asked.

"Yeah, I will be. I've just never killed anyone before," Soviar answered. "I guess I'm feeling a little jittery."

"It'll pass," Jackman said. "If it doesn't, come see me. I have some good stuff in my medicine cabinet to help with the shakes."

"I might take you up on that," Soviar said.

"You know where to find me," Jackman said. She hurried up the steps and made her way to the galley.

Livingston marched into the cockpit, seeing the swirling hyperspace lights shining through the viewing glass. Douglas Soto was in the pilot's seat, with Webb in navigation.

"Course is set for Glorric," Soto said.

"How long until we arrive?" Livingston asked.

"Two hours, roughly," Soto answered. "We'll come out of hyperspace roughly five-thousand kilometers from the planet, which will allow Webb to hack into the defense satellites before they can detect us."

"Good," Livingston said. "Once you're done, come back into the galley."

"Yes, Captain."

Livingston exited the cockpit and followed a short stairway which led to a corridor. He walked straight, passing the pilot's cabin as well as his own, and emerged in a large rectangular room. The galley was the most spacious area in the ship, being about thirty feet in width. In the center of it was a circular white table, covered in crumbs and a few stains.

The team had assembled in the galley. Neill helped himself to some rations, bitter tasting beans that supplied all kinds of nutrition. He winced as he swallowed a spoonful. Luke stood at the back corner, sharpening the curved bayonet blade of his rifle. It put the Vickel into a Zen-like state. After all, they were a species that valued the most skilled members. The more enemies a Vickel killed, the more respected they became. Those that became Generals usually had hundreds of kills to their name. Those that became Chancellors rarely had less than several thousand.

The U.G.S. was fortunate they were on their side.

After a couple of minutes, Soto and Webb stepped into the galley, leaving the ship on autopilot.

"Let's get right to it," Livingston announced. He looked at Webb, who placed a pyramid-shaped device onto the table. A blue light shone from the tip, and in moments, it displayed the image of an Earth-sized planet.

"This is where we're going. The Tarkadons call it Glorric. Its landmass is made of solid rock, with swamps scattered throughout the landscape." The schematic highlighted satellites circling the planet. "Webb will disable the defense systems, so they won't detect us coming in. Then we'll set down at region 5-2." The schematic zoomed in deep into the planet, focusing on a flat region set near a lake.

"What's the distance from there to the objective?" Park asked.

"Three-point-six miles," Livingston answered. "There are a series of outposts between the landing point and the objective. We'll disembark, and hit them one after another, as silently as possible. That'll be the easy part, since each one should be manned with only two or three troopers."

"I don't get it. Why hike there when we can just bombard the place from high above?" Ramos asked. Webb enhanced the imaged until it displayed a schematic of what appeared to be a mountain.

"What are we looking at?" Weatherford asked, glaring at the floating digital image. "I forgot to mention, I've already climbed Mt. Everest."

Webb enhanced the image. A green light marked a tunnel entrance which led a couple of hundred feet into the mountain.

"This is the first facility we're gonna hit," Livingston said. "This one is the most heavily defended, with reinforced steel doors that can withstand a battering ram rocket."

"Great. And we're expected to breach it?" Weatherford said.

"That's why you have me," Webb said. "For me, opening that door will be as easy as flipping a soda tab."

"Another thing I miss from home," Neill moaned, tossing the leftover beans to the trash incinerator. Luke intercepted the bowl and dumped the beans into the back of his throat, then belched.

"Amateur," Weatherford muttered. Webb rotated the image so everyone could see the entrance. Bright green lights marked manned turret guns. There were several of them, spaced out by fifteen feet.

"These are Riptide models," Livingston explained. "They're designed for defense against air and ground troops. Just one of these things can cut through our ship like cracking an eggshell."

"So? Have Webb shut them down with his little computer thing," Neill said.

"They're run manually," Webb said. "Not by computers. I can't hack them. And they've got energy shields protecting them from bombardment. These defense turrets aren't cheap."

"And they're mainly used for protecting high-value facilities," Livingston said. "And to answer your other question, I want those outposts neutralized because I don't want those troopers closing in on us from behind as we overtake the facility."

"And what do we do about those turrets?" Jackman asked. Webb grinned and raised a hand.

"Sometimes I feel you guys couldn't fight this war without me," he quipped.

"You just said you can't hack the guns," Neill said.

"Yeah, but I can hack the power generator that powers their plasma shields," he said. "Unfortunately, I'll have to get close to do it, as the energy emissions will disrupt the signal from afar."

Weatherford smiled and rubbed his hands together with excitement. Being the demolitions specialist, he always relished the opportunity to blow up Tarkadon technology.

"So, what do you expect me to use?" he asked the Captain, figuring he'd be asked to take out the turrets after the shields were lowered.

"Snipers," Livingston said. Weatherford cocked his head in disgust.

"Aw, come on!"

"Sorry, but I'm not looking to draw the attention of several hundred troopers scattered across the region. Well placed shots through the operator's viewing system will take each of them out before they have a chance to alert reinforcements. You'll get your 'blow-it-up' fix by planting charges throughout the facility, and detonating when we extract."

Weatherford crossed his arms and pouted. "Well shit, I won't even get to watch my own fireworks."

"You'll get over it," Livingston said. "So, to sum it up: We'll land, eliminate the outposts; overtake the facility, download any files from their computers while Jackman takes samples from their labs for analysis; Weatherford will plant explosives, and we'll determine the location of any other facilities on the planet."

"There's more?" Luke asked, his growly voice ear-piercing. To the human ear, he sounded agitated, though in reality, he was ecstatic to have a chance to engage more enemy troops and build his reputation.

"Maybe," the Captain answered. "The data we collected referenced a secondary lab. This one that we're hitting, however, is undoubtedly the primary facility where the majority of the tests are being conducted. We'll find out for sure after we've secured the site."

"Like with Boracan, security should be fairly light," Park said to the group. "These troopers haven't seen any action in months. They think they're safe from the war, since they're so far out in the Outer Rim. They're not expecting us. That said, be ready for anything."

"Any other questions?" Livingston asked. He watched the group, giving them time to address any concerns. There were none. Everyone understood their jobs. His eyes went to the back entrance and spotted Dr. Soviar standing with her arms crossed.

"What about me?" she asked.

"You'll stay on the ship with Soto," Livingston answered.

"I can handle a firearm," she said.

"I believe you," Livingston answered. "You can help us after we've secured the lab. With your training, you'll be able to identify any toxins that the Tarkadons are constructing on this planet."

"That's what you believe they're making?" Soviar said.

"That's the suspicion. The spread of disease can quickly wipe out an enemy force if implemented properly. Whatever it is, a government doesn't hold a Top-Secret lab in the middle of nowhere for no reason." Livingston checked his wrist-timer. "Alright, team. We'll be coming out of hyperspace in one-hundred minutes. Check your weapons and gear."

"Yes, sir," the team replied. All at once, they stood up from the table and went for the armory, while Soto and Webb returned to the bridge. Soviar stepped into the galley in order to make way for them. She was dressed in army green fatigues with black boots.

"Looks like a better fit than those prison clothes," Livingston said.

"Feels a lot better. That's for sure," Soviar replied. She cracked a smile, which only lasted a brief moment. "Captain, how likely are you to destroy these labs if you find them?"

"One-hundred percent. My team is the best there is," Livingston answered. "There's a reason we were chosen for this mission. Once we're done, we'll return to U.G.S. territory. Now, if you'll excuse me, I have something I need to see to. Help yourself to the rations and water. Sadly, it's mainly nutrition beans and water."

"Blech," Soviar replied, comically forming a disgusted expression.

"Yeah. It's healthy, but tastes like absolute shit," Livingston replied.

"You'd think, since they've sent you guys out into the far reaches of hell, they'd at least indulge you with decent food," Soviar commented.

"It's all part of the discipline," Livingston answered. "When we get back, I'll treat everyone to a Roarkmeli steak dinner. Now, if you'd excuse me."

He walked through the corridor and entered his cabin. Taking a seat at his desk, he pulled the recorder chip given to him by Jackman. He placed it in a display reader and watched as a plasma screen unfolded across the wall. He watched the footage of Jackman's team overtaking the east wall and converging on the barracks. After several tense minutes of blaster fire, it came to a sudden halt. As Jackman moved from cover, the recorder caught four red flashes shining through the windows. He watched as she arrived at the doorway, and gazed at Sergeant Park. In front of him were four dead bodies. Smoke trailed from each of their foreheads from a blast recently received. And as Jackman had noticed, there were no weapons anywhere near them.

An execution.

The stress he felt triggered the nerves in his face. He placed his hands over his mask and waited for the pain to dull. It would not be a pleasant conversation he would have with Park, a man he had served with for over six years. They'd saved each other's lives repeatedly in the conflicts at the Barrier Fields and ocean planet of Noctern. Every fiber of his mind wanted to overlook this issue, but unfortunately, his duty required him to confront it.

He stepped from his quarters and marched for the armory.

CHAPTER 6

"Come on ladies," Sergeant Park bellowed at the group. "I've seen five-year old kids with stick rifles look more intimidating than you clowns!" The team members ran diagnostic checks of each of their weapons, making sure each one was up-to-task. It was standard procedure, but extremely important, as residue easily built up inside the rifle barrels. They disassembled the dirty rifles, cleaned them, and put them back together. The most difficult of the bunch was Neill's 180 Viper minigun, which contained the most components. "Come on, Neill. It's not gonna fall apart at the slightest touch. Stop acting like you're playing with Lego and clean the damn thing."

"Don't knock Lego, Sarge," Neill retorted, while scraping residue from the inside of one of the barrels. Behind him, Adam Weatherford checked the explosives he would use to detonate the research facility.

"I don't suppose the Captain is looking to cover our tracks this time?"

"Negative," Park replied. "Discretion in blowing up the lab is not an issue. We don't care if the Tarkadons know it was us, just as long as it's *after* we're out of dodge. By then, we'll be done."

"Fine by me," Weatherford answered. "In that case, I'll pack the seismic-energy charges. That'll.turn the whole place into a crater."

"Fine with me," Park said. He heard footsteps coming from the corridor behind him. He turned and saw Captain Livingston approaching.

"How's it coming?" he asked.

"Dandy," Park answered. "As long as Neill doesn't screw up reassembling the Viper."

"I resent that, Sarge." The group chuckled. All except the Captain.

"Sergeant, I need to have a word with you," Livingston said, keeping his voice low and discreet.

"Yes, Captain," Park said. He followed Livingston to the cargo hold where they could speak in private. It was a dimly lit space, with a few secured crates that stored extra ammo and rations. Park noticed that the Captain looked uncomfortable. He was looking away, as though trying to figure out what to say.

"Zach," Livingston called him by his first name, "how long were you planning to remain in the service?"

"Sir?" Park cocked his head, surprised at such a bizarre question. Livingston waited for an answer. Park shrugged his shoulders. "About four years until I reach my twenty."

"That's not what I asked," Livingston said. Park registered the strictness in his tone. Finally, Park's face hardened.

"I plan on being here until this war is won. Sir."

"And how do you think we'll accomplish that?" Livingston asked. Park paused. He wasn't initially sure if he was asked a serious question or not.

"I…" he chuckled uncomfortably, "how else do we win wars? We persevere. Adapt. Overcome. Overwhelm." Livingston was still silent. Park was simply reciting the pledge from the military handbook. "What answer are you looking for, Captain?"

"How about an answer for this?" he said. He held up a portable screen, about the size of his hand. On it was the image of Park in the Tarkadon barracks where he executed the surrendering troopers. "What am I to make of this?"

Park shook his head. His eyes narrowed and nose wrinkled. The hatred that lied beneath had reemerged.

"It's called scrubbing the filth from the face of the galaxy," Park said. Livingston removed the image.

"This is *not* how we do things," Livingston stated.

"Why? Do we prefer more civil methods of killing?" Park replied.

"We've killed enough people in our lifetimes," Livingston said. "Enough to keep us awake at night. We don't need to add any more to the list when we don't have to. Fact is, those men were surrendering. You violated the rules of engagement."

"For the record, I sleep just fine," Park said. "They do this every single day. Hell, they take civilians as prisoners for target practice. I don't understand this idea that you can simply *make friends* with the enemy."

"You think this war will go on forever?" Livingston said. "Sooner or later, our two sides are gonna have to make peace. That involves us coexisting at some point."

"You don't make pacts with an invasive species. You *eliminate* it," Park growled. "Clearly you think otherwise. You probably figure we'll eventually shake hands with the Tarkadons and go about our separate ways."

"You know what I think? I think you, Sergeant, are so blinded by vengeance that you're becoming to be like the ones you hate so much." Park turned away, his eyes flaring with anger. "Don't act offended. You said it yourself, 'they do the same thing every day.'"

Park stood silent, watching the stream of light on the other side of the viewing glass.

"Maybe you're right. Maybe we should've blown up that Planetary Death Ray. We've should've taken if for ourselves."

"Come on, man, you can't seriously think like that," Livingston said. "Listen. I'm sorry for your father. The Tarkadons have many crimes to answer for.

Nobody's denying that. But exterminating a whole quadrant of the galaxy is not how we handle it."

"You're defending an empire that would gladly set a disastrous plague on our home planet," Park said. "Hell, look what they did to you. You have to wear that tin can on your face just to breathe properly."

"Refusing to stoop to their level of warfare is not defending them," Livingston argued. "There's a difference between combat and execution. There's a reason we have laws. We're not only defending our planets, but our principles. Principles you've forgotten."

"I haven't forgotten. I just no longer believe in them," Park said.

"And that's why, when we return, I'm recommending your transfer," Livingston said. "Due to your service record, I might be able to convince Command to keep you on long enough to complete your twenty. But you will no longer see combat after this mission. I'm sorry, Zach."

"If that's the way you feel, Trent," the Sergeant replied. The shakiness in his voice betrayed the feeling of contempt he felt. "Is that all?"

Livingston nodded. "See to the squad. Have everyone ready in the next thirty minutes."

"Yes, sir," Park said. Without saying another word, Livingston exited the cargo bay. Park listened carefully as the sound of his footsteps trailed off. Finally, he released his fury, and smashed a closed fist on one of the boxes. He struck again and again, denting the side inward.

He heard the hiss of an opening door. He looked over his shoulder and saw Dawn Ramos standing there. Park exhaled slowly and shook his hand.

"I'm fine," he answered her unspoken question. Ramos nodded and stepped forward.

"It's probably for the best," she said. Park stared at her questioningly. "I eavesdropped during your conversation. Moved away when the Captain left." She looked behind her to make sure nobody was around, then approached the Sergeant. He looked like the shell of the warrior he was. He looked...weak. Defeated.

"How can you say that?" he said after a couple of minutes of silence.

"Because I don't think you'll ever move on otherwise," Ramos said. She reached out and kissed him. For several seconds, they held each other close, long enough for Park to regain his mental strength and mask his emotions.

"Get your gear. We'll be coming out of hyperspace in an hour."

CHAPTER 7

Grit and sweat hit the floor as the soldiers strapped on their body armor. Battery packs slammed into the frames of blaster rifles, pistols, and Neill's enormous minigun.

"Alright, ladies! We are near our moment of reckoning!" Park's voice echoed through the armory. "I'll remind you again. The success of this mission will result in millions of lives being saved. The *right* lives! These Tarkadon pricks wanna use biological warfare on us. Goes to show that they're no good at actual fighting! In fact, they suck so much dick at fighting, they have to kill unarmed civilians for their troopers to muster any kind of body count. We're going down to Glorric, and when we meet the enemy, we will remind them why they're so desperate to create weapons of mass destruction, with a belly full of hot plasma, and the smell of their own burning meat. What say you?!"

"Sir, yes sir!" the group chanted.

"That's what I want to hear," Park said. "Now strap yourselves in! We'll be coming out of hyperspace in TWO!" Boots drummed against steel floor tile as the soldiers hurried to the fuselage. One-by-one, they took a seat and harnessed themselves in. Once the ship was out of hyperspace, Webb would initiate the disabling of the security satellites. Once that was complete, Soto would fly the ship down into the planet's atmosphere.

Dropdown was always a shaky ride.

"Neill! You know the drill! Get on the starboard rail gun!" Park shouted.

"Music to my ears, Sarge!" Neill climbed a small ladder to the upper level and made his way to the starboard weapons control. He strapped himself into the seat and activated the Viper 250 blaster turret. Though they depended on stealth, they always had to be prepared for the unlikely case of being detected. He cocked the joystick, panning the gun left, right, up, and down.

Weatherford took the port gun.

"All set," he radioed.

"Good," Park replied. He took a seat and harnessed himself in. "Captain, we're ready whenever you are!"

"Thirty seconds," Livingston replied. He stared at the swirling haze outside of the viewing glass, ready to witness it transform into a dull black vacuum. He was in the co-pilot seat with his hand on the *cloak-activation* switch, which he would flip the instant they came out of hyperspace. In the navigation chair behind him was Webb, who was set with his hacking computer.

"Ready in five..." Soto said. At the end of the countdown, the blue lights turned to white, then evaporated into black as the ship came to a sudden stop. "Holy shit!"

"Evasive maneuvers!" Livingston ordered.

Scattered around them was a world of scattered debris hurtling through the black vacuum of space. Scans had indicated no asteroid field in this sector of the quadrant, leaving Livingston puzzled as to its unexpected appearance.

Soto dipped the nose and engaged thrusters, steering the ship underneath an enormous barrel-shaped piece of debris. He arched back up, avoiding another fragment. And thus, he began the process of zigzagging his way out of the debris field.

"We've come out of hyperspace into some sort of meteor shower," Livingston announced into the comm, informing the team of the situation. Soto veered sharply to the right then drove the ship into a corkscrew motion. Livingston engaged the cloaking mechanism, then conducted a scan to navigate their way out of the debris field.

"Sir, I don't think these are rock fragments," Soto said. Livingston looked at the viewing glass, pinpointed a large hunk of debris with his eyes and studied it briefly before it spun out of view.

"Metal. Fragments of freighter hull. A ship has been blown apart out here," he said. He turned around. "Webb? You picking up any signals from the planet?"

"Negative, sir," Webb answered in a tense voice. "Then again, I'm having difficulty pinpointing them through all this shit."

"Standby," Livingston said. The scan completed, analyzing a route through the debris field by calculating the trajectory of every fragment in front of them. An energy screen streaked over the viewing glass and marked the path for Soto with a digital line that looked like a neon river winding through the field.

"Following projected route," the pilot said. "Getting us out of dodge." He steered up, then over to the left. Huge jagged pieces of shrapnel passed within mere feet of the hull. They accelerated deeper into the field, spotting interior components of the ship that was formerly composed of all these parts.

"Those are Class-M boosters," Livingston said, pointing at a large cylinder object floating overhead. Those boosters were the driving force behind thirty-five hundred foot Trek Freighters. Built for long voyages, these freighters carried heavy materials and ores used for constructing armored facilities, or hauling out debris. For a ship this size to be torn apart like this, it must have suffered a major collision, or had its proton reactor detonated from inside.

"Fifteen hundred meters," Soto said.

"What the hell did this?" Webb asked.

"No idea," Livingston said.

"This was a Tarkadon ship," Webb continued. "There are no other U.G.S. units all the way out here. No asteroid readings. That means they blew up their own ship. Why? What purpose would that serve? I don't get it."

"Corporal, we'll figure that out later," Livingston said.

"Seven-fifty," Soto continued. He continued weaving around the large chunks. Echoes of impact vibrated across the hull as tiny, harmless fragments peppered the ship. "Three-twenty-five. Two-hundred." The route leveled out, leading to a straight shot out of the field. Soto engaged the afterburners and sped out of the debris field. "Clear!"

Dead ahead was Glorric, a dark grey planet surrounded by thick clouds. Silver flashes of lightning streaked over the North Pole. There was hardly a speck of land that could be seen from orbit.

The computer pinpointed a line of security satellites that surrounded the planet. They were remote controlled structures, mostly disk-shaped with a capsule in the center for manual docking.

"Get to it Webb. Disable them before they detect us," Livingston ordered.

"I'm on it, Captain," Webb said. He went to work and focused his transmitter onto the satellite antenna. He prepped the signal blocker, only for his computer to flash *No target detected.* "The hell?"

"What's going on?" Livingston asked.

"I, uh, don't know," Webb said. He tried again repeatedly, only to find the same result. "The satellite's not responding."

"Are they blocking your signal?"

"Negative. There's no signal at all. The satellite's dead. Non-functional."

"Non-functional? I don't understand," Soto said.

"These satellites are operated from a control center on the planet," Webb explained. "To be active, they have to constantly receive a signal from a high altitude tower. If there's a void in the signal, the satellite shuts down until it is manually powered on. You can run a scan yourself, but I don't think there's anyone manning that thing."

Livingston conducted a scan. Webb was right. The satellite was vacant. With no signal from the control tower, it was just a dead piece of metal hovering over Glorric's atmosphere.

"You think they lost contact?" Soto said.

"Not sure," Livingston said. "Something weird is going on, though. Let's set course and prep for..." An alarm flashed on the sonar screen. "Proximity alert. Four spacecrafts emerging from hyperspace. Two kilometers to port and closing fast."

Soto flipped a switch, eliminating any trace of ion particles from the thrusters.

"Want me to make a go for it? Or should we wait?"

"Let's wait here," Livingston said. "Let them pass by. The cloaking device is on. They won't detect us, especially with this debris field behind us." He watched the screen as the four blips drew nearer. Ten seconds later, the ships' silver hulls reflected the sun's light.

They were Tarkadon Stingers, standard space combat vessels. They were small ships, only fifty-five feet in width. Their wings curved forward, giving the ships a crescent-moon shape. At the tip of each wing was an ion blaster. They flew in groups of two, the first row traveling fifty meters ahead of the other.

"Probably a standard patrol," Webb said.

"Keep patience," Livingston said. The ships began to circle the satellites, then looped back and began flying away from the planet. Right toward their ship. All three men in the cockpit waited in silence as the ships approached. Soto placed his hand on the accelerator. Something seemed odd about the Stingers' movements. They began to slow as they drew near...almost as though they knew they were there.

"Sir?"

The ships began to space out. Security monitors flashed on the console. Livingston knew the alarm all too well: the Stingers had targeted their ship. He activated the forward guns, locked onto one of the ships, and fired. Blue streams of plasma flashed from the forward guns and struck the nearest Stinger. In a flickering neon puff, the Stinger broke into a dozen jagged fragments of metal.

"Evasive maneuvers," Livingston ordered. Soto engaged the thrusters and looped to port. Green rays of energy streamed from the Stingers' guns, passing the ship and vanishing into the infinite distance. The Stingers initiated pursuit, firing all weapons.

All hands jolted in their seats as the ship jerked violently. Emergency lights flashed through the cockpit and tunnel.

"We're hit," Soto said. "We lost camouflage control."

"Like it was doing us any good to begin with!" Webb added. "How the hell did they detect us?" The ship shook from a second hit, this time from debris.

"Damn it!" Soto said. "They're driving us into the debris field!"

"Let them," Livingston said. He leaned toward the intercom. "Gunners! Time for you two to go to work. We have three Stingers on our ass." His mechanical voice sounded calm, yet strict.

"On it," Neill replied.

"Affirmative, Captain," Weatherford sounded.

Red blasters on each side of the ship rotated to stern and simultaneously fired red bolts at the enemy. The Stingers spanned further out, dodging rubble and energy blasts while relentlessly keeping up the chase. Green blaster fire dashed around the debris field, hitting large fragments and driving them out of their paths.

One of the fighters accelerated, making a straight line for the Recon-Valley as Soto steered to starboard, avoiding a rounded piece of hull.

Neill tensed in his gunner's seat as he centered the Stinger in his sights. He opened fire, striking the ship dead center, but not before the Tarkadon pilot got off a few shots of his own before exploding into a hundred metal scraps. The Recon-Valley shook as one of those blasts struck overtop.

"That can't be good," Neill muttered to himself.

The ship curved upward, then down again, its ion trail resembling the shape of a sea serpent traveling along an ocean surface.

The two remaining Stingers followed directly behind, whizzing back and forth to avoid debris. Livingston blasted the forward cannons, clearing a path for their retreat. Another impact struck the dorsal fin.

"Lateral controls lost," Webb announced. Right as he spoke, a piece of debris spiraled into view. Soto pulled up with all his might. Scraping vibrations traveled along the underside.

"Activate reverse stabilizers," Livingston ordered.

"Sir? While on full thrust?"

"I didn't stutter. Do it."

Soto pushed the marked lever forward into full gear. The ship vibrated as though caught in an avalanche as polarizing forces drove it both forward and back, whipping it into a spiral.

In less than a second, the ship had turned around completely. Both Stingers veered in opposite directions. Livingston targeted the one on the right and fired. The plasma cannons struck the port wing, severing it from the main body. The Stinger spiraled out of control, trailing golden sparks until smashing against a piece of hull.

The Recon-Valley continued its spin. The starboard rail gun blasted at the remaining Stinger, but missed. Soto deactivated the thrusters, diverting the power to stern stabilizers, which slowed the ship's spin. After stabilizing, he reengaged the thrusters, sending the ship after the last remaining Stinger.

Soto dodged to starboard then down, hooking under a cubical piece of engine. He immediately veered to port as a flickering piece of reactor core shielding whipped into view.

"Damn!" he muttered.

"Captain, I'm reading damage to engine-two. Not only that, but we have structural damage near area three and four. Up top. The hull's holding on by a thread," Webb said.

"That's why we have to get this last fighter first," Livingston said. "Soto, apply full power."

He could barely see the Stinger through the array of material. He armed the Heavy Reactor cannons and attempted to lock on. The targeting screen flickered repeatedly, the digital crosshairs struggling to keep track of the Stinger.

"You're gonna use the cannon?" Webb asked. "The force generated from that blast will make this debris field look like it's in a blender!"

"That's the idea," Livingston said. "Soto, set a course out of here. Be ready to go in ten seconds."

Soto plotted the course, then got on the intercom. "All hands, hang on tight. We're coming out fast."

"Just for the record…" it was Ramos' voice, *"Weatherford, you suck at shooting."*

"Appreciate it. What a blessing it is to have friends," Weatherford replied.

"Cut the chatter," Livingston said. He focused on the Stinger, ignoring the increasing pain in his facial nerves. The targeting system tried again to lock on, but failed as another piece of debris got in the way. Finally, the Captain shut down the tracking mechanism and switched to manual controls.

"Course is set," Soto said. Another moment of silence passed. Livingston found an opening and fired the cannon. The ship shook with reverberating force as the ion cannon launched an enormous streak of hot blue energy. It passed through the debris field at light speed, detonating a thousand meters away.

"GO!" Livingston said. Soto turned to starboard and engaged afterburners. The cannon blast expanded into a flaring aberration, spewing lightning strikes in all directions. Metal fragments broke into smaller pieces. The Stinger pulled up, desperate to avoid the blast, but failed to avoid one of the lightning strikes which punched through the stern. It spun out of control then smashed along a river of debris, gradually breaking apart until there was nothing left to identify it as a ship.

"Target down," Livingston said. The view ahead cleared as the ship sped out of the debris field. The three of them shared a sigh of relief before Livingston glanced back at Webb. "Damage report."

"Captain, we're gonna have to set down on that planet and fast," Webb said. "Our life-support system took a hit. We're losing oxygen supply. If we stay in space longer than an hour, we'll be permanently out of breath."

"Damn it," Livingston said. He ran a scan of the planet, searching for their intended landing zone.

"Without cloaking, we can't make our original landing destination without being spotted," Soto said.

"I'm aware." Livingston brought the landing site onto the screen, which marked the locations of the outposts according to the data Webb downloaded. "Here! There's canopy to the west, only a quarter mile from our landing zone. It'll be thick enough to provide cover."

"Let's hope we're not spotted on our way down," Soto said. He plotted the course and initiated atmospheric entry.

CHAPTER 8

Fog and smoke swirled around the Recon-Valley as the landing boosters gradually lowered it into a field of small trees. Landing gear protruded down and splashed into the wet marsh below.

"Everybody out," Livingston announced.

The team assembled at the drop center, with Sergeant Park's verbal goading filling their ears. The doors came down and the team filed out. They fanned out and immediately secured the surrounding area.

Only Doctor Soviar stayed behind. Her skin was pale; no doubt she was immensely unnerved during the recent conflict. Livingston passed her by on his way to the ramp.

"Doctor, you will stay here with Soto," he said. "Understand?" Soviar nodded, not saying a word. He looked over to the pilot, who stood at the back of the small chamber. "See what you can do with repairs, if there's even anything you *can* do."

"I'll try, sir. But life-support—there's not much I can do without replacing the whole unit. We might have to steal a Tarkadon vessel to get out of here."

"That'll make going home a lot more fun," Weatherford's voice echoed from outside.

"Keep an eye out," Livingston said. "If you have to make a run for it, do it."

"Yes, sir," Soto said. Livingston stepped out into the world of Glorric. The sky was dark with a shade of green. To the north were residual flashes from the lightning storm. His boot splashed into a small puddle filled with weeds. Beneath that puddle was solid granite. Fog swirled around the team and swallowed the ship, obscuring it from view.

The team fanned out, with Neill taking point. Behind him was Weatherford and Luke. The Vickel stopped and knelt down to observe the stem of a nearby bush. Brushing away some of the leaves, he saw how the roots seeped between tiny cracks in the earth.

"Planning on picking up a side gig as a botanist?" Weatherford quipped.

"Stow it," Park hissed. The team completed the sweep of the marsh, then reassembled near the ramp. "Looks like this area's secured sir."

"No sign of aircraft? Ground patrols?"

"Negative sir. Nothing. No signs of foot patrols either," Park answered.

"Webb, what's the distance to the nearest outpost?"

"Two-point-two miles northeast, sir," Webb replied. Livingston glanced at the map, then back up at the sky. He couldn't help but find it strange that they made the landing undetected. And how was it that the Stingers located them despite their stealth technology? Not only that, but if the satellites weren't functional, certainly one of the Tarkadon pilots must've gotten a signal down to the Command Post here on Glorric. But if they had, he had no doubt they'd be met with resistance no matter where they set down.

None of these circumstances added up.

"Sir?" Park's voice intruded his thoughts.

"Sergeant Park, move them out," Livingston said.

"Neill, Weatherford, take the lead. Luke and Jackman, stay to the left. Ramos, Webb, watch our six. Standard formation, twelve-foot spread. Watch your footing. Go."

The team moved silently, keeping a slow pace as they emerged from the thick marsh. There was a clear valley of rocks, with only a few scattered trees. Confirming no enemy presence, they quickened their pace and converged on the nearest guard post.

CHAPTER 9

"Neill, scout ahead," Park ordered. They could see the shadowy silhouette of the guard post in the dark blue sunlight. It was an odd design, almost resembling a tin can. It was two stories high, its metal exterior showing signs of rust. One thing Neill noticed in particular was the silence. He could see the power generator, but there was no humming sound coming from it. There were metal barriers surrounding the structure, with standard machine turrets on each side.

Neill wrapped his finger on his minigun's trigger as he slowly approached. So far, he saw no movement. Weatherford, Jackman, and Webb took the left flank, keeping low to not be seen. Several yards back, Ramos found some high ground where she would take sniping position. She gazed at the structure with a thermal imaging scope.

"I see nothing," she whispered into her mic. Livingston stepped forward until he was crouched near Neill. Moments later, they smelled the hot breath from the Vickel.

"Luke, Neill, on me," Livingston said. "Three, two, one…go." The three of them rushed the front entrance, while Jackman led her group around to the back. Both teams took breaching positions. Livingston armed a stun grenade and opened the door slightly. To his surprise, the locking mechanism hadn't been engaged. He tossed the grenade inside and slammed the door shut. A white electrical flash shone through the cracks below, accompanied by a dull *pop*.

Livingston's team entered first, smashing the door inward and blasting lights into the dark room. The main section of the shack was a large radio monitoring station, with powered down computers sitting on the front desk. Jackman's team entered, saw the Captain, who pointed to a small stairway at the back of the room. She proceeded upstairs, hugging the wall with her rifle pointed upward.

The stairs led to the crew quarters, which was empty. There were still personal contents left behind, such as a personal computer, reading devices, vitamins, spare clothing and uniforms, and various other belongings. They checked the second room, which was in the exact same condition.

"Clear," she radioed.

Park and Ramos moved in, joining Luke and Neill inside the perimeter barriers. The three infantrymen took watch outside while the Sergeant entered the building. His flashlight met with Weatherford and

Jackman's. Webb took a seat at the computer desk and attempted activating the monitor.

"Is there no power in this place?" he asked.

"Negative. Generator is shut down," Park said. Livingston was at the back of the main room, inspecting the small armory unit. It was a sealed mechanical box with a manual lock on the door. Livingston broke the lock with the butt of his rifle and opened it. Inside were racks for four rifles, two of which were missing.

"Jackman, how many bunks were upstairs?" he asked.

"Two. That's the standard personnel for these types of outposts," Jackman answered.

"There's no roller outside either," Park said.

"Then I must conclude that our friends left in a big hurry," Livingston said. "The question remains; why? When securing a vast area such as this, all stations have to be manned twenty-four hours a day."

Weatherford checked the kitchen area which was adjacent to the armory. He checked the pantry and refrigeration unit, seeing nothing but soggy nutrition cubes and spoiled milk.

"Hell, if I had to eat this shit, I'd make a run for it too," he said.

"Perhaps they were alerted to our arrival and are out looking for us," Jackman suggested.

"Unlikely," Livingston said. "They have assault teams on standby for such duties. Also, if they were onto us, we'd have seen signs of it between here and the ship. But we haven't seen anything. There's no reason this outpost should be vacant."

Webb stood up from the desk. "I can't get on this thing without a power source."

"Don't worry about it," Livingston said. "Let's move on to the next one."

"Another two-mile hike on the way!" Weatherford said. "Can't say we're not getting our exercise."

"No one asked for your commentary," Park hissed. The team followed Livingston out through the front entrance, where Ramos was staring out into the horizon. The Captain noticed a look of suspicion in her eyes, and a slight uneasiness in her body language.

"Something wrong, Private?" he asked.

"You hear that?" she said. Livingston listened for a few seconds, then shook his head. "Exactly. A planet with as much flora as this would typically have its fair share of wildlife. Yet, we've seen or heard nothing. No animals. Birds. Hell, even the plants look wilted." She pointed to a line of bushes that grew a few yards past the barriers. The leaves had a soggy appearance to them, vastly different to those they saw where they landed.

A distant rumble echoed through the sky, drawing their attention to the north. The lightning flashes were brighter, the clouds thicker. The storm was rolling their direction.

Luke clicked his tongue, then growled in his Vickelian dialect.

"Sorry, I don't speak dinosaur," Neill said.

"He's suggesting that if the Tarkadons were building a bio-weapon, perhaps it's possible an outbreak occurred," Webb suggested. He then noticed Neill's confused stare, then groaned in frustration. "I took a semester of Vickelian back in Fort Riker."

"Yeah...doesn't explain why the prick won't just speak *English*!"

"Ugly dialect," Luke growled.

"If there was an outbreak, they might have evacuated their forces," Ramos said. "Which would explain why we haven't seen anybody."

"Except those Stingers," Park pointed out.

"It that's the case, shouldn't we leave too?" Weatherford asked.

"Okay, knock it off," Livingston said. "And use your brains. We can't leave until we can commandeer a ship, unless Soto gets lucky and manages to repair the Recon-Valley. Listen up; we will proceed with the mission as planned. There should be a hangar bay somewhere on this planet, likely near the command center. Let's move to the next outpost, then secure the lab. After we've downloaded the data and set the charges, we'll find the hangar bay and get the hell out of here. Sergeant, move them out."

"You heard the man. Move like you're going to a strip club," Park barked to the group. Taking standard patrol formation, they proceeded west toward a series of rocky hills.

****

They moved in silence for an hour, while keeping a watchful eye on their surroundings. Livingston continued to monitor the storm, which gradually appeared larger. He estimated that it would be another few hours before arriving over their current location.

"Fuck," Neill groaned.

"What's wrong, Private?" Livingston said. The heavy weapons specialist stepped to the side and lifted his boot.

"I stepped in...something," he muttered. On the bottom of his foot was a slimy substance. It was black and oily, dripping like tar from the soles of his boot. He shone his light where he had stepped, finding a pile of that tar-like substance...mixed with thick red fluid. He panned the light further out, seeing shredded clothing lying about, the fabric coated with the black tar.

"Fan out," Livingston ordered. Neill and Luke moved over the apex of the hill. Even the reptilian felt a tad nauseous as he looked at the large valley of rocks, and dozens of rotting bodies spread all over it.

"Holy shit," Webb said. Livingston approached the lead and saw the graveyard. The group slowly moved onward, shining their light on each corpse they passed by. Every single one of them was covered in energy burns, with each of them having received a blast to the head. Some bodies wore prisoner jumpsuits, while others wore Tarkadon uniforms.

Livingston immediately noticed the condition of the skin of each corpse. Each body was in a strange state of decay. The flesh had turned grey, the veins black as though filled with oil. The same oily substance covered each one, glistening as the flashlights passed over them.

"They've been shot in the head. All of them. Even the troopers," Weatherford stated.

"Perhaps there was a riot?" Ramos suggested.

"Why would they shoot their own guys?" Ramos said.

"The prisoners probably did it. Broke out of their cells, created an uprising. Got themselves a few guns. Had a firefight," Neill said.

Luke growled, spraying saliva as he struggled to form English words.

"There are no guns here," he said, pointing at each of the bodies. His observation piqued Livingston's interest. He was right, there was hardly a single weapon to be found. As the team examined the area, they had found only three.

"Why did they shoot their own people? In the face, no less?" Webb said. He leaned down for a closer look at one of the bodies. The Tarkadon corpse was laying on its back, its face erased into scorched fragments from blaster fire, leaving no identity. Scorched brain and flesh matter caked the rocks around it, creating a horrid smell that permeated the air. The exposed skin on the neck and hands resembled wet tissue paper, the black veins looking like worms crawling underneath it.

"Everyone keep an eye out. Jackman, you're the medic. What is that in that guy's blood?" Jackman kneeled at one of the prisoner's corpses, making sure to keep any of the substance from getting on her skin and uniform. She stuck a syringe into the mixture then ran an analysis with the cell-scanner.

"Inconclusive," she said.

"Inconclusive?"

"It's some sort of pathological strain and it's intermixed with the host's cells. The recorder has detected proteins wrapping around some sort of genetic code, but it can't identify what it is. Whatever this stuff is, it hasn't been previously recorded in any medical record in the U.G.S, or any other sector of the galaxy that I'm aware of. It has probably infested all the vital organs. There's no way of finding out more without surgical scanners and trained staff."

"But what is it doing? Just eating away the cells?" Livingston asked.

"No, it's not breaking them down. It's more like it's mutating the cells," Jackman answered. She tossed the syringe away. "I would recommend not touching any of these bodies."

"You don't have to tell me twice," Webb called out. The Captain stepped away from the corpse and approached the tech expert.

"How far are we to the next outpost?"

"Another mile."

"And the distance of the research lab from there?"

Webb pointed southwest at a large mountain.

"You remember the schematics? That's the mountain they built the facility under," he said. Livingston studied the landmass. It was a big rock that dominated the horizon. He estimated it was five miles away at least.

"Sergeant. Let's continue onward," he said.

"You heard the Captain, ladies! Get your ugly asses moving. On the double!" Park said.

The soldiers moved in twos and went west, Neill taking the lead once more. Livingston gave one last look at the corpse. His eyes noticed something about the fingers. They were slightly elongated, the tip of the bones nearly punching through the fingertips like spears.

Mutating the cells, Jackman had said.

He noticed she was still standing next to him.

"This is why they've been trafficking people," she said. "They're running all kinds of strange experiments on them."

"Whatever it is, it looks like it came back to bite them in the ass," Livingston said.

CHAPTER 10

Scorched plasma burns filled their nostrils as the team trekked west. Joints started to ache from walking over solid, uneven ground. The valley had been marked heavily by some sort of conflict. They passed a few more bodies of various species, each strangely malformed by the same infection. Like the ones they passed at the hills, these corpses had been shot in the head.

A few hundred meters later, they passed by the remains of a roller. It was overturned onto its right side, its engine having imploded where it had smashed against a huge boulder. Rock and engine fragments littered the surrounding area, as though launched from an explosion.

"They had to have been flying at full speed to do that much damage," Weatherford whispered. Ramos walked around to the top section of the roller and gazed into the driver's seat, only to realize there was no seat left. The engine had caved in completely, crushing the driver into pulp. Two arms stretched from the folded metal. They were stripped to the bone.

Ramos turned around and dry heaved, prompting Park to hurry to her side. She nodded, signaling she was okay, then nudged an elbow back to the roller. Park went to take a look, then saw the bone hands.

"Oh God," Weatherford said. "Sarge, this is getting weirder and weirder."

"Did the virus, or whatever it is, dissolve this guy?"

"No," Luke said. He pointed a claw at the ground below the arms. There were shreds of uniform clothing entombed in a pool of dried blood. The sleeves had been ripped from the arms, meaning the same had likely been done to the skin and muscular tissue.

Jackman took a look, then noticed Livingston glancing in her direction.

"Don't ask me for an explanation, Cap, because I don't have one," she said.

"Burned away, perhaps?" Webb suggested.

"No burns in or around the vehicle," Park said. "It's almost as if someone took a pocket-knife and decided to—"

"We get the idea, sir," Ramos said, swallowing hard. She took another breath, which only seemed to worsen the nausea, as the odor of rotting flesh was rife in the air.

She took several steps onward, then froze. Her combative skills took over. Her ears picked up faint sounds coming from ahead. Warping sounds...blaster fire!

"Contact," she said. The team fell into a wedge formation, separating ten meters from each other. They moved out for several yards, clearing a series of rock mounds. Five hundred yards to the west was the next outpost. The world around it was bright red, as blaster fire blazed across the area.

The team knelt into firing positions, while Ramos used her sniper scope to study the situation.

"What do you see?" Livingston asked.

"Roughly a dozen Tarkadon troopers facing off against...I think escaped prisoners. I'm not sure."

Livingston lifted his thermal binoculars to his visor and watched. He saw the troops standing inside the perimeter barrier. Two were operating defense turrets, blasting away at what appeared to be several unarmed humans. He watched as their figures jolted violently after absorbing the blasts, and fall to the ground. One of them managed to rush past the gunfire, supposedly uninjured, and tackled one of the soldiers. The skirmish went to the ground, with bodies tussling violently. The thermal imaging displayed brief red flashes which he presumed was blood. Other troopers engaged on the rebel, ravaging him with dozens of blaster bolts. Immediately afterwards, two of the troopers took their injured comrade into the compound, then stepped back out to join the fray. After several repeated bursts, the machine gun firing ceased. All besiegers had been dropped, and for a moment, Livingston believed the conflict to be over. Right as he started to remove the glasses, he noticed the troopers branching out. They stood over each corpse and shot them in the head before proceeding to the next.

"Want us to take them?" Ramos asked.

"Can't leave them between us and the ship," Livingston said. "Sergeant Park, take Webb and Neill and flank left. Jackman and Weatherford, you guys flank from the right. Move around the structure and secure the back entrance. Luke and I will take center. Move fast, but keep low. Their attention is elsewhere at the moment, and they're not expecting us. Ramos, when I give the word, snipe the gunners."

"Aye-aye, Captain," Ramos said.

"And team, pay attention: let's try and take one of these troopers alive for interrogation. You read me?"

"Loud and clear, Captain," Weatherford spoke for the group.

The team split up and converged silently onto the outpost. Ramos rested on her stomach and disengaged the safety on her sniper rifle. Luke and Livingston continued straight, keeping low as they weaved between a few large rocks. They took cover behind a small stone ledge, which led to flat ground with no cover.

To the south, Sergeant Park's team dropped into an army crawl, gradually moving into flanking position. They were directly in the troopers' line of sight, while they continued checking the corpses. They could hear nervous chatter between the enemy soldiers. While they couldn't make out words, it was clear tensions were high.

Livingston watched carefully for another minute, then checked the positions of his teammates with his binoculars.

"Okay, Ramos," he radioed. "You're up."

"About time," she muttered. She adjusted her sights and focused on the center machine-gunner, after gauging the distance between him and the other. She placed the crosshairs over his chest and squeezed the trigger. The blaster bolt soared into the compound, piercing the trooper's chest. All eyes looked toward the gunner as the blast drove him back against the building. By the time they recognized the smoking hole in his chest, another blast streaked down, hitting the second gunner through his left eye, ripping his skull straight across.

Park was the first to engage. He sprang to his feet and charged the outpost, popping off shots from his rifle. Two of his blasts caught one of the troopers in the midsection. The trooper, gagging in pain, dropped his weapon and fell to his knees, holding his gut in place.

Ramos sniped another who went for the machine gun. The bolt struck him in the chest, sending him into a spin before he dropped dead on the ground.

Livingston and Luke moved in, the Vickel launching large yellow bolts of energy from his heavy blaster rifle. His shots found a trooper's center mass and ripped it to shreds as though hit with a stick of dynamite. The troopers backtracked to the building, which proved to be their fatal mistake, as they were now boxed into a shooting gallery. They fired back, hardly able to see their enemy through the fog.

Livingston fired, hitting one through the forehead. Another trooper went for the machine gun. Livingston fired repeatedly, sending six blaster bolts into the enemy's chest.

Jackman's team closed in on the right and hooked around to the rear of the building, just in time to intercept two troopers making a desperate retreat.

"Freeze!" the compassionate Jackman shouted. Refusing to surrender, the troopers turned their rifles on her and fired, missing by miles. She returned fire with a three round burst, cutting one of them down the middle. Weatherford shouldered his shotgun and hit the other, sending him reeling back head over heels for several feet.

"Should've listened to the lady," he said.

Red hot energy zipped back and forth, erupting into orange flame wherever they landed. Another trooper fell, his chest nearly aflame from taking numerous hits.

The three final troopers retreated back into the facility. The manual latch slammed hard into its slot and was followed by the beating of scrambling feet as the troopers readied their defenses. Livingston took breaching position alongside the door.

"Everyone on me," he said.

"Move in," Park ordered the men. Neill and Webb hopped the three-foot steel barrier and took breaching positions alongside Livingston and Luke. At the same time, Weatherford and Jackman came from around the corner.

"They've got the back entrance locked," Jackman said. "We set a couple claymores outside the door in case they try to make a break for it."

"Good." Livingston pounded a fist on the door, keeping clear of the viewing window. "Listen troopers! There's nowhere to go. Surrender, and I ensure that you will receive fair treatment." He was answered with distant shouting from within.

As the rest of the team prepared to breach, Park backed toward the injured trooper whom he had shot in the gut. "I'll secure this prisoner," he said to the Captain.

With nobody looking, he turned to the injured trooper. He secured his sidearm and rifle, then proceeded to make sure there were no other weapons within reach. The trooper shivered in agonizing pain, his exposed intestines billowing smoke. It was a fatal wound, thus making it a mercy to put the young trooper out of his misery. The thought brought a smile to the Sergeant's face.

The Captain doesn't want me killing unarmed prisoners, he thought. He looked the trooper in the eye and shrugged his shoulders. The trooper looked him in the eye, blood dripping from his mouth. He tried to form words, but only gagged in considerable pain.

"Can't do nothing for you son—unless." Park glanced back at the Captain to make sure his actions weren't seen. As expected, Livingston was focused on the troopers in the compound. He then drew his pistol and pointed it at the trooper's temple. "You tell me what I need to know, and I'll put an end to your misery. Blaster bolt to the stomach? Ooh." He shivered. "With no medical transport around, you're looking at an excruciatingly slow death. You think the pain is bad now? Just you wait, son." He grinned ear to ear. The subtle trembles in his face might as well have been screams.

Livingston shouldered his weapon and listened to the noises within the complex. It was obvious the troopers were barricading themselves in the back of the main room. Unfortunately, it did not appear they had any intention of surrendering. After clearing his throat, he decided to give them one final opportunity.

"Tarkadons! This is your last chance. Place your weapons on the ground *behind you*, place your hands behind your head. Take a knee and cross your ankles!"

"Eat shit, you worm loving filth!" one of the troopers shouted.

Livingston wrinkled his nose. "Have it your way, then." He glanced over his shoulder. "Weatherford, plant a charge on the door."

Weather removed a disc-shaped explosive from his vest pocket and aligned it with the internal latch.

"Want me to set a timer?"

"Thirty seconds. I want to give them a final chance to surrender," Livingston said. Weatherford set the timer and moved back behind Luke.

The troopers assembled in the back of the main room and took firing positions. Their injured comrade was on the dining table, his eyes glazed over in death. Blood dripped from the many gashes in his ribs and neck received from the mad prisoner who attacked him.

"Navy filth!" one of the troopers barked. "We will obey the High Command. Do not allow yourselves to be taken prisoner!"

"Yes, Sergeant," the other two replied. They had torn the refrigeration unit clear from the wall and placed it between them and the door, using it as cover for the inevitable invasion. Exhausted, angry, and covered in blood and soot, they waited with rifles pointed at the doorway.

The Sergeant gave one final glance at the dead trooper on the table, specifically at the Lieutenant insignia on his upper arm. Until ten minutes prior, he had been the last surviving officer, which now left the Sergeant as the highest rank...above two infantrymen.

The blood had formed a large pool under the table, which largened from the steady streams that fed out from the wounds. The Sergeant returned his attention to the door. His two infantrymen stood in front of him, each peeking around opposite corners of the refrigeration unit.

He steadied his breathing and readied his mind, focusing on the wisdom fed to him from years of propaganda. It would be an honor to give his life to the cause, even if he didn't fully understand his own government's intention or endgame.

A loud splattering sound disrupted his focus. Droplets of blood struck his pantleg. The table legs were scraping against the metal flooring, propelled by shifting weight.

The Sergeant turned. The Lieutenant was now standing, head cocked to the left, those pale eyes staring right at him. The Sergeant froze. He had heard the stories of people coming back to life, but he never believed it. It couldn't be true. Only the supernatural could achieve life after death, if such a thing existed. Even when he had to turn his gun on his own men, he believed he was putting sick people out of their misery. Not people who were already dead.

Yet, here he was, literally staring death in the face. And still, he couldn't believe it.

"Lieutenant?"

The officer stood in a puddle of his own blood, motionless as a statue. Then, as though fueled by demonic possession, the Lieutenant sprang to life. Clawed arms lashed out, grabbing the Sergeant by the throat. It leapt on him like a cat, driving him to the floor, while pressing its fingertips deep beneath the skin.

The two infantrymen turned, seeing the Sergeant on the ground, throat now torn wide open. The Lieutenant drove his face downward and bit into the gash, shaking its head to rip the flesh free.

It looked up, face bloodied, and saw the two troopers spinning on their heels. It darted to the one on the left with inhuman speed, driving him across the room and into the radio console. The trooper screamed, firing several shots into the ceiling before losing his grip on the gun.

His companion closed in and fired a shot into the crazed Lieutenant's shoulder blade. The 'officer' turned around in a blurring motion. Its glazed eyes were wide open, the lips revealing bloodstained teeth. Another shot hit its neck, but did nothing to stop it. The Lieutenant sprang with outstretched arms, driving the trooper backward. He struck it with its rifle, which did nothing to stop it. A swing of its arm knocked the gun away, and those jagged fingers found his neck and shoulders. They dug in like fishing hooks, curving under the skin before pulling outward. The trooper screamed in agonizing pain, feeling his flesh coming apart like putty.

It leaned down and bit him across the face, shredding his left cheek and nose. It chomped repeatedly, its hands digging further in.

The last trooper rolled off the radio console just in time to see his friend savagely torn apart. Fountains of blood painted the walls a dark red. The Sergeant was on the floor, staring lifelessly at the ceiling. Pieces of meat flew with each tearing motion.

In one quick motion, the officer perked up. It cocked its head, looking up and around like a bird, then rotated on its heels. Still kneeling, it glared at the infantryman. Strands of meat dangled from between its teeth as it snarled. And the trooper had no misgivings about thinking of it as 'it'. There was nothing human left.

Panic struck, and the trooper dashed for the door. The beast leapt from its crouched position, slamming hard into the console. It turned to follow him, bloodstained hands knocking over electrical equipment.

The trooper screamed and retreated to the west exit, unlatched the lock, and raced out the door. The ghoul was just a step behind him. With a bounding leap, it closed the distance, landing on his back as he stepped out.

His foot came down on the landmine, which ignited with a red flash and a deafening boom, shredding both the trooper and his attacker.

"The hell's going on in there?" Weatherford remarked. A few moments ago, they had heard nothing but hurrying feet and a few scattered insults. Now, it sounded like a full-fledged brawl had erupted. A few moments later, they heard the claymore's detonation on the other side.

Livingston turned to Jackman and Weatherford, then nodded his head, signaling for them to move around the back.

The charge detonated, blowing the door wide open. Livingston tossed in the stun grenade, waited for the loud *bang*, then breached. Smoke from the claymore had entered the room and swirled into a vortex. He saw the Corporal come around the other side, stepping over pieces of trooper.

There were two bodies, each ravaged by the blast. They had been launched several meters from each other. The blast had imploded their torsos, splintered bone, and ruptured every organ.

"Clear out here," she said. "Two hostiles KIA."

"Noted," Livingston said. He and the others stared at the carnage in the room. Luke and Weatherford checked the bodies, then looked back at the Captain with flustered gazes.

Luke growled and coiled one of his claws. "They weren't killed with a blaster."

Weatherford nodded in agreement. "I've seen enough of this shit to know this wasn't done with a rifle. But it doesn't look like it was done with a knife. It almost looks…like…they were attacked by a jaguar or something. Look at that. They've had their jugulars ripped out. And is that a tooth?!"

Luke leaned in and pried the white object from the infantryman's neck.

"Correct," he confirmed, flicking his tongue.

"Whatever happened, it took place in the span of seconds," Webb said.

"But who, or what, did this?" Jackman asked. "We saw them retreat in here. It doesn't appear anything else broke in. There's no sign of forced entry we didn't cause. No upper floor either."

They all looked to Captain Livingston. He had no answers to provide. Not even hints. He was at a loss just as they were. It was another moment that he was grateful for the helmet, which obscured the puzzled expression on his face.

Pain flooded the injured trooper's insides like magma rising within a volcano. Sergeant Park took glee in every twitch, gag, and bulging reflex in his face as the injuries took their toll.

"Man, I bet you'd kill for some morphine right now," he taunted quietly. The trooper looked at him, shaking. Those eyes focused on his pistol, which wavered back and forth. Park looked at it, then back at the trooper. To his surprise, there wasn't even a hint of anger. Just a silent plead for his misery to end. "You should be proud of yourself. A three-shot burst to the gut would kill most men. Immediately, I mean. It says a lot that you're still breathing. Then again, I guess those other guys would be considered the lucky ones." Park smiled and stood straight. "Do your intestines feel like taco meat yet? Bet if you coughed right now, you'd lose some lung tissue."

The trooper shook.

"Tell me what I want to know. Where is your home base? What planet is High Command located. Tell me now, or believe me, I'll poke you in the gut with hot sticks, and supply you with enough adrenaline to keep you even the slightest bit alive if need be."

The trooper gagged, then swayed back and forth on his knees. Park grabbed him by the hair to keep him sitting straight. Finally, he drove the muzzle into the gaping cavity in his gut. The trooper convulsed, wheezing in a level of pain he never knew was possible.

Park drew the gun back then turned the trooper's head to face him.

"Spit it out."

After several moments of heavy breathing, the trooper spoke.

"Ral'Mega," he whispered.

"Ral'Mega," Park repeated. "Which system is that in? I swear, if you lie, I'll put every Tarkadon through this hell you're experiencing. Man, woman, child, you're all filth to me."

"Steerus Star syst—" the Tarkadon ran out of breath, but it was enough for Park.

"Steerus Star System," Park said. "I appreciate it, Trooper. You've appropriately demonstrated how weak and pathetic you and your people are." He stood straight and backed away. The trooper wheezed in protest as the Sergeant holstered the pistol. "Oh, sorry. Can't afford to waste a blaster bolt. Gotta conserve ammo to, you know, kill the rest of your buddies and—"

A flash of red zipped across the valley and struck the trooper in the back of the head. Park staggered back then looked to the hills.

Livingston hurried out of the compound, rifle held at the ready.

"What happened, Sergeant?"

Park looked back at him, still caught off guard by what just occurred.

"The prisoner drew a weapon," Dawn Ramos called out. She stepped out of the fog bank with her sniper rifle in hand. "Had no choice. Had to take him out."

"That's fine. You okay, Park?" Livingston asked. The Sergeant lowered his rifle.

"Dandy, sir," he said. He searched his mind for anything he could use to change the subject. "What's the status on the hostiles? I heard blaster fire and an explosion."

"Not sure," Livingston said. "They were all dead before we even set foot inside." Jackman stepped out and stared at the bodies. They were all torn up, having been blasted in the face. Their skin was covered in the oily substance and the veins turned black. Like the bodies they found earlier, there were several malformations in the bodies, especially the mouths and fingers.

"Not all of these people were prisoners," she said. "Look. There's infected people with Tarkadon uniforms. They were shooting at their own soldiers."

"Oh, come on, it's obvious there was some kind of outbreak here," Weatherford said. "Hell, we're probably carrying whatever it is. Captain! It's your call, but I think we should get the hell out of dodge right away."

"You know what else is obvious?" Livingston said. Weatherford groaned, then looked away.

"No ship. No, I haven't forgotten."

"There's no point in staying here," Livingston said. "The best way out of here is to continue the mission as planned. We will move toward that mountain and secure the base. There'll be a data-log in there. If we find it, we can locate the hangar bay and hopefully find ourselves a ship. You hear me?"

"Yes, sir," the group replied.

"Good. Move 'em out, Sergeant."

"Yes, Captain," Park said. He cleared his throat and raised his voice. "Come on, you bunch of cows. You think I'm gonna let you stand around and milk this job? You're not getting paid by the hour. Move it out."

As the team filed out and moved west, Park noticed Ramos staring at him. Her eyes contained a fiery disdain which she could not verbalize due to rank. It wasn't simply disapproval she felt; she was sickened.

I saw what you did. I thought such cruelty could only exist at the hands of terrorists and crusaders. Not those from a uniformed army. Not my own Sergeant, and CERTAINLY not the man I love.

The words flooded Park's brain like telepathy.

"Get any information?" she asked. Each word carried its own sting.

"Enough," Park answered. "Move out, Private."

"Sir…" her facial muscles tensed. "Yes, sir."

CHAPTER 11

The air was black and silent, with the exception of distant lightning and thunder. After a quarter mile, the path took the team to a steady incline full of razor-sharp rocks and oddly formed plants. Every leaf was diseased and wilted, its roots exposed from the cracks in the rocky surface, as though trying to escape the contamination beneath.

The black tar was everywhere. The mountainside resembled the aftermath of an oil spill. There were a few bodies, though not many. Some had been stripped away to the bone, like a carcass torn apart by ravenous dogs. Others were in a similar state like those at the compound, intact but diseased and riddled with blaster wounds.

The team found a level patch of land, paved by the Tarkadons for vehicle passage. The strip circled around a patch of gargantuan boulders that protruded from the side of the mountain like coral reef. The path straightened beyond the curve, leading dead ahead into a wide flat region occupied by six heavy-duty turrets, layers of steel defense barriers, which guarded a gaping hole that led deep into the mountain. The turrets were large armored structures, cylinder shaped, and standing ten feet high. At the top of each gun was a ball that was used to rotate the barrel. All six were pointed down, indicating they were powered down.

The team moved forward as though charging a fully defended fortress. Neill and Luke hopped over the first barrier and provided cover as Livingston, Jackman, and Weatherford moved ahead to secure the next. Park, Ramos, and Webb circled to the left, checking the trenches in search of hidden enemies.

Off to the sides, between the trenches, were reinforced steel hatches. They were bomb shelters, intended for the defenders to take cover in case of an airstrike. Park descended into the first trench and inspected the controls on the hatch. It was locked tight, unable to be opened except from within the base. Judging by the buildup of residue on it, like the rest of the defenses, it had been locked shut for a long time.

The Sergeant looked to his commanding officer. "Nothing," he said.

"Proceed into the cave," Livingston said. The soldiers ignited spotlights on their helmets and rifles and aimed them into the mouth of the cave. The tunnel was fifteen feet wide, its interior walls made of smooth metal which contrasted the rough appearance of the rough rock mountain around it. The spotlights illuminated overhead light casings that ran along the ceiling, which had either been deactivated or had deprived their power source.

The team split into two and entered the tunnel. After a hundred meters, the tunnel entered an enormous chamber. At the center of this chamber was a large, rectangular elevator pad, located between two vacant guard posts.

Sergeant Park walked the perimeter, finding stairwell entrances that had been devastated by explosives.

"There's no way we'll be able to walk down there, Captain," he said. His voice echoed through the chamber and down the tunnel. "The only way into the facility is down this elevator, or to locate some type of back entrance."

"Webb. Check the console. See if you can activate this elevator," Livingston ordered.

"On it," Webb said. He hooked up his device to the terminal and ran a diagnostic. "Station's on reserve power. I'm running a bypass to divert power to the main elevator. And. Here. We…Go."

White lights lit up around the platform, and the control console came alive. Webb proceeded to run another bypass to access the security frame. The console screen flashed green, while a light formed around a diamond-shaped button which would activate the elevator.

"Load up," Livingston said. The team assembled on the elevator and gave one final glance into the enormous chamber before the elevator lowered. They passed through three hundred feet of reinforced steel before slowing to a stop in another large dome-shaped chamber.

On the north end was a set of sliding doors. They were made of two-inch steel, originally dark grey in color. The door on the right had been knocked off its frame by a tremendous force, its center crushed inward, turning the door into a bowl. Both the doors and the tunnel they guarded had been coated with thin layers of the strange oily residue. On the floor were the remnants of footprints. There were hundreds of them, as though a stampede of humans had raced all at once for the very elevator they stood on.

Jackman proceeded to take an air reading with her air quality scanner.

"AQI reads seventy," she said. "Moderate, but there are signs of pollutants."

"Move up," Livingston ordered. They moved by twos, with Weatherford and Park being the first to enter the busted door. Behind the entry was a fifty-foot tunnel. On the other side was a sign reading *Processing Lab.*

They quickly pushed through to the other side. There were two guard posts on each side of the entrance, and in the center was a walk-through scanning device. The room was a lobby full of desks and medical charting equipment. A glass door on the left had been smashed, the fragments covered in residue and dried human blood. In that room were syringes and countless bottles of various vaccines, antibiotics, and disinfectants.

No wonder they call it Processing, Jackman thought as she explored the room. The Tarkadons would bring their prisoners through this room and evaluate their health and behavior, scanning for toxins and diseases that would interfere with whatever they were going to pump into their bodies.

There were no bodies. Just blood, as well as a few blaster burns in the walls. Livingston moved to the far-left corner, checking three glass-sealed cubicles. Each one had two seats: one for the doctor, the other for the patient. It was obvious who sat where, as the patient's seat had metal shackles attached to the armrests. At the far end were open cabinets with spilled sedatives and broken syringes lying about.

Just another part of the 'evaluation'.

Livingston proceeded to the back corner and studied numerous blaster burns on the wall. Directly below them was a mucky pool of blood, which had been intermixed with the strange oil substance.

Where's the body? If a riot took place, why take the time to move it?

"Move on to the next room," he ordered. At the back of Processing was another corridor. The sliding doors were already open, though the sliding gears appeared to have been tampered with. Not to keep them open…but to keep them shut.

They entered a corridor that had been riddled with deep grooves, as though marked by a goliath beast with razor claws and titanic strength. Here, the blaster burns were much more frequent. Depleted battery packs littered the floor, along with a couple of blaster rifles, whose frames were smothered in human blood.

Weatherford raised his shotgun and peeked around the broken entrance. He signaled *all clear* and proceeded in.

The team entered the atrium for the Main Chemical Lab and fanned out. All eight soldiers stared in awe at the enormous room in which many of the horrendous tests had been conducted. It was a thousand feet long at least. Red flashers flourished overhead, illuminating steel holding cells, enormous surgical machinery, and the many desks where the scientists conducted their work. On all four sides of the room were second-floor platforms. Some were clearly used as security guard posts, as they contained nothing but a chair, desk, and rifle rack. Others were used for other testing. They contained advanced computers and mechanical equipment that he did not recognize, nor fathom the purpose of. The Captain noticed a green glow coming from each of the chambers that lined the center of the lab. It wasn't an electrical light. Looking hard enough, he could see the individual particles rolling about in the air like a fog.

The soldiers hustled along the perimeter and secured the lab. Like with processing, it was vacant, with signs of violent conflict. Several of the glass chambers had been ruptured, the contents forming a black pool on the floor. Chairs and desks were overturned, computers smashed, rifles left unattended.

Jackman approached one of the glass chambers at the center of the room. There was a rotten smell in the air which intensified as she drew near. She pointed her rifle light through the door.

Propped up against the wall was a rotten corpse. It was shirtless, the flesh peeling from the bone like a banana. The meat had a gooey texture to it, appearing as soft as gelatin. The jaw was hyperextended, the cheeks nearly gone. Above them was a blaster burn where the nose had been.

"Christ." Neill's voice made her jump. She caught her breath and proceeded to the next chamber. That one was empty, except for the strange green mist that floated inside of it.

Corporal Webb boarded a hydraulic lift on the left side and elevated to one of the second floor platforms. He stepped onto a smooth steel surface and inspected the nearby machine. Mechanical arms were built onto a seven-foot slab, which contained restraints for the subject's arms and legs. One of the restraints had been ripped away entirely, the other three forced open. Slimy footsteps crusted on the floor, leading all the way to the ledge. Webb's imagination completed the picture, envisioning an enraged patient leaping twelve feet down. He looked at the substance that marked the footprints. The patient was barefooted, indicating that whatever this stuff was, it was secreting from his skin. He looked at the mechanical arms that arched over the slab. Some of them contained surgical drills and twelve-inch needles.

"What in God's name were they doing to these people?" he whispered.

Livingston's voice broke the silence.

"Webb. Come back down here and access the main computer."

"On my way," Webb answered. He got back on the lift and came back down. As he stepped off the platform, he noticed the Vickel staring at a row of large coffin-sized containers that were set along the back wall. "What the hell are those?"

"Don't worry about it. Worry about that terminal. Find out where these corridors lead to," Livingston said. On each side of the lab were two sealed entrances. In addition to being locked electronically, the frames had been fused together. Webb proceeded to the computer and ran his security bypass, which allowed him access into the mainframe. He scoured the program for the interior map and security system. Meanwhile, Weatherford and Ramos backtracked to Processing, where they found the welding torches discarded randomly near the initial entrance.

"Doesn't look like it was set here on purpose," Weatherford said. The fuel cannister was half full. He tested one of the torches, shooting out an inch of blue flame. Ramos hesitated in picking up the other. The shaft was smothered in blood, and its cannister was marked by an oily handprint. Even Weatherford appeared disgusted. "Don't bother," he told her, shaking his head. "I'd rather we don't risk it. Wash it off; spray it with an ocean of disinfectant...I don't care. I don't trust anything in this place."

"I hear that," Ramos said. When they returned to the Main Chemical Lab, they noticed their Captain inspecting the strange row of containers. They resembled sarcophaguses from ancient Egypt that preserved mummified pharaohs. The difference was that these sarcophaguses were made of a thick metal that Livingston could not identify. Each one was hooked to a series of cords and tubs. Some of them resembled IV lines; others were clearly electrical.

"Any idea what those are for?" Ramos asked.

"They're designed for shipment," Livingston said.

"What's in 'em? Pathogen?"

"No. They'd be airtight," Jackman said. "There'd be no use for whatever those tubes are."

Luke ran his claw along a tiny slit on the side, then attempted to pry the thing open.

"Negative," Livingston said. Luke backed away. "We don't know what's in this thing. If it's contagious, I don't want to risk letting it out."

"Oh, we're looking at quarantine when we get home, I promise you," Weatherford said.

"Probably," Livingston concurred. "Right now, I want those doors open. Weatherford, let Ramos do the welding. I want you to begin planting explosives in here and in Processing."

Ramos took the torch from Weatherford, then gazed at the enormous laboratory.

"You think you have enough explosives to destroy all of this?"

Weatherford smiled and shoved the cannister into her arms.

"Girl, I'll have this whole mountain coming down on this place," he said. He tossed his pack from his shoulder and opened it. Inside were over a dozen charges. He held one up and armed it. "Two of these alone are enough to turn this entire lab into scrap metal." Ramos eyed its oval shape.

"Looks like you ought to be playing football with that thing," she said.

"I'd be lying if I said we never did that during off hours," he quipped. He hustled into one of the far corners of the lab and planted a charge.

Ramos took the torch to the right corridor. With a hot blue flame, she cut through the patches, sending tiny snippets of metal floating to the floor.

Livingston and Park approached the main computer. Webb continued to punch in numerous codes, bringing up Top Secret files.

"I have a name for you," he said. "How do you like *Star Virus*? Has a nice ring to it, doesn't it?"

"What the hell is it?" Park asked.

"Don't know," Webb said. "I'm no scientist. There's nothing but equations on many of these files. I can download it, but you'll need someone else to translate it."

"Doctor Soviar might be able to do that," Park said.

"Maybe. But it's not necessary," Livingston said.

"I disagree," Park said. "It's up to you, but I advise we try and bring back hard samples of what we find in here. She's a scientist, so she might know how to do that properly. Plus, she might be able to help us make a report on our findings. I don't know what most of this shit is." He pointed at the various machinery.

Livingston took a moment to think. *At the very least, Soto should bring the ship near in case they had to make an escape.*

"Webb, can our comms get a signal out of this mountain?"

"The portable radio can. I've already boosted the signal," Webb answered. Livingston took the radio and extended its antenna.

"Raven-Valley, this is Captain Livingston. Do you copy?"

"Loud and clear, Captain," Soto replied.

"What's the status on the repairs?"

"Oh, it gets better and better. I've got fried circuits. There's no fixing life-support. The thrusters are damaged and there are at least three areas where the hull is compromised. Sir, I can confirm that this ship will NOT be leaving this planet."

"Copy that. Soto, are you able to fly it over to the big mountain on the west?"

"What's the distance?"

"Roughly six or seven miles."

"Yeah, she'll hold together for that," Soto answered. *"As long as we don't encounter any other resistance. On that note, what's the status of the Tarkadon's stronghold. I'm not gonna get blasted out of the sky, am I?"*

"No. But I do want Dr. Soviar here. I have a few questions to ask her."

"Copy that, Captain. We'll be lifting off in five."

"Copy." Livingston lowered the radio. "Neill. Luke. Take the lift and spot for Soto when he gets here. Use flares if you need to. Have him set the ship down on the southeast barrier."

The two giants hurried back through the corridor. A moment later, they heard a metal clang as Webb retracted the security locks on the north corridor. Another clang echoed behind them as the south door unlocked.

Ramos stepped back from the north door and began work on cutting through the patches on the south.

"Where does that lead to?" Livingston asked Webb.

"Genetics," Webb answered.

"Copy. Weatherford, you and I will explore Genetics. Sergeant, you and Ramos explore the south corridor once Webb gets it open. And you," he pointed at the tech, "wait here for Soviar. I need her to look at some of these files."

"Yes, sir," Webb said. Livingston unslung his rifle and approached the north corridor. Webb hit a button on the computer, opening the door. Livingston and Weatherford aimed down the long corridor, confirming no threat, then proceeded inward.

CHAPTER 12

Livingston hated narrow tunnels, especially when he approached a juncture. In enclosed spaces like this, he was the most vulnerable. Every time he spotted a bend in the corridor, he envisioned an enemy soldier waiting around the corner. And on many occasions, that turned out to be the reality.

Out of all the times he infiltrated deep corridors, this one was probably the worst. There was a presence in the air, as though something was watching him. The drone of the air current did little to ease his nerves, and the smell was worse. It was the smell of rotting flesh, and something else. He could only describe it as a thick, soupy smell, which seemed to fit with the quality of the air. It was heavy, like he had entered a swamp.

Weatherford had the good sense to put a rebreather on. Even that didn't keep the smell out of his nostrils.

They cleared the juncture and took the left turn. Twenty feet ahead of them was Genetics. Broken lights sparked as the reserve power continued its attempt to feed power into them. The doors were crumpled and peeled back like flaps of dead skin.

Upon entering Genetics, they saw large cages to the right. The bars were bent and covered with slices of skin. On the floor were drops of blood surrounding human teeth.

They proceeded further in. On the floor were two lab scientists, dead and decayed. One of them held a blaster in his hand, which was positioned less than a foot from his head. A self-inflicted wound? Livingston glanced at the other. The corpse was on its back with a gaping hole in his brow.

"Looks like *Frankenstein* killed *Ygor* and turned the gun on himself," Weatherford said. *Why?* was the unspoken question. Livingston placed each step carefully. His light landed on discolored walls. The mixture was thick in this room and was covering almost everything. It had formed black blobs on the floor near the desks and cages.

There was a corner in the wall up ahead to the right, where the room combined with a second, larger laboratory. They proceeded and turned the corner. There were four enormous slabs, positioned at forty-five degrees. Each one held a dead prisoner. Three of them were human, the fourth a species known as Crullen, a tentacled-faced alien. Its normally green skin had turned brown, its eighteen-inch tentacles frozen in coiled positions. The humans stared back with white, soggy eyes, their mouths slack, fingers clenched. Their grotesque appearances visualized the agonizing death they had clearly suffered.

"Christ, what the hell were they doing to these people?" Weatherford said. He shined his light on the machine, particularly the huge syringes attached to the mechanical arms. "They were injecting these people with something. What was it?"

"Whatever they were creating, it was both liquid and aerosol form," Livingston said. He panned his light over at a ten-foot tall, pressurized gas chamber. Inside was another corpse, which had been put to death with a blaster bolt to the head. Weatherford looked at the way the door had been smashed open. The reinforced glass had burst outward, the steel frames marked with nail scratches.

"This was busted out from within," he said. "Call me crazy, but I don't think this guy broke out on his own. I think there were others in here." Livingston nodded. The room was spacious enough for at least six people. Maybe even eight.

The Captain continued walking through the lab. His light reflected off a series of glass containers. Inside were small test animals preserved in formaldehyde and water solution. He looked at the first one, which contained a rat-like creature with bug-like eyes and an elongated snout. He had seen these creatures before, but something was off about this one's appearance. Its skin was blistered, its claws elongated. Even its teeth seemed sharper than the average specimen. Normally, they were flatter, designed to chip wood. There were other specimens of equal size; lizards; squids; each a malformed version of its former self.

At the back of the lab was another corridor.

"What was that?" Weatherford said. Livingston aimed his rifle at the open tunnel and listened. For a few moments, there was silence. Then, he heard it: a faint echo of what sounded to be someone in pain. Weatherford looked at the Captain. "A survivor?"

"Perhaps. Or a Tarkadon trooper. Only one way to find out," Livingston said.

****

Sergeant Park and Ramos entered the south corridor and followed it to a small stairway. At the bottom, they found the galley and kitchen area. The walls had been scorched by flamethrowers, the food supply completely destroyed.

"I guess somebody wasn't a fan of the menu," Ramos said.

"It wasn't the food they were trying to burn," Park said. He shined his light down near the dining section, where several human corpses had been burnt to the bone. Their black skeletons almost appeared alive, frozen in twisted postures, charred pieces of tissue and clothing hanging off of their ribcages. It reminded him of Catholic sketches he had seen depicting hell with the dead rising from the earth in flames.

At the kitchen entrance was a juncture. They followed it into another corridor on the left all the way to staff quarters and offices. There were enough beds for thirty scientists and a few commanding staff, all of which were empty. There were not nearly enough to house all the soldiers on site, which meant the barracks was separate from this facility; likely near the hangar bay, wherever that was.

Park found the Station Commander's door. It had been left open. Station Commanders were *required* to keep their doors locked at all times, due to the sensitive information contained in their computers. Park stepped into the room and saw the Commander lying in the corner, propped up against the wall.

At least, it was whatever was left of the Commander. His uniform had been ripped to shreds, as though put through a blender. His flesh was even worse; minced, shredded, pulled apart. Rotting intestines were looped on the floor, dark brown in color from exposure. Park found himself staring at the corpse. His mind struggled to piece together what had happened. It looked as though he'd been attacked by a lion. But one thing was for sure; whatever did this, it wasn't what killed him. The blaster pistol in his hand and the exit wound on the top of his head made that clear.

Park looked behind him to the opposite wall. There were faint blaster burns in the wall. Such faint burns were caused by decreased energy, which usually happened if the blaster bolt exited through its intended target. He took the pistol from the Commander's hands and checked the battery.

"Saved the last one for yourself, didn't ya?" he said.

"Oh, Jesus," Ramos exclaimed. Park glanced back and saw his lover backing out of the office. "What the hell did that? It's like something…ate him?" It came out as a question, to which Park simply shrugged.

"I'd ask him, but…" he shrugged again then stood up.

"Zach?" she said, her voice low.

"Not now, Private," he said. He was sure to address rank, hoping to end the argument on official terms. Ramos shook her head and clenched her jaw, keeping her arguments in as long as she could contain them. A blinking light on the desk caught her attention. "What's that?"

Park took a look, then smiled. It was a portable hard-drive, which had been wired to the office computer. About the size of a football, it was the size of an old-fashioned iPad. A blue light flickered, indicating it was in *powered-down* mode. He tapped a button on the side, which brought the screen to life.

Download complete.

"Well, look at *that*!" he said. "Looks like the jolly Commander here was in the process of downloading classified files before bolting for the exit. Explains why the door was left open. Dumbass should've barricaded himself in here. Probably could've held out for a few days at least. Punk's got himself his own ration bar and hell," he opened a hinge-door at the back of the office, "his own personal shitter!" He unhooked the portable unit and carried it out of the door.

"What are you doing?" Ramos asked.

"What does it look like?" Park said. He proceeded to slip the data into his pack. "This could contain vital intelligence. They want me out of the war. Fine…I'll stay out. Officially, that is."

"So…what? You planning on going mercenary after you get out?"

"Can't win with the diplomatic talking heads mucking things up," he said. "In case you haven't noticed, this is a weapons-testing site. There's not just bio-weapons being worked on here. With this info, I can find the location to other Death Rays the Tarkadons may have."

"How brave you must feel, dedicating your life to the war effort, even after military service." Park didn't appreciate the sarcasm. "So, you're not giving that to Livingston?"

"Nope. It'll just end up in some tech's lab, the data passed further up the chain. And nothing will be done in the end. If they don't wanna finish this war, I will. I know how to infiltrate enemy ships. I know how to find passage to Tarkadon space."

"So…is there *any* information you're willing to share with the group?" Ramos said. Park turned and stared her in the face, the same look he gave any unruly subordinates. Once again, it was an attempt to win the argument by pulling rank. Ramos didn't back down this time. "I saw what you did, back at the guard post. What'd you find out from that trooper?" There was a brief pause. "You think I didn't watch you? You were getting some information out of him. Something you didn't want to share with Livingston."

"None of your concern," he said. He started walking off again.

"You do know my sniper scope had a recording device," she said. Park stopped again. "It may not pick up audio, but Livingston might not take kindly to seeing that footage of you torturing the prisoner."

Park looked at her the way a bull eyed a wrangler before charging.

"Ral'Mega," he said. "That's where their High Command is located."

"Ral'Mega," Ramos said. "And you're planning on doing what with this information, exactly? You haven't told the Captain, so whatever it is, it probably won't go well with the Military."

"My mind's working on it," he stated.

"And you're confident that information was accurate?"

"I always know when someone's lying to me," Park retorted.

"Yeah…was he a Colonel, by any chance?" Ramos said. Park opened his mouth to speak but stopped. He stared into space, slowly realizing his mistake. "Nobody here would know that kind of information…save for maybe the dead Commander fella. Zach, you've allowed yourself to become so jaded, you don't even have good judgement anymore. Any infantryman out of basic would know some cock-a-doodle-doo trooper isn't gonna know shit." Park didn't say anything. His face flushed while his mind went in circles.

How did I fuck up so bad? If anyone else had done the same, he would've had them whipped.

Ramos stepped up to him and placed a hand on his face.

"Zach…turn that device over to Livingston," she said. "Do it, and I'll overlook everything else." They stood silently, gazing at each other. "Please." It came out just above a whisper. Park looked away. He was never one to accept defeat. Unfortunately, he was at a crossroads. It was clear Dawn would not be with him if he continued on this current path.

Finally, he considered the path she would rather have. Moving on from his hatred, living a normal life, maybe have a family. He ran his hand over his chest and felt the silver emblem on his necklace. *Mau'lena.* He thought of their conversations of building a home on the grass plains and living out the rest of their days in paradise. With a military pension, which would be gracious for a Sergeant in Special Forces, they could easily afford it.

At that moment, Ramos pulled her matching necklace from beneath her collar. It was a deliberate move, and it worked. Park took the device from his pack and held it out to her as a sign of good faith.

"Thank you…Sergeant," she said. Her voice took on the role of a military operative. She tucked the necklace back and stood ready with her blaster rifle.

"Get that to Webb," Park said.

"Yes, sir," she said.

****

Weatherford rested his finger on the trigger as he and the Captain arrived at the end of a small stairwell. Electric wires sparked from a broken fuse box somewhere to the left. Otherwise, the chamber was entirely dark. They entered the room and pierced the darkness with their lights.

The room was as large as the lab they recently inspected, but this was nothing like it. This was where they stored the prisoners. All around the perimeter were holding cells, each barely enough to fit two prisoners. Each

84

bunk was barely enough to contain an average-sized man, much less some of the larger species they captured. There were dozens of holding cells across the room. In the center was a dining area and a few guard stations scattered about, with an elevated post on each corner of the room.

Containment doors had been ripped open. Blaster rifles were scattered on the metal floor. The soldiers each took a side and moved down the room, inspecting each holding cell for any survivors. They met at the center of the far side.

"Anything?" Livingston asked.

"A couple of bodies in a fucked-up state. Like—like the others. Molded skin, but not like normal decay," Weatherford answered.

"Same," Livingston said.

"It doesn't look like there's a way out of here," Weatherford said. "I swear we heard something."

"Shhh," Livingston hushed. Weatherford clamped his jaw shut to control his volume, then mouthed *my bad*. They proceeded to inspect the bodies and weapons in silence. Then, finally, they heard it again.

There was no doubt this time it was a human moan. It was coming from the corner, left of the entrance. They shined their lights but saw nothing. Livingston raised his beam to the elevated guard post. There was movement.

"Contact," he said. He raised his voice. "Show us your hands." There was no response from above. "Show us your hands." Again, there was no compliance. No sign of aggression either. Then again, any kind of non-compliance could be a sign of malintent. Livingston wasn't going to wait. "Weatherford. There's a panel attached to the hydraulic. It's battery powered. Lower it. I'll cover you."

Weatherford moved to the panel, keeping his shotgun pointed at the platform above. As he hit the switch, the person let out another moan...followed by a high-pitched squeal. They heard him battering the metal floor, as though rolling in pain. Weatherford backed up and stood a couple of meters to the right. The person was a prisoner, or at least he was wearing a prisoner jumpsuit.

"Sir? We're U.G.S. Special Forces. We're here to help," Weatherford announced. The platform reached the bottom. The prisoner was in the fetal position, shivering intensely as if in Antarctic weather. Weatherford approached, lowering the shotgun slightly. "Sir, speak to us. Are you in pain—"

"KILL ME!" the prisoner screamed. He was suddenly on his hands and knees, looking like a rabid dog. Their flashlights streamed onto diseased skin, broken teeth, disjointed fingers, and pupils that had turned forest green in color. He yelled again, "KILL ME!" Bloody saliva sprayed from his gums, along with the oily mixture.

"Sir, just wait. We have a medic on our team. We'll have her come take—" The prisoner leapt from the platform and rushed him. He sidestepped and swung the shotgun barrel low, catching the prisoner below the knees. Momentum drove him into a tumbling fall, which knocked over tray tables and spilled their contents onto the floor. "That's your warning," Weatherford said.

"Please," the prisoner groaned. "Kill me."

"Negative," Livingston said.

"You have to! I'm already dead. Kill me now!" He groaned loudly, then convulsed in agony.

"Livingston to all units, we have a situation here in Containment, past Genetics…" As he spoke, he noticed the prisoner reaching for something on the floor. It was silver…a knife. "No…sir, don't you even think about it."

He was way past that point. The prisoner sprang to his feet and, baring all his teeth, charged the Lieutenant. Both soldiers opened fire, ravaging the prisoner with blaster fire. He spun and fell, his skull split open.

"Holy fuck," Weatherford muttered.

"Lieutenant?! We heard blaster fire!" It was Sergeant Park's voice. After a few seconds, they heard running feet coming down the corridor. A minute later, Sergeant Park arrived with Ramos and Jackman. They lowered their rifles after seeing the Captain and Weatherford standing at ease, then gazed at the dead patient.

"What the hell happened?" Ramos asked.

Livingston stepped back, took a moment to process what just occurred, then replied. "He was a survivor. He rushed us. There are signs of genetic testing in Genetics, and it looks like this guy had been subjected to it. He was, uh—" he took a closer look at the dead prisoner, "covered in that stuff we found the other bodies in. It looks like it's secreting through the skin."

"Yeah, we saw it on the way here," Ramos said.

"Are you okay?" Jackman asked. Livingston pretended not to notice her concerned expression.

"We're fine," Weatherford spoke for him. He glanced around the room again, then at the Captain. "So, what's the plan from here? Should we try and see if there's any lower levels? Want us to collect samples?"

"Negative. Just images. Then return to the Main Chemical Lab," Livingston said.

Neill's voice suddenly burst through the commlink. *"Neill to Captain. We've got Soto inbound."*

"Copy that. Bring the doctor to the main lab. I wanna know what she can tell us. Meanwhile, Webb, try and figure out where that hangar bay is. Livingston out."

"This shit isn't normal, Cap," Weatherford said.

"No, it's not," Livingston said. "Whatever they were doing, it turned on them. And whatever it is, we can't let it leave this planet. Do me a favor: plant another charge in Genetics. Whatever this stuff is, I don't want it getting out of here."

"With pleasure, sir."

CHAPTER 13

Soviar took in the cool wet air as she stepped off the Recon-Valley. Directly ahead were the station's defenses, all shut down and abandoned.

"Welcome to Paradise Resort," Neill called to her. "Here, you'll get to enjoy a variety of luxuries, such as a bed-and-breakfast…if you enjoy slabs. You'll experience an exotic view, meet lovely new people, get a massage at our high tech—"

"Okay, John," Soto said.

"Thanks," Soviar said, rubbing her temples. She was slow to approach the tunnel. Her eyes seemed fixated on the derelict defenses. If felt like she was entering a haunted mansion.

"You okay there, Doc?" Neill asked. For once, he wasn't being obnoxious.

"Yeah. I'm fine," she answered.

"You don't have to go in there. I'll message the Lieutenant if you're uncomfortable. He's a good man, he'll understand."

"No!" She was even surprised at the suddenness of her reaction. "Sorry. Thank you. I'll be happy to help." She proceeded toward the tunnel, leaving Luke, Neill, and Soto glancing at one another.

"Ooookay then," Neill said. Soto nodded. The doctor was acting a little detached since they'd arrived.

Then again, she was in a prison camp for a month, barely survived a massacre, and now she's on some weird planet some hundred million lightyears from breakfast, going towards the big black tunnel of death.

"I'd probably be on edge too," he said to himself. Luke remained with him to keep watch, while Neill escorted the doctor. She was quiet during the entire elevator ride. On the walk to the Main Chemical Lab, she was visibly antsy, especially after seeing the devastation in Processing.

"My God," she muttered, looking at the busted doors and residue. She held her hands up to make sure she didn't touch anything. "You guys didn't do this?"

"We *are* that good. But unfortunately, we can't take credit," Neill said.

They entered the Main Chemical Lab. Webb was seated at the Main Central computer. On the screen were an array of digital files, some of which stated status logs, research reports and findings, updates in chemical formula, and many other things that Webb did not understand.

Standing behind him was the Captain, who turned around and saw Soviar.

"Thank you for coming," he said. Soviar stepped over to the computer.

"You found this lab like this?" she asked.

"Correct. Didn't fire a shot...well, not until we reached the holding chambers. There was a crazed patient who forced us to shoot him."

"My God," she said.

"Doc, can you tell me what they were developing? It looks like some kind of pathogen, but I'm not clear what it's supposed to do. If it was something like smallpox; something just designed to kill and spread, I'd just blow up the place and be done with it. But this is different. I've seen chemical weapons put to use. They're not like this. I think they were developing a mutagen, but for what purpose, I have no idea."

"Let me take a look," Soviar said. She took Webb's seat and began scouring the files. Each one contained several terabytes of data pertaining to past research and equations. *"Regmaten. Torring Solution. Rophine?!"*

"What's that?" Webb asked.

"That's a cell regeneration drug. It was designed to repair tissue damage. But it was canned after it was determined that it caused rapid cell reproduction. I thought it was still in the experimental stage," she answered. "If you inject that into a person's bloodstream, it could cause cancers. But they're not doing that, they're injecting it into this virus."

"Why would they do that?" Jackman asked.

"For the virus cells to reproduce faster," Livingston said. "They were making a plague."

"It gets weirder," Soviar continued. "It looks like they've added a drug called Rahm."

"And that is...?"

"It's a drug designed for tissue repair in the brain," Soviar said. "It's supposed to trigger the neurons, but has limited effect."

"They're putting a brain drug into a virus?" Weatherford spat. "They trying to cure Alzheimer's as they kill everybody?"

"Doctor, what use would a drug like that have in this kind of compound?" Livingston asked. "Being a brain enhancing drug, it won't have its intended effect if the body's full of toxic compounds."

"No. Unless..." Soviar's voice trailed off. "Its only purpose would be to jumpstart the brain after death." She leaned back in the seat, bemused at what she was reading. "That doesn't make any sense. Not with those other toxins added in there. At best, it'd reactivate the brainstem. Maybe some of the prefrontal cortex."

"So, they're killing them…and bringing them back to life?" Weatherford asked. His serious expression cracked into a smile.

"You'll want to download this information if you're looking to take something back to your base," Soviar said.

"What else is there, Doctor?" Livingston said. Soviar started looking through the files. Many of them were daily adjustments to the serum, namely dosages of the many individual components. What followed were what seemed like a hundred novels worth of notes. "They've cataloged everything. And I mean, *everything,*" she said.

"Well, my superiors aren't going to care about all of that shit," Livingston said. "We need something concrete that the dumbest politician can understand."

"Hang on, I think I found something they might find interesting," Soviar said. Several dozen files flashed over the screen before she stopped at a video log file. She clicked one of the folders and watched the feed.

The footage was from Genetics. Several scientists stood around one of the slabs, which contained a patient, restrained at the arms and feet. His voice flooded the speakers as he pleaded to be released. The mechanical unfolded like squid tentacles. Two of them carried large syringe needles, the vial filled with a glowing green fluid. The patient let out a bloodcurdling scream as the needle entered his neck.

The scientists began rattling off data, such as time, reactions, and fluid amounts.

"*Let's up it to ten milliliters of Star,*" one of the scientists said.

"Star Virus," Webb muttered.

"*Skin discoloration at forty-one seconds,*" one of the scientists said.

"*Eye color at fifty-three seconds,*" another said. "*Cell reconfiguration has begun.*"

The patient began to convulse on the slab. The scientists injected sedatives into his IV lines, which resulted in a brief slowdown before the patient convulsed again.

"*Heart rate elevating.*"

"*Scan shows bone splinters. The cellular structure is altering.*"

The patient's screams became so loud that Soviar had to tone down the speaker volume.

"You think they'll understand *that*?" she remarked.

"What the hell are they doing to him?" Jackman asked. Soviar didn't immediately answer. She looked over a few more files, read the list of chemical compounds, then fast-forwarded to the next chain of events.

"*Day two. Patient 34 deceased, two hours, eleven minutes. Monitor is now reading new brain waves. Scanner reveals minute activity in prefrontal cortex.*"

"There's the Rehm working for you," Soviar muttered.

"What the hell is that on his skin?" Jackman asked. She leaned over Soviar's shoulder and zoomed in on the body on the slab. The high-definition image revealed the prisoner's tan skin had turned a dark grey. The wet texture reflected the lights in the room. "That stuff wasn't on him in the previous footage."

"That's because it's been several hours," Soviar said. "The virus has had more time to overproduce. The residue you see is the waste left over from the membranes."

Neill glanced over at the crusted surface of the desk he was leaning on, burped up some bile, then backed away.

The footage continued. The scientists backed away in a mixture of joy and shock as the head began to move. The eyes opened and the fingers unclenched. The soldiers noticed the bony appearance of the fingers. They had grown nearly another inch or so in length, their tips like needles.

The body turned its head slowly, like a child seeing the world for the first time. Then, in the blink of an eye, it became a ravenous beast, lurching at the nearest scientist with gaping jaws. Teeth clamped down in numerous bites, while its sickly snarls filled the audio.

Jackman looked sick. "They've brought people back to life?"

"That's what it looks like, Corporal," Soviar said. She opened up a series of notes pertaining to the test subjects. She spent several minutes reading through them, then closed it. "Yep. It reanimates the brain—ish."

Soviar turned in her seat.

"Your suspicions are correct," she said. "They've developed a mutagen; a virus, that once it enters the body, it attacks the cells and turns the host into a carrier. Once the transformation is complete, it proceeds to reproduce more cells, and uses the body to spread the virus to a new host."

"So, this virus has an intelligence?" Livingston asked.

"Don't know about calculated intelligence. But in living organisms it takes, it restarts the brain. Jumpstarts it. According to the notes, they've had subjects come back to life in a matter of minutes, while others took hours. The person is dead, but living, with no purpose but to mindlessly spread the virus. To do that, the virus triggers the basic drive for all living species."

They looked back at the footage, as a reanimated corpse continued to snap at the doctors. It snarled, shaking its head and arms as it tried desperately to get at the guards. It was clear what instinct the virus triggered.

The instinctive need to feed.

Livingston had seen enough. He turned toward Sergeant Park, who had begun working with Webb to withdraw data from the portable unit he had taken from the Commander's office. They wired it to one of the secondary computers and began accessing it.

"Looks like we'll need a password," Webb said. "Oh…here we go!" He typed in a code, bypassing the security access. A series of files came up, mostly security design for the fortress as well as plans for other facilities. Webb cracked a smile. "What would you guys do without me?"

"I'll see to it you get promoted when we get back," Livingston quipped.

"Yeah? Make me a Captain?"

"In your dreams," Livingston retorted. They went through a blockade of files, many of which detailed plans for research facilities on other planets. Most of them were in the construction stages. Additionally, there were battle plans detailing the intended targets for the Star Virus. "We can check this stuff out later. Does this thing have any details for the other security outposts…and a hangar bay?"

"Hang on," Webb said. He punched several keys and brought up a map of the settlement. "Found it. Looks like they have a base roughly twelve clicks north of here. They've used construction equipment to flatten out a small region. Won't take us long to get there if we use the Recon-Valley."

"You wanna chance that, Lieutenant?" Park asked.

"Yes," Livingston. His tone displayed definitiveness. He did not want to stay on this diseased planet any longer than they had to. "Complete the download of all necessary data. Then pack it up and let's get the hell out of here."

"Sounds fine with me." Webb secured the portable terminal and returned to the main computer. Soviar was still seated there, going through files. "Excuse me, Doc, but I'm gonna need to steal this seat so I can—" he glanced at the file on the screen, titled *Brute,* "What the hell's that?"

There was a single edited video log for the Brute file, which displayed a Tarkadon soldier receiving a dose of a serum, administered by scientists. The clip jumped to footage of the soldier performing inhuman feats. One scientist took a metal bar, tested its strength by shattering a stack of bricks, then handed it to the soldier. He took the bar and, without displaying any kind of strain, bent the bar into a loop. The soldier's muscle mass had visibly increased. However, due to a series of tattoos on his neck as well as a scar on his brow, it was clear it was the same soldier.

"What the hell? They're testing the virus on their own men?"

"A different strain," Soviar said. "This one focuses on muscle generation. But…it looks like it didn't go as planned." The clip moved on to the next segment, which contained a video log from one of the head scientists.

"This is Doctor Kettig. This report is to be given straight away to Major Liskai. Project Brute must be delayed until we can find a way to counteract the adverse effects of the serum. Within three hours, the patient complained of visual delusions. Thirty minutes later, he experienced bleeding due to a rupture in his kidneys. We need more time to find a way to control the mutative properties of the compound. Otherwise, it proceeds to mutate the host to the point they're no longer...human."

The footage then showed the trooper, completely malformed, assaulting two troopers. With ease, he ripped one of them in half, splattering the camera with his innards before proceeding to pound the other into the floor. Blood completely obscured the image, leaving the viewers to simply listen to the grinding sounds of body parts mashing into the floor. That sound was soon replaced by blaster fire and the shouting of various other troopers.

"Damn," Webb said. *I might want to download that as well.*

Soviar stood up from the seat and made way for him. Webb sat down, only to jump back up as the room flashed dark red and an ear-shattering alarm rang out through the entire facility.

CHAPTER 14

"Ow, damn it," Soto snapped. The reflective panel popped off a series of sparks as he tried to repair the wiring. It proceeded to spark even after the wires fell away from each other. "So much for fixing the cloaking mechanism."

"Just reroute the power," Luke said.

"I already tried that," Soto said.

"Use spare parts," Luke said.

"Look, genius, why don't you give it a shot?" Soto said. Luke growled something in his native language, which caused Soto to shake his head. He looked over at the Vickel. "You said something mean, didn't you?"

The Vickel bared his teeth in a hideous attempt at smiling.

The levity lasted a moment, as high-pitched alarm sirens filled the air. Soto and Luke raised their weapons and looked around for any sign of hostile presence. So far, there was nothing, on ground nor in the air.

Luke grunted a series of growly words and looked at Soto, who simply shrugged.

"I have no idea what it is?! Do I look like I've built this place?" Soto placed his headphones on and adjusted his mic. "Sergeant Park. I've got alarms blasting in my ears out here."

"We're aware. We think we might've tripped an alarm somehow while accessing the computer. We'll be coming to you shortly. We have coordinates to the hangar bay. Prep the ship for takeoff and await our arrival."

"Affirmative, Sergeant," Soto said. He hurried outside and yelled to Luke. "Help me close these panels. We're about to make a fast getaway." Luke holstered his blaster and sprinted around the bow to secure the open panels, while Soto performed a final fusion needed in the port engine. "Come on. Come on. Come on," he muttered repeatedly.

****

"Get that alarm shut off, Corporal," Livingston barked. Webb frantically tapped keys to scour the computer's security systems. The swirling red lights flashed in his eyes, inducing a feeling of disorientation and madness. Soviar covered her ears and backed away from the computer, bumping into Neill. The gunner grabbed her by the shoulder and led her to the center of the room, grouping with Park, Ramos, Weatherford, and Jackman.

"I got it," Webb shouted. He tapped a flashing button on the screen, ceasing the alarm. Another alarm immediately replaced it, this one sounding like a ringing bell. After several seconds, it subsided. The team embraced the silence like a cool wind on a hot summer's day.

"Damn…that worked better than a hot mug of Joe," Weatherford said.

"Is that download complete?" Parked asked, his tone expressing sheer impatience.

"Sorry, Sarge. Got a little distracted," Webb said. He clicked a few buttons and resumed downloading all the necessary files. "Almost done."

"Alright. I'll wait here. Sergeant, move the team out," Livingston said.

"Wait…sir?" Weatherford called out. He stepped toward the metal sarcophaguses at the back of the lab. "I hear something."

All eyes went to the steel tombs. They were vibrating, shifting a few millimeters side-to-side. Deep within, a distant growl reverberated from each one. Next was a sizzling sound of air, identical to those during the opening of a pressurized door.

"Private, get your ass away from those things!" Park yelled at Weatherford. Thin white clouds zipped from each coffin as the front section shifted forward. Weatherford backed away and the group spread out. Suddenly, all nine coffins burst open, revealing the horrors they contained. Each coffin contained a hellish fiend; products of Tarkadon experiments, previously human; now, horrendous monsters with greenish-black skin, glowing green eyes, claw-like fingers, and gaping jaw that gaped to impossible proportions.

For a brief moment, they appeared to be rotting corpses waiting for all eternity, staring out into the world with glowing, dead eyes. Several words rang through Livingston's mind all at once: Ghouls; demons; zombies.

All at once, they came to life, leaping from their containers, effortlessly ripping the medical cords from their bodies. Like famished canines, they charged the fresh meat in the lab. The squad opened fire. Blaster bolts zipped across the room, punching through ribcages and torsos. But the ghouls were unfazed, despite vital organs being ravaged.

"Holy fuck!" Weatherford shouted. He fired a shotgun blast, throwing one of the creatures back. It flipped over a table and hit the floor, only to stand back onto its feet. Innards trailed at its feet as it sprinted for another assault.

The team dispersed as the monsters invaded the center of the room. As they backtracked, Ramos threw an impact grenade at the gathering of beasts. The resulting explosion shook the room, shattering equipment and body parts. The explosion caught three of the creatures, reducing their rotting bodies to chunks. Others were knocked down, their bodies ravaged by shrapnel. There was no concern for injuries, no sense of disorientation, no fear, nothing.

They were dead already.

They sprinted and attacked the group at random, forcing the team to spread out across the room.

"They're not dying!" Webb shouted. He leapt up across a computer table as two of the creatures closed in. They folded over the desk, grasping for him unsuccessfully. Blaster bolts struck their shoulders, spraying oily matter onto the floor. With smoke sizzling from their wounds, the ghouls turned around and bared teeth at Ramos, then proceeded to chase her toward one of the elevated platforms.

As they ran after her, another series of blaster fire cut into them. Park gritted his teeth as he sprayed energy into one of the undead, striking its left ribs and shoulder. Bone and meat fell away in charred scraps until the arm broke away entirely, separating a few inches below the shoulder. The limb hit the floor and flopped, the fingers continuing to coil as though grasping invisible prey. To the creature, it was nothing but a mere scratch, as it continued chasing after Ramos. Park could see the tiny remainder of its arm outstretched. The damn thing was still trying to grab her with its non-existent limb.

Backtracking to the front of the lab, Livingston shouldered his weapon and fired, hitting an advancing ghoul in the torso. Jolting with each blast, it kept coming at him. Coiling hands lunged at him, grazing his vest as he jumped out of reach. He aimed low and fired, rupturing both of the ghoul's knees. It fell forward with a grunted snarl, then proceeded to crawl after him. He pressed the barrel down to its head and squeezed the trigger, erupting the skull into a sizzling mess of pink and grey brain matter.

The blood hadn't even finished its splatter before he heard Soviar screaming across the lab. She staggered back against a wall, with one of the creatures closing in on her. She lifted a chair and thrust it out, blocking its jaws as it leaned in for a bite.

The Captain aimed carefully and fired a single shot. The blaster bolt entered through its temple, blowing a perfectly round hole in the side of its head. The 'life' instantly left the undead creature, causing it to slump at Soviar's feet.

"Headshots!" he yelled. "Only take headshots!"

"Late for the party, aren't ya Cap?" Weatherford shouted. He fired a shotgun blast, popping the head of one of the zombies like a balloon full of sludge. It was his second kill.

Sergeant Park tapped the trigger, striking Ramos' pursuers in the back of the skull. They fell to the floor, their driving force eliminated as quickly as blowing out a candle.

Silence engulfed the lab.

"Son of a..." Webb finished his statement with a sharp exhale. The troops reloaded and assembled at the main computer. Webb, eager to leave, checked the downloading process. "Oh, good, it's finally done."

"Yeah, it helps if you have something to kill the time," Neill remarked.

"Knock it off, Neill," Park said.

"Nice of you to join in there, big guy," Ramos said. She walked past him and tapped his minigun.

"Oh, shut up. It takes a few seconds to charge up, and by then those things were on us," he said defensively.

"Hey," Livingston said. His loud mechanical voice and faceless expression brought the confrontation to a close. He walked over to Soviar and helped her to her feet. "You okay, Doctor?"

"Yes," Soviar answered. She looked around the room, amazed to see the team unharmed. Her eyes went to the corpses that were ravaged by the grenade. The bodies had been burst open entirely, the arms and legs broken into fragments. Dark fluid leaked in thin streams from each piece, forming a lake of blood and secretion.

Ripples in the pool caught her eye. The rings streaked out from a head which had been severed from one of the bodies during the blast. Its neck was attached to a chunk of upper chest. Bones stretched out from the body fragment like tree roots. The head was marked with shrapnel and burns, though the skull was unfractured. The jaw snapped, the eyes rolling back and forth in search of prey.

"That's fucked up," Neill said. He drew his sidearm and shot the head through the eye. He glanced at Ramos and smirked. "There. I got one."

"Those coffins were meant to be dropped on enemy territories. The security system we triggered must've opened them," Livingston said.

"No shit. We got the live demo of what they were doing here," Weatherford said.

"I don't know what I did to trigger the system," Webb said.

"I'm not accusing you, Corporal," Livingston said. "But it would be nice if you packed up your gear so we can leave." Webb shoved the portables into his pack, zipped it tight, then collected his gun.

"Ready when you are, boss," he said.

There was no need to bark further orders, as the team filed out the back door in unison. They assembled on the elevator platform and activated the lift.

"Stand by, Soto, we're on our way up," Livingston said.

CHAPTER 15

Soto started the engines. The port engine rattled violently as it came to life, shaking the Recon-Valley. He routed minimal power to it, testing the durability of the damaged shaft inside. No warning lights came on. With a little luck, it would hold together for the journey to the hangar bay.

Luke watched the damaged engine carefully, then looked to the cockpit window and nodded at Soto. He moved back, passing through thick walls of fog as he watched for the rest of the team. Any minute now, he would see the shining elevator lights streaking out through the tunnel. After a few seconds, he could hear the mechanical hum as the lift completed its elevation. Those lights flashed and the team hustled out through the tunnel as quickly as they could.

Between it all, he heard something else. Beyond the engine's groan and the team's approach were the sound of additional footsteps. There were many of them, scraping along the rocky surface. He looked back and forth, unable to see through the thick fog that billowed around them.

"I hear something!" he growled.

"It's just the team you hear," Soto said into his commlink.

"No. Not them," Luke answered. He pointed his claw to the arching patch around the west rock wall. The sounds of footsteps grew louder and more frequent. Luke could hear other sounds. They were living sounds, like animalistic growls. They were difficult to pinpoint, as they seemed to be coming from everywhere.

The scraping grew more intense over the hill. Luke watched it carefully, his lower jaws baring teeth. Whatever was causing the sounds it was living, yet, the movements didn't appear organized like a military unit. It almost seemed like a wild animal, or a pack of them, was climbing the other side of that hill. Whatever it was, Luke didn't like it. He raised his weapon and approached the sound.

As he investigated, the team approached the rear trench and began moving across the planks. Livingston could see the Vickel taking a few cautious steps toward the rocky incline. His weapon was charged and ready to fire,

"What's the problem, Luke?" Livingston said. The Vickel didn't have to answer. The Captain could hear the sounds himself. There was something over the hill…and yet…it sounded like it was coming from below. "Weapons ready," he warned the team. Everyone could hear it, and after the events in the lab, they were ready with hairpin triggers. Park and Weatherford flashed lights into the trench.

Nothing. Yet, the snarls and scapings were unmistakable. There was something below their feet. Livingston began to sweat under his helmet, something he would never admit to his team. However, it was evident by the tone in his voice, and there was nothing he could do to stop that.

"Everyone, on the ship now."

The team filed onto the bridge and began to move across. At that moment, the hissing and snarling was overshadowed by several mechanical creaking sounds. The Sergeant shone his light back into the trench and panned it to the far end. With a loud whine, the hatch doors slid open. Immediately, the growling and hissing grew louder across the defense area. Park looked back to the opposite end of the trench. The bomb shelter had opened there as well.

Scrawny hands with elongated fingers reached out from within, and in less than a second, four infected corpses hauled their bodies free from their entrapment. Dripping with black fluid, they raced across the trench for the fresh meat above.

"Son of a bitch!" several troops yelled as they opened fire at once. The creatures were like hyenas, clawing their way up the trench walls. Two of them had their skulls imploded by blaster fire, while the remaining two made it to the edge. One of them made it to the top, turned to face the team, and screamed with its claws outstretched. Its mouth stretched twice that of a normal human's, the teeth rotten and serrated. The Tarkadon uniform was nearly falling off its chest, exposing the bite marks it had received in life.

Livingston sent a blaster bolt through its eye socket. The second one made its way up top. Corporal Jackman fired a burst, hitting it in the neck and lower jaw. The creature spun, then, with no indication of pain, turned to face the team again. Its lower jaw hung from its face by a few tissue strands, which seemed to stretch like gel as the jaw weighed down. It began to charge.

The Corporal fired another shot, this time putting the blaster bolts through its face. As she caught her breath, the growling grew louder. The team looked up ahead. Between them and the ship, over a dozen creatures emerged from the two trenches, each of them marked by gashes and bites received before taking shelter in the bomb shelters, where they soon became trapped when the power was shut down. Some of them trailed intestines as they moved, which dangled from ribcages that had been torn outward.

"Fucking alarm opened all the hatches," Weatherford said. He looked to the one on the right as several infected corpses started darting out. He pointed his shotgun and fired repeatedly. He caught one as it emerged, blowing its head to shreds of pink and black. The next one caught the blast in the neck. It lurched backward from the force, its head peeling off its mangled neck. With a sticky peeling sound, it detached entirely, biting at the dirt as it rolled away.

"We're gonna have to go through them," Livingston announced. "Go."

"Don't hit the damn ship!" Park shouted. They pushed forward across the bridge and spread out. They fired at will, the hot energy bolts cutting through infected flesh. Creatures climbed out from the trenches and rushed the team, feeling no pain from the hot energy that punched through their chests and shoulders. There was no rhyme or reason to the way them moved, other than the fact that they wanted to sink their teeth into their new prey. They moved with great speed, making head shots hard to land. Red energy streaked past their targets, whizzing far into the horizon.

They closed in on the squad like a stampede of wildebeests, forcing them to spread out. Weatherford slammed a fresh battery into his shotgun. As he did, one of the zombies closed in. He thrust the butt of his weapon out, striking it along the temple. It fell backward into the path of another, slowing it down long enough for Weatherford to shoulder the shotgun and aim. The blast caught the top of its head, which erupted into wet, infected matter. He pumped the weapon and aimed down at the first. It sat up, its gums splitting as it screeched. The blast blew its face clean off. It fell back, its head reduced to a bowl containing brain and residue.

"Ha! You like that you piece of walking pus!" He fired a shot, which struck one in the chest. He pumped the weapon and fired again. With all the gunfire, he didn't catch the sound of claws scraping against rock behind him. Pebbles trickled into the trench, knocked free from the body weight of an undead fiend pulling itself over the edge.

Weatherford fired another blast, blowing the skull off another zombie. He pumped the weapon and aimed again. At that point, his brain registered the hot breath touching the back of his neck. His eyes widened, and he started to turn. The creature struck first. It thrust both hands out, the fingertips lancing through his ribcage like arrows. Weatherford gasped in pain, then proceeded to scream as the fingers curled inside of him, grasping inches of organs and tissue. His attacker pulled him forward and pressed its mouth to his neck. The jaw clamped down, shredding skin, arteries, and muscle.

Livingston and Jackman turned toward him simultaneously. Weatherford struggled in the zombie's clutches, his shotgun wavering far out. The Captain grabbed the medic and pulled her away. Less than a moment later, the shotgun went off, sending a spray of energy right where she had been standing. The Captain rushed to help the Specialist, but it was too late. The creature fell backward into the trench with Weatherford in tow, landing between two others who had delayed in emerging from the bomb shelter.

They converged on the helpless Specialist, whose screams intensified as they dug their hands into his body. They ripped flesh away with razor-sharp teeth, spewing blood from each wound. One grabbed his left hand and clamped its jaws over his index and middle finger, severing both of them with a loud crunch. As Livingston reached the edge of the trench, another had emerged from the hatch. It reached out and wrapped its hands around his head and jaw, then pulled with all its might. Weatherford struggled, flapping his arms and legs in agony. Then all at once, his body went suddenly limp, simultaneous to a wet, crunch sound from his neck. The head detached, the fiend holding it like a trophy before biting into the cheek.

Livingston shouldered his weapon and shot each one in the head. They each fell over the bloody mess that had been Weatherford's body. There was one more shot to take. He fired a round into his severed head, liberating Weatherford of an eternity of spending his afterlife as one of these things.

He spun on his heel just in time to put a blast through another corpse sprinting his way. As it fell, another scampered out from the trench directly ahead and came for him, only to be cut down by Jackman. Several others approached and began to swarm the team. They were everywhere! Several groups of troopers must have taken refuge in the shelters, not realizing at the time that they were locking themselves away with others who had been infected. What were supposed to be safe havens became death traps.

"Oh God!" Doctor Soviar gasped. She held her blaster out, unsure where to shoot. There were too many targets, all moving randomly, yet all at once.

Livingston ran to the right, blasting an approaching ghoul along the way. Adjusting his rifle to full auto, he unleashed a wild spray of blaster bolts into the horde. One of them caught a blast to the head, while the others were drawn his way.

"Get everyone to the ship!" he yelled to Park.

"But sir…"

"That's an order," Livingston said. "All except you, Neill. Take position over there, and I'll draw these bastards into a crossfire where you won't have to worry about hitting the ship."

"Yes, sir," the gunner said.

"Go! Go!" Livingston yelled to Park. He backtracked to the edge of the trench, firing at the horde. With the undead drawn toward the Captain, the team hurried toward the ship. A few zombies didn't fall for Livingston's diversion, instead preferring to go after the team. They were met with a volley of gunfire that cut them to pieces.

Neill scampered up the hill on the left and took position. As he readied his gun, he noticed two creatures quickly moving up after him. They looked like insects, their necks twisting in odd shapes as they moved on all fours.

"Shit, shit, shit," he muttered. They were too close for the minigun, which forced him to draw his sidearm. As he did, he saw the flash from yellow energy striking between the two corpses. The shot exploded like a grenade, launching both bodies apart. Livingston glanced across the defense line, seeing Luke perched up on the hill. Smoke lifted from the muzzle of his heavy blaster. Neill gave a quick nod of appreciation, then proceeded to rotate the barrels of his minigun. The horde was almost on top of the Captain. Unless he made some distance, there was no way Neill could kill the horde without getting him too.

Livingston reached the edge, continuing his spray while keeping an eye on his team as they hurried toward the ship. Over twelve undead corpses converged on him. Blood and slime trickled from their bodies and mouths as they reached with bony hands.

Livingston turned. He would not reach the walkway in time. There was only one chance: to jump. The undead were right behind him. With no time to think of a different strategy, he jumped as far as he could, tossing his rifle ahead of him. He reached out as he descended, crashing into the opposite trench wall. To his surprise, his hands caught the ledge.

Neill unleashed the fury of his minigun. Thousands of rounds minced the group of walking corpses with ease. Pieces of meat flew into the air as though launched from a grinder. A large grin creased the gunner's face as he watched the cause-and-effect of his blasts. After several seconds, he released the trigger, and looked at the puddle of pulverized bodies.

Livingston hauled himself up and collected his rifle. He gave one quick look at the aftermath, then gunned down a couple of corpses that had fallen into the trench during their pursuit. He shared a thumbs up with Neill, who returned the gesture.

They met in the center and trekked across the walkways, crossing each trench before finally arriving at the entry ramp. Luke approached from the right, continuously glancing over his shoulder.

"What's wrong, Luke?" Livingston asked. By the time he finished speaking, he heard it. Snarls. Footsteps. Rocks shuffling about. A moment later, the top of the hill was crawling with an unfathomable number of corpses. Drawn by the alarms, they had climbed the steep hillside. Their screams filled the air as they raced down the inner side, coming right for the ship.

Livingston closed the ramp.

"Go, Soto! Take off!"

The pilot lifted on the control. The turbines roared to life, the vertical thrusters lifting the ship upward. The Recon-Valley ascended several meters before a loud clanging sound burst from the port engine, followed by an array of sparks.

"Fuck!" Soto yelled. Emergency lights flashed as the ship dropped. It hit the ground, flattening several corpses that had assembled underneath it. The horde advanced, crawling over the ship like ants. They pounded on the ship with their fists, gathering onto the wings and tail thrusters.

Livingston hurried into the cockpit and took a seat.

"What's the matter?"

"Fucking port engine, Captain," he said. "I put too much power into it too fast. Shaft was bent. Probably broken in half by now." He lurched backward in his seat as several undead began piling onto the nose of the ship. Their hands smeared their residue over the glass. They leaned forward, putting their rotting, soulless eyes directly in front of the pilot. They proceeded to pound the glass with all their might. Countless fists struck the glass with inhuman strength and endurance.

Livingston watched the cracks rapidly traveling across the panel. It was a matter of seconds before they would be inside.

"Divert all energy from Engine 2 and hit the afterburners!" Livingston said. Soto didn't argue, despite knowing that engaging the afterburners while only a hundred feet from a mountain could spell certain doom. But doom was already looking them square in the eye. At least smashing onto the rocks would be a quick end.

Soto drew a quick breath and hit the afterburners, then felt himself being driven into the back of his seat as the ship shot forward. Livingston pulled up on the controls as hard as he could, pointing the bow up to a forty-five degree angle. The Recon-Valley blasted upward, scraping its underside against the rocks.

The ship arched over a long valley, its twisting motion throwing several of the undead from the hull. They hit the ground below, splattering like mud pies. Livingston and Soto fought for control of the ship, but the starboard engine could not supply power to stabilizers and thrusters at the same time. Livingston activated the comm.

"Get strapped in if you're not already. This won't be a gracious landing." He set a course for the hangar bay. Already, they had passed a few miles. At their current speed, they would arrive in a matter of minutes.

The sound of scraping brought his attention back to the viewing glass. One remaining corpse reached down from overhead, holding on tight to one of the rifts in the hull above. A moment later, another one reached down. There were at least two corpses crawling down the glass, obscuring their view. They pulled themselves lower until their upside-down faces gazed at the prey inside. They salivated, their black spit trailing high into the air.

"Cap?" Soto said.

"Maintain course," Livingston ordered. The creatures proceeded to pound the glass. The cracks widened.

"I can shake them off," Soto said.

"Don't do it. She can't handle the stress," Livingston said. The creatures struck in unison. Finally, a flake of glass shot inside, nearly grazing Soto's face. He stared at the flesh-eaters, intensely grabbing his controls. Livingston saw the look in his face. "Pilot! You follow my orders."

"I can do it," Soto said. Ego and fright were assaulting his senses with a ferocity mirroring the creatures' attack on the glass.

"Negative," Livingston said. "We will make it." Soto's grip tightened. Beads of sweat trickled from his brow. Another flake of glass, the size of a nickel, broke free. The ghoul tried sticking its mouth through the gap. Its teeth separated, the long, green tongue slithering inside. Its breath filled the cockpit. "Use your blaster," Livingston said. "Make sure you get its brain."

Soto drew his blaster and thrust the barrel into the open mouth. He squeezed the trigger and watched as the zombie was instantly launched from the glass, its grip lost with its life. The other one moved to the gap, then with no thought of consequence, it tried sticking its head inside. Soto fired again. The wind caused its brains to plaster over the glass, while the body was flung over the top. Soto caught his breath, then holstered his weapon.

Soto relaxed, ignoring the heavy draft pouring in from the panel. He looked over at Livingston and nodded. Through that blank mask, he could read his Captain's thoughts. *Always trust my judgement.*

"You were right," Soto said out loud. It was the closest he could get to making an apology. The Captain nodded.

"You did good, kid."

"Thanks, I—" Soto looked up at the sight of streaking lights. Green lasers cut through the air, grazing their hull. Two Tarkadon Stingers zipped down from a thousand feet above. Their shots struck the ground below and erupted, throwing chunks of rock across the landscape.

Soto jerked the control to the left, evading another wave of blasts. The Stingers angled themselves wide, then closed in from opposite sides. They were caught in a crossfire. Soto had nowhere to go but down.

"Brace yourself, Cap," he said. He took the ship into a plunge, bringing it between a valley of rocks. Several lasers crossed overhead. One of them caught the starboard thruster, while another struck the port wing. The ship shook and fragmented. One way or another, it was going to come apart. Soto leveled the ship as best he could then descended as though landing on an airport runway. "Crap." Unable to swerve over a large boulder, he elevated again, grazing the top of it. He lowered the ship again and touched down as gently as possible. Metal groaned and electric panels sparked as the ship scraped against the planet's surface.

The ship fishtailed, rolling onto its starboard side. The wing snapped like a toothpick, the engine splintering into shards encased in energy flame. The debris spread into a swamp where most of the flames sizzled out in the water. The larger plants, however, lit up like a furnace, causing the fire to build, then spread rapidly to adjacent flora.

The Stingers circled overhead then gained altitude. Several thousand feet in the sky, they each performed a spiraling loop, bringing them down toward the wreckage for one final assault.

A crack formed down the center of the Recon-Valley's hull, traveling from the nose to the dorsal fin. From there, it traveled to the portside of the fuselage. An ear-piercing groan filled the air, followed by a crack, and the ship splintered into fragments.

Screams filled the airlock, where the team had strapped themselves in. The wall tore away completely, making way for racing winds and rubble. Finally, all fragments of the ship slowed to a stop, with the cockpit landing two hundred feet ahead of the rest of the ship.

The team waited in silence for a moment, glancing at themselves and their companions. Remarkably, other than a few bumps and bruises, nobody had been injured in the crash.

"Damn. Soto's good," Webb said. The silence was overtaken by the drone of two approaching Stingers.

"We're not out of this yet, ladies," Park said. "Move it out! Come on! Come on! Let's go! Move it!" The soldiers grabbed their weapons and hurried out of the broken ship and ran into a field of burning debris. They saw green lights flickering above, followed by an explosion behind them. The fuselage erupted, sending bits of metal whipping into the swamp nearby. The shockwave shook the earth and echoed for miles.

Park glanced back and forth, making sure all of his soldiers were accounted for. The orange glow of the flame glinted off of their faces and uniforms. That glow, along with the scrapes and burns they now wore on their faces, gave the appearance that they had walked straight out of hell.

The Sergeant looked up. The ships had traveled far into the distance and were beginning to circle back. He looked at the Recon-Valley's wreckage. The fuselage had been completely destroyed, as had the mess hall, sleeping quarters, planning room, storage, and engines. However, the back of the ship appeared to have been broken away.

Park looked back. The thrusters had broken away and began to burn over a hundred yards back. Between them and the ship was another compartment of the ship: the armory, as well as portions of storage compartment. Without saying a word, the Sergeant sprinted to the wreckage.

Weapons and ammo had been scattered about, many of them damaged beyond use. Stepping over a series of busted rifles and the rack that had contained them, Park searched for a large metal container.

Several small explosions made him jump back. Battery packs had begun exploding into large bursts of plasma, their cores having been ruptured during the crash. He backed away and looked again. After several seconds, he found what he was searching for: a large metal container containing a rocket launcher.

As the Sergeant closed the distance to the weapon, the team branched out to reduce the risks of being picked off by the approaching ships. There was nowhere to hide, with nothing to provide cover from the inevitable storm of energy that was moments from starting.

"Fuck! Where do we go?!" Soviar cried out. She was bruised, frightened, and disoriented. The world was a blur of flames, oddly shaped plants, black residue, with the drone of turbine engines growing louder with each passing second. She looked up into the distance and saw the two ships completing their turn. Their guns took on a green glow as they charged. "They're coming back!"

Neill and Ramos stood side-by-side, looking at the threat, then at each other.

"Fuck it," Ramos said. She found a relatively flat surface, lay on her stomach and propped up her sniper rifle, while Neill spun the barrel of his minigun.

Either we drive them off, or we'll get blown up. Fact is, if we do nothing, we'll get picked off eventually.

He pressed the trigger, sending a barrage of blaster bolts soaring straight toward the enemy. He waved the barrel in a small circle, spreading the volley to increase the likelihood of striking one or both of the Stingers.

It was like flying into a sudden storm, with high winds blowing the rain horizontally. Except these raindrops were made of hot energy that burned at a thousand degrees. Sparks flew off the hull as several bolts made their mark. Both ships separated, their green lasers flying high over the team.

Neill kept the barrage going, focusing on the ship that angled to the left. Smoke trailed behind it. The gunner had inflicted several hits, though the spacecraft remained functional.

"Damn," Ramos said. "They broke away before I could make my shot."

"Eh. You would've missed anyway," Neill quipped. He felt her jab his shoulder. Suddenly, a stream of blue caught their attention. Plasma bolts ripped from the forward cannons, still attached to the fuselage, and struck the fleeing ship in the back. It spiraled out of control and smashed down into the rocks, its core erupting like dynamite. Neill squinted from the blue and green flash, then realized what happened, as did the rest of the team.

Luke roared triumphantly, while Webb and Jackman proceeded to cheer loudly at the other end of a huge pond.

"Nice work, Cap!" the medic shouted.

The console spat red sparks in the Captain's face. The reserve fuel cannister for the computers died, resulting in the computer powering down.

"Good shooting, boss," Soto said. The pilot had a long gash running from his forehead to his nose, thanks to a panel that fell down from the ceiling. Livingston tore his straps free and helped Soto out of his seat. "I can stand," the young man protested.

"Good. Let's get out of here," Livingston said. They walked through a curtain of wires and panels which hung from the ceiling, then exited out the back of the cockpit where it had separated from the rest of the ship. Up ahead was the rest of the ship, which had been completely destroyed, and to the right was his squad. Their cheers were distinct, especially with Luke's Vickelian dialect and Neill's vulgar contributions about why women loved the Captain.

"…Because he can time his shooter just right!" his voice carried.

Livingston shook his head and helped Soto forward. The sounds of whirring engines overtook the cheering. He looked to the south and saw the burners of the second Stinger as it began to elevate. The plan was obvious: it would try and bombard them from high above, out of range from Neill's minigun.

"Captain? You hear that?" Soto said. Livingston listened carefully. There were a series of groans in the distance, mixed with the sounds of tearing and growling. They looked toward the crashed Stinger. Its flames lit the horizon a dark blue, and in that glow were countless humanoid figures swarming around it. Attracted to the light, the infected corpses converged around the Stinger, unfazed by the fire that engulfed some of them. They pulled the pilot's body free and proceeded to tear into it.

What alarmed Livingston was not that the sight of the herd, but that the snarls he heard were much closer. He unslung his rifle and raised it.

Water splashed as multiple corpses scampered out from a muddy pond, dripping bacteria-filled saliva from their jaws. The Captain fired his rifle, hitting the first one through the nose. Soto drew his pistol and fired at the next one, first hitting it low in the collarbone. He adjusted his aim and placed a shot in its forehead.

They backed up as several more emerged from behind the bushes. They were biting the air, eager to sink their teeth into anything. The two soldiers backed up as fast as they could, firing with the best precision they could manage. Three more dropped with smoking holes billowing smoke from their skulls, while six more dashed out and converged.

Livingston fired, successfully killing one. He fired again, only for nothing to happen. The battery was spent, rendering his rifle useless except as a club. He reached for a fresh battery, but was unable to go fast enough, as the nearest zombie was upon him. He thrust the rifle out and struck it in the jaw, knocking it to the ground. He drew his sidearm and fired a bolt into its temple, then turned to aim at the next one.

Two others were rapidly coming at him. His shot went wide as the first grabbed at his arm. He spun on his heel, using its momentum to throw it to the ground. He completed his turn to face the next one. Running at full speed, it tackled him to the ground, knocking his pistol from his grasp.

Soto yelled out as he saw the Captain go down. He fired another shot at an approaching corpse, but fired wide. It was his last shot. Overpowered by fright, he flung the pistol and ran as fast as he could, blindly going toward the wreckage. Three creatures followed him, running at equal speed. The only difference was that Soto was dazed from the crash and was already getting winded; something the creatures could never experience. They could not get fatigued. Their hunger could not be satisfied. They were weapons; unthinking, unsympathetic, with one objective…to kill.

Sergeant Park busted the lock and opened the compartment. The rocket launcher was undamaged, but had only one round. There were probably others scattered throughout the crash site, but with the Stinger beginning its descent, he had no time to look for others.

He activated the targeting system and loaded the rocket, then hoisted the heavy weapon over his shoulder. He pressed his eyes into the visor and aimed high, zooming in to the max to allow the sensors to detect the incoming Stinger. It came into view, its weapons charging. The digital crosshairs flashed red, then green, indicating the target was locked.

Park squeezed the trigger. His body shook as the rocket was launched with tremendous velocity, quickly shrinking into a dot in the sky as it ascended toward its target. That dot turned into a bright flash. The rocket struck dead center, ravaging the cockpit and sending the fighter into a spiral. It came down like a flaming meteor, smashing several yards north of the Recon-Valley's cockpit.

The ground rumbled under Livingston's back, the resulting flash glinting in his visor. It lit the dark-green skin of the creature that was on top of him, scraping its claws uselessly against his breastplate. He punched it in the face, shaking a tooth loose. He tried again to strike, only for the creature to throw its body weight on him.

Drops of residue splashed over Livingston's helmet as the creature lowered its jaws to it. Its teeth scraped over the steel, searching for any soft flesh to tear. The Captain pressed his palm to the biter's throat, pushing it away from his face. It tilted its head and bit down, trying desperately to get at his wrist.

He looked to the side and saw the other zombie righting itself. Its jaw clicked, its glowing eyes pointing right for him. It bellowed and approached the helpless Captain, its arms cocking back to impale him.

A blaster bolt streaked across its face, exploding the front of its skull. Faceless, the zombie collapsed.

The team charged, with Luke taking the lead. With a mighty swipe of his claw, he ripped the infected corpse off of Livingston and smashed its skull against a rock. As it hit the ground, he turned toward the bushes and blasted at numerous undead corpses that emerged. Another sniper blast streaked from far back, hitting one of the zombies chasing Soto.

Neill ran to the Captain and helped him up, while Webb, Jackman, and Luke created a firing line. Their shots connected with the skulls of a half dozen creatures as they emerged though the swamp.

They looked ahead toward the Stinger wreckage. In front of its glow was a mass migration of infected bodies moving in their direction.

"They're attracted to the flames," Livingston said. "There's too many. We need to pull out."

"I can take 'em," Neill said.

"No! They'll overwhelm us," Livingston said. "Let's move. Where's Soto?"

"I got him, Cap," Ramos radioed. The sniper was perched on her rock, following the pilot and his pursuers with her crosshairs. She had

already eliminated one and had two to go. Soto had reached the fuselage. He weaved between several burning fragments, then found a piece of wing partially intact. He jumped as high as he could and found a fissure, which he used to grasp and haul himself high. Slime-covered hands grabbed his boots and pulled down.

"It'd be nice if you'd hurry up!" he radioed.

"Hang on," Ramos said. She focused in on one of the creatures and fired, exploding its head. She panned right and found the next one. It was struggling to keep a grip on his leg as it leaned forward to bite. She applied pressure to the trigger, only for Soto to jerk his leg, shifting the creature to the side away from her crosshairs. "Hold still!" she said. She could hear his rampant breathing through the headphones. The pilot stopped struggling, allowing her to focus in on the ghoul. Its jaws yawned open and neared his ankle. As it began to close its jaws, a blaster bolt punched through the back of its head, creating a fountain of skull and brains.

Soto breathed a sigh of relief and lowered himself from the wreckage. He looked over to Ramos, who was now standing up, and gave her a thankful salute.

"Thanks," he said.

"You're wel—LOOK OUT!" Ramos screamed. Several hands reached from beyond the flames and grabbed Soto by the arms, shoulders, and neck. All at once, they dragged him backward behind the debris.

All team members raced toward the wreckage, with Luke and Neill providing cover fire with their heavy weapons.

Soto twisted in agony as fingers pried their way into his flesh. Teeth clamped down on his neck, arms, fingers, and face. There were tens of corpses gathering, having approached the wreckage from the east, their presence obscured by the smoke and various distractions.

The pilot gagged as fingertips pressed into his stomach and pulled outward. A fountain of blood spurted out, encasing the zombies as they grabbed intestines and stomach tissue.

Livingston was the first to arrive on the other side of the wreckage. He had his rifle reloaded and pressed against his shoulder. In front of the muzzle was a horde of infected corpses, each devouring various body parts.

"He's gone, Captain," Park said.

"No," Ramos shouted. She started to cross the wreckage, only for Park to pull her back.

"Captain, we have to move!" Park shouted. The undead were everywhere, closing in on the flames. Neill's minigun cut through several of them, sending body parts spiraling several yards across the landscape. His LED reader flashed red, indicating his battery pack was getting low.

Livingston pointed to a hill to the west.

"Let's go that way and hook north after we reach that big rock," he said. With a little luck, they would be obscured by the fog and canopy long enough to make some distance.

Luke led the way, quickly engaging with a small group of zombies that had moved between them and their escape route. He brought his gun down like a hammer, crunching its head down into its neck.

Luke thrashed another zombie, knocking its head clean off its shoulders, then kicked another, driving it down hard. The back of its skull imploded into its brain. Another swipe split the top of another's head, which came off like the lid of a jar. With the undead out of the way, and the main horde distracted by the flames…and Soto's body…the team raced through the canopy. Splashing through a few shallow ponds, they disappeared into the fog.

CHAPTER 16

The next two miles was a long and grinding trek through hard ground and wilted swamps. They kept a slow pace to avoid gaining the attention of any hordes lurking nearby, and there was no question whether there were undead corpses wandering out of sight. Their moans were unending. The sound of feet splashing through water had the usually confident team on edge.

Livingston stood at the edge of a shoreline and watched his team as they stepped out of one of the murky swamps. By his demeanor, it appeared he was simply accounting for all of them while providing cover. In actuality, he was measuring their morale.

It was low, and for obvious reasons. The team seemed so much smaller without Weatherford and Soto. Ramos was the most distraught, and her stern sniper expression failed to mask it. Park walked behind her. His eyes were like black holes of hatred. Hatred for these infectious monsters. Hatred for those that created them. And with that hatred came disdain for those who showed any mercy for them. That disdain was evident with a brief glance at the Captain. It was brief, but it was there; that look of resentment. Livingston had seen it many times before; it was part of being a commanding officer.

Boots squashed globs of black oil as they continued on. Five hundred yards past the swamp, they came across an abandoned security outpost. The team secured it, confirming no enemy presence, Tarkadon or otherwise, then settled within the perimeter to take a breather.

"Ten minutes," Livingston said. "Webb, check the armory for ammo. Luke, scout ahead. We should have another mile to go before we reach the hangar."

"Yeah. Maybe we'll find some more Stingers waiting for us," Ramos said.

"Pardon me, soldier?" Livingston's mechanical voice had a sharp hiss to it, like a snake. Ramos inhaled deeply.

"Nothing, Captain," she said, turning away. She took a seat next to Neill, who sat on a smoothened rock and loaded his final battery pack into the Viper.

"I still don't get how those guys knew we were here," he said. "You think we missed a few troopers back on Boracan? Maybe some were hiding out and overheard our plans?"

"But then…how did they detect our ship when we first arrived?" Jackman said. "Our stealth capabilities were second to none. Yet, they knew exactly where we were."

"The bigger question is how many are still on this planet…and whether those fighters are part of the defense squadron, or part of a cleanup operation," Livingston said. "Regardless, we can't let them get this stuff off the planet."

"Yeah, but your man Weatherford had the detonator," Dr. Soviar said. "We can't detonate the explosives without it. You still intend to destroy that lab?"

"I do," Livingston said.

"How?" she asked.

"We'll dock at one of the security satellites," Livingston replied. "We'll turn it around and direct its laser toward the base. Those things can cut through a Class-3 Battle Cruiser. It'll have no problem punching through that rock. The blast will detonate the charges, and the rest will be history." Soviar, Neill, and Jackman each nodded in agreement, while Park continued his stern glare. Livingston's nerves began to throb in his face. "You have a problem, Sergeant?"

"I say we let them keep this damn virus," Park grunted. "Look around. You can see how well they're capable of controlling it. If they're stupid enough to try and weaponize it, I say let them. Let them infect their own planets and populations. They'll make this war easy for us. This might actually be the answer to it all."

"You can't be serious, Sergeant."

"Hell yes, I am, Captain," Park said.

"Then you're a fool," Livingston said. Park bit down on his tongue to prevent him from making an obscene retort. Unfortunately, he was bound by rank in this exchange, though that was gradually meaning less and less to him. The Captain continued, "If this virus gets out, it could spread well beyond the reaches of this quadrant. A military population might be able to fend it off if they know what they're doing, but what if it comes into a civilian population? It'll spread like wildfire. Transports will carry the disease to other planets and infect their populations as well. You think that won't carry into U.G.S. space?"

"You think those things will be able to pilot ships?" Neill said. The wrinkled look on his face indicated he was suppressing a laugh.

"I don't know," Livingston said. "Doctor? Do you have any theories?"

Soviar shook her head. "I haven't had a good enough chance to study the documents and video logs. I don't know if the undead are mindless zombies or if they can evolve beyond that. I know they have enough intelligence to tell the difference between a steel hull and glass, as you saw during the flight. And they will search for any weak point in their target to bite or claw into. As we've seen, they were quick to overpower the military forces guarding this place. Who knows, maybe they could learn how to use weapons and fly ships, especially if they've done it in life."

Livingston nodded, while Park shook his head.

"Sounds like a bunch of guesses to me," the Sergeant said.

"Educated guesses," Livingston said. "Regardless of how the hosts may or may not evolve, I think the virus will simply spread during evacuation efforts if planet populations are exposed. You think civilians won't try and get infected loved ones to safety, especially if the Tarkadons decide to exterminate everyone who's been even slightly exposed? And you know that's how they'll handle the situation."

"If they even know what this thing is," Jackman added.

"They don't," Ramos said. Her voice was drawn out and tired. "As much as I'd like to see this Star Virus bite the Tarkadons in the ass more than it already has, the Captain's right. We have to destroy that lab." She noticed a glance from Park. Though brief, it gave away a sense of betrayal. How dare she side with the Captain over him? This was not her idea of a breather. Her body was resting, but her mind was racing more than ever. Needing to separate herself from the conversation, she stood up and entered the compound.

The smell of cooked turkey immediately filled her nose. Webb looked back, a shit-eating grin creasing his face. He was in front of a heating unit. On the counter beside him were pieces of sliced bread and a pint of Tarkadon gin.

"Wow, I see you've struck gold in the weapons cache," she said.

"There's nothing there," Webb said. "Found this stuff in the freezer. The unit was shut down, but it was still cold enough to preserve the meat. It'll be wasted by tomorrow."

"How can you eat?" Ramos said. She was looking at the oily footprints on the tile floor. Webb shrugged.

"It's what people do when they're alive," he said. "Besides, I'm so sick of ration beans, I'd like to eat something of substance before we head back." Ramos took another whiff of his meal. To her surprise, her stomach began to rumble.

"Is there enough for two?"

The door flung open before Webb could answer. Park stepped in and glanced at the Corporal, then motioned for him to leave. Webb looked at him, then back at the pan. The food was almost done. But Park's hard expression was clear. Without saying a word, Webb stepped outside. Park shut the door behind him.

"No weapons or ammo," Ramos said.

"You think he's right?" Park said. Ramos sighed. "I'm not pulling rank. I'm asking for real." Ramos shook her head. Park missed the point entirely; she was tired of his rage against the Tarkadons.

"I thought you were getting past this," she said.

"I thought so too," Park said. "But you saw what they've been doing. They're building weapons of apocalyptic proportions. You don't think we should use it against them and bring an end to this?"

"I think you need to settle your grudge," she said. "You can't kill half the galaxy. Just focus on what we've talked about before. Let's get out of this unit and settle for a normal life."

"What normal life will there be if the Tarkadons keep doing what they're doing?" Park said.

"They fail every time," Ramos said.

"Until they don't," Park replied.

"So…what's your plan? Send a few walking corpses on a shuttle for the nearest planet? Then send another out after that and hope you get lucky? You don't even know where the High Command is."

"No, but I bet there's something on that portable terminal that'll tell us where some bases are," Park said.

"Goddamnit, Zach!" Ramos snapped. "I'm tired of this. I'm done. I'm not doing this anymore!" Park forced a blank expression, but inside he was trembling. She had addressed her concerns many times, only for them to revert back to this same conversation. Only now, there was finality in Ramos' voice.

"Dawn," he said. His voice trailed off. He didn't know what else to say. She started walking for the door, bumping his shoulder along the way. He turned, that blank expression now a rare form of desperation. "I'll retire early." The words seemed to come out automatically with no prior thought. Ramos stopped, her hand clutching the door handle.

She was deep in thought, her eyes staring at her blurred reflection in the metal door. She then turned to face him, and without speaking a word, she removed the necklace. She placed it on the desk, gave it one last look, then without even glancing at the Sergeant, exited the compound.

Park approached the desk and gazed at the emblem. It took a moment for his mind to realize what had just happened, and when it did, the cycle of blame and deflection began, only for it all to come back to him, his actions, and obsessions. Now, he was faced with the consequence.

It only took moments for his mind to reach the stage of bargaining. Maybe he could salvage the relationship. There had to be a way! She was the only one that managed to rekindle any humanity inside him, and only now did he realize how important that was to him.

He placed the necklace in his pocket then stepped outside. Ramos was already across the field, following Luke's path. It would do no good to go after her now. The best tactic would be to wait and let her cool off.

"You okay, Sergeant?" Livingston asked. Park saw the Captain staring at him, then realized his discontent was plain on his face.

"Negative, Captain. I'm fine," he said. "Uh…you're right. We should destroy the lab." He spoke loudly, hoping his voice would travel far enough to be heard by Ramos.

"Glad to know you're on board," Livingston said. Park took a seat on one of the rocks, while Webb tiptoed back to the building.

"What's that smell?" Jackman asked, sniffing.

"Smells like ham…no…turkey! Thressen turkey! I know that spicy smell from a mile away," Neill said with excitement. He followed Webb into the compound. His voice grew louder when he entered the kitchen. "You son of a bitch. You were gonna hog this shit up and hope the rest of us wouldn't notice!"

"I was gonna share!"

"Uh-huh, sure you were."

Jackman chuckled at the exchange, then watched as Livingston stepped away. She saw from the way his hand went up to his helmet that he was in pain. She followed him a hundred feet out, opening her pack along the way.

"No thank you, Corporal," he said, not bothering to look back.

"Your nerves are lighting up like sciatica in the face," she said. "I know the stress of the situation is making it worse." She held up a small syringe filled with pain medication.

"Negative," he said.

"Captain, I know you need it," she continued.

"Save it for the others," Livingston said. "That's an order." With a sigh, Jackman walked away. The Captain watched the horizon, specifically the atmosphere for any aerial activity. If there were ships flying around, they'd be difficult to spot through those rolling clouds. The lightning flashed brighter dead ahead. Silver streaks of electricity reached for thousands of feet, sparking the ground they touched.

They were cutting it close. Livingston estimated that the storm would hit around the time they arrived at the hangar bay.

He heard footsteps approaching from behind.

"Corporal, I told you to—" he looked over and saw Dr. Soviar behind him. "Oh, excuse me, Doctor." She laughed.

"I never properly thanked you for getting me out of that prison camp," she said.

"No need," he answered.

"No, there is," she said. "What you're doing here, I really appreciate it. It can't be easy being so far away from home for...how long has it been?"

"Too long," he answered.

"You don't seem bothered," she said. "You have anyone back at home?" Livingston shook his head. "No? Nobody?"

"Not much time for mingling when I'm out here much of the time. Besides, not many women want to be with a man who's practically a droid," he replied.

"I know the type of helmet you wear. Is it to help you breathe or prevent infection?"

"Both."

"How bad is it?"

"It'd be painful and difficult to breathe if it came off," Livingston said. "It wouldn't kill me, though I'd probably wish it would."

"Clearly you're in pain already," Soviar said. "Why won't you take the meds?"

"Because I need to manage the pain on my own," Livingston said. "I've seen plenty of people get hooked on pain medication. I'd rather be in pain."

"Nice excuse. Too bad it isn't true," Soviar said. The Captain turned to look at her. "I know what she was offering you. It was *Angelus Alas*. You'd need to inject ten of those needles each day for a week to get addicted. No, something tells me it has something to do with the lovely Corporal down there." She waited for an answer, then smiled when none was produced.

"Regulations wouldn't allow it," Livingston said. "I'm a Captain. She's a Corporal. That's it. Besides, she'd be foolish to wanna be with someone whose face has become minced meat."

"See, I'd believe your rank excuse if you had left that last part out," Soviar said.

"I appreciate your impute, Doctor. But right now, I'd rather focus on getting my people out of here. No offense, but your dating advice doesn't help with that."

"It does if you apply it right. After all, you've got to give yourself something to live for," Soviar said. She walked back to the compound, intentionally ending the conversation on that note. Livingston watched her walk away, then looked ahead at Jackman. She was placing a bandage on Webb's leg after tending to several scrapes on Neill's neck. She was always a caretaker at heart, preferring to preserve life rather than extinguish it.

"Captain?!" Livingston looked back and saw Ramos and Luke hurrying over the small hillside. Both of them were clearly alarmed, the Vickel breathing heavily. Infected blood dripped from the barrel of his rifle after having smashed a few skulls. Ramos shook some blood free from her knife then sheathed it.

"We've got problems."

CHAPTER 17

"Well, shit," Neill whispered. He crouched low, keeping three meters apart from each of his teammates as they observed the horde staggering about in the distance. There were at least sixty of them, with a few stumbling in and out of a nearby swamp.

"I estimate there's another dozen or so in the pond," Ramos said. "We were lucky not to attract their attention when we ran into these clowns here." She gestured at the four dead corpses lying behind them. Each had been stabbed or bludgeoned in the head, the brain destroyed.

"Skill. We Vickels do not believe in filthy luck," Luke growled. Livingston watched the herd through his scope, then gazed a quarter-mile left. He could see traces of the hangar facility just past a large group of boulders. The landscape resembled an empty campfire, with the center flattened and a giant rock perimeter surrounding it. The Tarkadons had cleared out the space early in the construction phase. Unfortunately, the south road that led directly to it was paraded on by the undead.

"What's the plan, Captain?" Webb asked.

"We'll keep off the road," Livingston said. "Keep these hills between us and them. If we come across any infected, kill them as silently as possible. Don't shoot unless absolutely necessary. We know they're drawn to noise. That's why that crowd converged on the mountainside; the alarm drew them in."

"How far can you see?" Webb asked. "Can you tell if there are any ships?"

"There's no way of knowing that until we get there," Livingston said. "Come on, ladies. Get your act together. It's time to move."

Webb watched the horde for another moment through a pair of binoculars, then stood up. His boot crushed the stem of a wilted plant that had grown through a fissure in the rock. Its leaves had been reduced to mush, the wooden stem folding over like a paper straw. All around it was the residue. He looked back at the creatures and the state of the swamp they congregated by. The plants looked like something from a haunted house story. Wherever these corpses went, they brought the disease with them.

"Could the plants spread it too?" he thought out loud.

"I don't know," Soviar said. She was kneeling to his right, watching the horde with a scope borrowed from Neill. She wore a fascinated expression on her face, as opposed to the distraught looks she exhibited prior. "It's possible. Who knows; the virus might mutate some of the flora and use spores to produce more virus strands. It might even mutate and take on new properties."

"Let's theorize later," Livingston said.

"Come on, Doc," Webb said. Keeping low, the team moved down a long stretch of rocks along the back side of a long crest of rock towering fifty feet high. Beyond it was several hundred yards of jagged ground with scattered patches of rotted marshlands. What Livingston hated the most was the fog that drifted between it all, which would make it difficult to spot wandering corpses.

They walked in standard formation, keeping several feet of distance between each other to reduce the chance of being spotted. Third in line was Sergeant Park, whose gaze was locked on Ramos. As they walked, he subtly quickened his pace, just enough to gradually catch up with her without looking too obvious. He could hear the necklace rattling in his pocket. With each jingle, he felt his desire to speak to her grow overwhelmingly. He didn't care if the whole squad knew or if he'd be kicked out of the military at the cost of his pension and benefits. He couldn't take the fact that she was leaving him. It was worse than any injury he sustained in battle. Only now did his revenge on Tarkadon seem meaningless.

His stomach tightened. Unable to take it, he doubled his pace, crunching pebbles under his boots. Ramos looked back and saw him approaching.

"Not now," she whispered.

"Private, I need to speak with you," he said, keeping his voice down.

"No," she said. "Don't press the issue, or I'll report you to the Captain."

"Like he cares right now," Park whispered. Ramos grimaced. *More like, 'like YOU care right now.'*

"Zach, stop," she said. Park glanced back. There was plenty of fog obscuring them from the rest of the team. He grabbed the necklace and extended it to her.

"Hear me out," he said. "We'll blow up the lab and go home."

"I wish I could believe you," she said.

"I mean it," he said.

"You mean it now," she whispered. She noticed the awkward glance from Luke, who then proceeded to patrol as though he couldn't hear their conversation. "Give it a couple of days and you'll go back to your obsessions. I'm tired of it all. The stress of war is bad enough. I don't need this in my life."

"No, I won't," he said, raising his voice.

"Park! Ramos! Cut that chatter," Livingston barked through the commlink. The Sergeant switched it off then stepped in front of Ramos, blocking her way.

"Sergeant—Zach," she struggled to keep her voice below a whisper. "You're losing your mind! This can wait until we get off-world."

"I can wait...if you're actually willing to talk," he said. Ramos squeezed her weapon in frustration. What she really wanted to grab was his neck. She couldn't believe what he was doing; he was actually trying to win her back...by pestering her as they trekked through an infected wasteland. He had lost all sense of discipline, as well as any regard for the situation and the rest of the team. These were not the qualities of a Sergeant in Special Forces. In fact, she'd seen better self-control in new recruits.

She didn't know how to answer. She didn't want this conversation to go on, especially here of all places. But she didn't want to deal with him on the confines of the ship either. She at least wanted to wait until they got back to their home world to settle the aftermath of their new separation. It seemed the only way to get him to drop the subject was to lie.

"Well?" he continued. Ramos sucked in a breath of air. Her blood felt like it was about to boil. She switched on her commlink.

"All units stop." Immediately, each squad member stopped in their tracks.

"What's going on up there?" Livingston hissed through the comm.

"Captain, please come up to my position," she said. Park's eyes flared.

"What are you doing?" his voice was like that of a murderous beast. He heard the Captain approaching from behind. Without looking back, he gave up and marched ahead, preferring not to be there for the conversation. "I'll scout ahead," he reasoned.

Livingston watched the Sergeant go past Luke, then disappear into the fog.

"What's going on?" he asked Ramos.

"He's not stable," she replied. Livingston shook his head. *As if I didn't have enough problems.*

"I'll deal with him when we—"

"Best thing right now is to keep him separated from me. You see, we are, well—were..."

"I know," Livingston whispered. Ramos looked surprised, then slowly nodded. Of course he knew. Hell, most of the squad probably knew at this point. What were they really going to say? It's against regulation? Like Livingston gave a shit about that a hundred million lightyears behind enemy lines?

"The life's gotten to him," she said. "It's warping his mind. Back at the compound, before we got to the lab, he tortured a Tarkadon soldier to get information. I put him out of his misery before Park could do worse. The guy was already fatally wounded anyway. Then at the lab, when we found the portable terminal from the Commander's office, he was gonna keep it for himself. Said he'd start his own mercenary operation after quitting the service. I convinced him not to and threatened to report it to you if he continued with his plan. Thought I broke through to him, until hearing his talk of using the virus in our favor in the war." She sighed. "I—uh, broke it off today, which was my mistake. Not the breaking off, but the timing. Now he's obsessed with winning me back. He's on a downward spiral, Captain. And it's only gonna get worse."

Livingston absorbed the information.

"Right now, let's focus on getting out of here," he said. His voice was gentle, giving her a hint of sympathy. Behind that tough exterior was a heartbroken woman. Chastising her for her mistakes would accomplish nothing, especially in the current circumstances. Livingston spoke into the comm, "All units, resume patrol. Sergeant Park, where are you?"

The Sergeant had forgotten to switch his commlink back on as he walked. His hands gripped the weapon tightly as though attempting to suffocate it. He had screwed up with Ramos and could not take it. To make matters worse, he would now have to deal with Livingston. A migraine set in, making his temples feel as though they were being pinched together through his brain.

He wandered through a fogbank then came onto the edge of another pond. All around it were bushes that stood as tall as him, wide as pine trees. Their leaves sagged like wet tissue paper, secreting the residue into the water below. Some of these bushes had been uprooted like weeds, the rock around them smashed to bits, as though someone had smashed a giant hammer over the area.

Construction vehicle? It was the only thing that made sense. That is, until he remembered the smashed doors inside the lab's corridors.

He noticed something floating in the pond. Park looked closer, keeping his eye along his rifle. He saw a hand, then a head, then the squashed body it had been attached to. The center of its back had been caved inward between the shoulders, smashing the spine. There were no signs of burns, energy or power. Whatever caused the injury was physical, as though a big rod had been forced through its back. At that point he noticed the shape. It wasn't like anything caused by a spear or any other pointed object. It wasn't circular, rather elongated, perhaps twelve inches long; almost like a giant boot print.

Suddenly the head lifted up from the water and snapped its jaws. Park jumped back and pointed his weapon, but managed to keep from squeezing the trigger. The corpse wiggled in the pond, its head lifting high, but the rest of its body too mangled to operate. It snarled and bit, but could not pursue him.

Park let out a sigh of relief, then drew his knife. He figured he'd kill it. Why not? He took a step toward it then stopped at the water's edge. He watched it flop for another moment, then focused on the ragged Tarkadon uniform it wore.

You know what... let the bastard rot. Serves him right.

He figured he'd been out long enough. Not like he could stay away from Livingston and Ramos forever. He turned around to head back, just in time to see the outstretched arms of a rapidly approaching corpse.

Park shrieked and thrashed the knife. The blade cut along its face, splitting the cheeks all the way back to the tendons. The jaw widened. Slimy hands clutched his shoulders. Park sneered and drove the knife through its eye socket. The arms went slack, and the creature dropped.

Bushes rustled and water splashed behind him. Park turned around as two more zombies stumbled out of the pond. They bellowed, launching black bile, and accelerated into a full sprint upon seeing him. Park threw a kick into the first one, knocking it back. The other one closed the distance and swiped its arms like whips. He backed up, allowing it to miss, then launched himself at the creature. With all the force he could muster, he drove the knife into its eye socket, killing it. The other one had already recovered and came at him again. Slithery fingers found his shirt collar, then his skin. Park shrieked and spun on his heel, striking it in the face with his elbow. The zombie didn't let go.

The fight ended up in the water, with the living attempting to keep the claws from penetrating his flesh, while keeping those jaws back as well. On top of all of that, he had to do it without attracting the attention of others.

Park felt the water coming up to his shins. He pressed a hand against its chest, desperately keeping it back. He felt its skin folding where he pressed, the residue oozing onto his hand like pus. He tried to stab it but couldn't get his arm over those of the creature. They thrashed back and forth, the rifle swinging from its sling.

The corpse leaned in, the teeth clamping down a centimeter from his nose. Its breath flooded his nostrils, the tongue waving back and forth like a black worm. It forced him back further in another attempt to bite. Park felt his boots hit something solid. A moment later, he felt a tightness over his left ankle. He glanced down and saw the disabled corpse in the water, biting into his boot. Its jaw applied intense pressure, slowly sinking the teeth through the leather.

Park shrieked and tried to shove his attacker away, only to be outmuscled. Growling incessantly, it leaned in to bite.

The Sergeant dropped the knife and grabbed his rifle. Holding it one-handed like a pistol, he aimed it down at the floating corpse and blasted a hole in its head. He then pressed the muzzle to the attacker's right knee and fired repeatedly. Blaster bolts sliced through the kneecap, severing its lower leg. Suddenly unbalanced, the ghoul fell into the water. Park, overcome with adrenaline, shouldered his rifle and fired several bolts into its face. He squeezed the trigger again and again until there was no head left.

"Sergeant?!"

Panting heavily, Park backed out of the pond as his teammates assembled around him. Neill and Webb checked the bodies, while Jackman approached the Sergeant with her med-pack.

"Are you injured?"

"No!" he snapped. Jackman held up her hands and backed away. Livingston stepped forward. Judging by the speed of his march, irritated was barely scratching the surface of describing how he felt.

"Sergeant, you understand the meaning of low-profile?"

"Captain?!" Neill called out. He was pointing toward the pond. Livingston followed his finger, then saw the dozens of bodies stumbling through the water. A moment later, they charged, screeching like possessed spirits.

"Disperse!" Livingston shouted. He shouldered his rifle and fired the first shot.

CHAPTER 18

They were like a swarm of bees, moving in all directions at once with no sense of guidance. Blaster bolts dropped a few, but their speed and ever-changing trajectories made accurate headshots near impossible.

The soldiers scattered. Blaster bolts zipped everywhere. In a matter of seconds, the team had broken apart. Luke held his own to the best of his abilities, trying to slow the horde with as many heavy blasts as he could manage. Ramos threw a couple of grenades into the bond, exploding several undead with each blast. Livingston remained on the front line until he heard screams coming from the right. Three of the things had swarmed Jackman, whose battery had run out. She stumbled back in fright, then tripped over a rock.

He rushed the group, sending red energy into each of their skulls. The last one fell over her, provoking another scream. She quickly realized it was dead and not biting her, then kicked it off. Another blast struck another that approached, dropping it. A moment later, the Captain arrived at her side and helped her to her feet. She reloaded her rifle just in time to shoot at another group that came at them.

Each time they put one down, another would take its place. It was as though they were spawning out of nowhere. The world around them had become a blur of diseased bodies swarming out from the water.

Corporal Webb ran blindly through the fog, unable to see more than a few feet ahead of himself. He saw Ramos up ahead but lost her in the fog. He could see several blaster flashes strobing beyond the mist, accompanied by the sound of splattering blood.

Human shapes took form through the fog. Webb dug his heels into the ground to stop. In under a few moments, they were all around him, their arms reaching in grabbing motions. Webb shrieked and blasted one in the stomach. Its innards spilled out like sewage. The blaster continued shooting as he raised the barrel, the bolts cutting it dead center until one finally found its brain. The tech fired again and hit the next one with pinpoint accuracy. He spun on his heel in a dance-like motion, cracking the gun against another, denting its temple inward.

Right behind it were several others. He sprayed blaster bolts in a panic until the battery ran empty. He chucked the weapon then attempted to flee, succeeding only in running headlong into the grasp of another creature. He felt its hot breath, then the razor edge of teeth closing over his face.

Webb screamed in agony, then thrust both hands against the fiend. It staggered away, tearing several inches of flesh from his face. Webb proceeded to run, while a red waterfall spilled from where his left cheek had been. After a few steps he was lightheaded and losing balance. His run degraded into a stumble. His body shook as the congregation of undead collided with him, tackling him from behind. He faceplanted into the rock, barely conscious enough to feel himself being spun onto his back.

Teeth and claws raked his body, shredding his uniform and the flesh underneath. Only when the fingers punched into his stomach and coiled around his innards did he finally feel the pain. And the pain was intense, inducing a high-pitched scream that traveled into the stormy sky.

They bit his flesh like piranhas, never bothering to pull their mouths from his body. They simply bit and bit again, allowing the repeated motion to perform the chewing necessary to swallow the flesh. Others moved over his shoulders, attracted by the blood that gushed from his face. They pried their fingers into the wound, bending their knuckles at his jawline. One decided to pull. Webb felt his mouth hyperextend. There was a crack at his mandibular notch, and his jaws detached from their joint. His cheeks peeled apart during the tugging, his tongue flipping wildly between it all, until another ghoul bit down on it and ripped it clean out.

"Get behind me! Get behind me!" Neill screamed, cocking the rotator on his minigun. He had backtracked forty steps, shooting a few corpses with his sidearm. His voice reached only a few of his teammates, as the whole group had spread all over the area. He raised the weapon and brought it down like a hammer, crunching a corpse that came at him head on. Its head snapped back, the skull having taken a wrinkly shape, oozing brain matter through the cracks.

Park blasted several, then ran back behind Neill. Luke was right behind him, swatting back to knock away a zombie that was directly behind him. In his other hand, he had grabbed Soviar and lifted her over his shoulder, her hair waving wildly as he carried her behind the gunner.

Neill glanced around for the others. Livingston and Jackman had retreated over to the right. He couldn't see Ramos or Webb. The horde had split apart, though many of them were hard to see through the fog. All he could see for sure were fifteen or more infected corpses directly between him and the pond, with at least six more stumbling near the shore. He rotated the barrels then opened fire. His blaster bolts were like red-hot machetes. They cut through their spongy bodies with ease, creating black piles of rot along the ground.

After eliminating that group, he aimed to the right and blasted several that converged near the Captain and medic. Limbs spiraled like batons as they detached from their bodies. Blood spouted from each corpse, adding a black mist to the fogbank.

"Fuck, there's more!" Soviar said, pointing at the pond.

"More! To the east!" Luke growled. Neill looked. The Vickel was right. Several yards past Livingston and Jackman came a wave of walking dead, dripping with residue.

"Cap! Get out of there!"

Livingston heard the moans and footsteps. He didn't even have to look to know what was coming. He grabbed Jackman by the arm and ran toward the group, angling to the side to allow Neill to fire into the horde. He waved the barrel back and forth as though sprinkling a garden hose, tearing the enemy to shreds. Livingston and Jackman ran a tight arch toward the others.

Park and Luke had formed a firing line beside Neill. Soviar was facing the opposite direction, firing her pistol at several that approached from behind. She hit two with pinpoint accuracy, but ran out of shots before she could get the four that raced over their bodies. The Captain and medic opened fire, popping all four heads in a hot red stream, then joined the defense line.

The air was hot, stale, and wet from the combination of moisture, rot, and plasma. Livingston studied the landscape to access the situation and get a headcount. He immediately realized two of his people were missing.

"Where's Ramos and Webb?" he said.

"I lost track of Webb," Neill shouted over the drone of his weapon. "Ramos is back there somewhere." He nudged his head backward to gesture at the landscape behind them. Park was the first to look. The area was swarming with corpses, going at varying speeds. Out in the distance, he could see tiny red sparks. Blaster fire.

"No! No, no no," he said.

"Sergeant, wait," Livingston said. Park ignored the order and ran west, plowing through walkers as he went. Livingston saw a duo racing toward him from behind. He aimed carefully and shot each one, though Park never noticed in his crusade to save Ramos.

More were coming in from the hills and pond. There were more infected than there was ammo to stop them. As far as Livingston could tell, there were far less behind them than in front.

"Let's go! Follow the Sergeant!" he ordered. Neill lifted his finger off the trigger and pointed the hot barrels skyward, then ran behind his team. Jackman took the right side, carefully picking off a few uglies along the way. Luke, being the fastest, was at the front of the line. He swiped his claws back and forth, easily knocking any zombies out of their path. Even with their enhanced speed and strength, they could not outmatch the ferocity of a Vickel. Two hundred yards behind them, a tsunami of infected corpses descended the hillside. Some branched off, inspecting the bodies lying about in search of fresh flesh, while others followed the sound of running feet and blaster-fire.

The squad passed a few hundred meters before they found a dozen creatures kneeled in a tight circle, gorging themselves on a fallen victim. Blood had formed a dark red pool around them, which splashed with each jerking movement. Intestines and clothing material were thrown about like confetti.

One of the undead looked back, its face caked in blood. Its teeth clenched down, slicing the wet meat between them. Staring at the soldiers, it sprang to its feet and screamed, only for Luke to take its head off with a swing of his gun. The other creatures sprang from their feeding frenzy, only to be met with a volley of blaster-fire.

The victim had been pulled apart, the flesh stripped from the bones. Ribs protruded, appearing like the sides of a bowl containing entrails and blood. Any identity had been peeled from the face. Only the bag, which had fallen nearby, gave them any sense of who the soldier was.

Webb.

There was no time to grieve. Livingston grabbed the pack and led the team on. There were another series of flashes through the fog, and the echoes of Sergeant Park yelling out.

"Dawn!"

Ramos screamed as she swung her rifle like a club, bashing another zombie in the face. It was the fourth one in a row, after retreating for what seemed like forever. Like everyone else, she had gotten turned around during the attack. With the undead swarming around her, she ran as fast as she could, shooting any that drew near. But her battery had run out, and every time she attempted to reload or draw her sidearm, another set of claws reached out to grab her.

She struck repeatedly, shuddering with each impact. With one final blow, she pancaked the creature's skull.

Immediately, another one approached from behind and lunged. She turned just in time and raised her weapon horizontally, blocking its jaws with the barrel. She lifted a knee into its groin, but it accomplished nothing. The claws reached under the gun and grabbed at her shirt, ripping a strip off her mid-region. Gritting her teeth, she knew she would not outmuscle it. It pressed in again. As its weight came forward, she sidestepped and rotated her hips, then thrust the gun in a semicircular motion. The maneuver redirected the creature to the ground.

She stomped as hard as she could, hearing a loud crack as her heel connected with its skull. The creature vibrated with each hit, until finally, the skull broke open like a ceramic pot, spilling brains and black ooze.

Ramos staggered, completely exhausted. With shaking hands, she ejected the empty battery from her blaster rifle and grabbed her last remaining one. More footsteps approached. Many more of the undead were coming at her in a full sprint, directly ahead.

She slammed the battery pack in and fired a wild spray. One of the targets was hit in the head, while the others only caught bolts to the chest and stomach. It slowed them down long enough for Ramos to make a dash for safety. It didn't take long for them to close the gap. They would be on her with a few more steps. She looked for anywhere she could go and saw a large group of boulders at her two-o'clock. With every last ounce of stamina she could muster, she ran for those rocks, and with a bounding leap, she climbed onto the largest one.

She scraped her boots against the side, pushing herself over the top. The three creatures behind her crashed into it. Groaning loudly, they raked their claws against it, nearly grabbing her boots. She stood up and aimed down, blasting one in the skull. Then a second. The third, to her amazement, was already mid-way up the rock. She shot it between the eyes, the back of its skull exploding outward into grey shards.

Ramos collapsed onto her knees, completely spent. She breathed hard for several seconds, then forced herself to move. This rock was no sanctuary. Hell, all it did was delay the zombies long enough for her to get a shot.

That point was proven further when she saw another one climbing the opposite side of the boulder. It hauled itself up, jaws baring down on her thigh. She thrust her muzzle into its mouth and fired. It fell away, only for another to take its place. And another. And another. They were climbing over each other like bugs.

A series of blaster bolts flashed, accompanied by several wet splashing sounds. The undead collapsed into a rotting pile. Ramos looked in the direction she had run from. Out of the fog came Zach Park. He kicked one final zombie, knocking it to the ground, then picked up a bowling ball-sized rock and slammed it down on its head. He proceeded to check the immediate area for others. So far, they were clear, though it wouldn't be that way for long. They could hear others wandering from the northwest, as well as the big horde that approached from the east.

Park and Ramos shared a gaze, the former expressing relief that she was okay. Ramos let a small smile slip through. He had run through thick hordes of demonic beasts to get to her. Maybe he was genuine in his declaration of ending his crusade.

A downdraft swept over both of them. Spotlights spat rays of white over the area and panned around. Both soldiers looked up and saw the Tarkadon dropship hovering ahead. Thirty-feet from bow to stern, it rotated in place, with two turret extensions protruding from the open fuselage.

The light found Ramos and the guns opened fire. Park screamed in fury as one of those blasts punched through her midsection, throwing her backwards onto the ground. The gunner continued firing, the bolts crashing into the rock where she had stood.

Park fired at the gunner, his bolts exploding into red fireflies as they collided against the hull. The gunner rotated the turret, shining the light on him. Before he could fire, the Sergeant found his mark, sending a bolt through his chest. The gunner leaned over, handing slack from his harness. He continued firing, hitting another trooper that attempted to pull his comrade from the straps.

The ship rotated, the ventral guns glowing green. Park ran to the right as fast as he could. The cannons struck down, blowing a crater into the rock. The force of the blast launched Park head over heels until he hit the ground on his back, several feet later. His hands were empty, the blaster nowhere in sight. His head and back throbbed and his ears rang. Blindness was added when the spotlight panned over him. He heard the thud of the gunner's body hitting the ground, then the clipping of a harness over his replacement.

"There he is!" one of the troopers shouted.

"Nail that sucker," another said. Park squeezed his eyes shut and waited for the inevitable. He heard the firing of a railgun, yet, there was no heat or bombardment. Hearing the screams and the groaning of a damaged engine, he looked up. Thousands of bolts streaked at an upward angle, ravaging the gunner and the fuselage behind it.

"Ye-hah!" Neill cheered. He panned slightly to the left, hitting the cockpit window. The glass shattered and the insides burst into flame. The ship spun out of control, zipping overhead and crashing a thousand feet to the southeast.

The dropship rolled for another twenty feet before settling, with a few of the troopers getting thrown out then crushed under its hull. Only five of the twenty troopers on board survived. They climbed out the starboard fuselage, all red with bruises and scrapes.

A horrid stench overcame the smell of burning fuel. Next came the sound of racing feet and biting jaws.

The horde swarmed the dropship, forcing the troopers to flee. One was immediately caught off-guard, and was defenseless against the many hands that seized him. The zombies grabbed him by the legs and arms, while others focused on his center. With a gag that bubbled blood, he felt bones detach somewhere near his lumbar region, followed by the tearing of flesh. His waist separated from his ribcage, both halves trailing blood and intestines, which the undead helped themselves to.

The others fled, quickly being diverted in different directions as they were intercepted by zombies. They blasted rifles and pistols, dropping a few as they went. But it was as useful as splashing a cupful of water away from an incoming wall of ocean. More undead stampeded their way to the fresh meat, cornering each trooper.

Two of them had climbed on top of the ship, hoping the elevation would be their saving grace. That hope faded in seconds as several zombies began clawing their way onto the ruins. The troopers hyperventilated, realizing they had just trapped themselves. They shot their guns, picking off the first few that climbed up. Others quickly took their place and teemed over the ship, overwhelming the troopers. One jumped in a Hail-Mary attempt to flee, only to land in a crowd of the things. They descended on him, biting his flesh and tearing his limbs free. The other made his last stand on the ship, firing off another few bolts before he felt teeth shredding the back of his neck. Then another set of jaws came down on his brow, the teeth scraping his skull. The zombie, favoring his head, pressed its attack while its brethren feasted on the rest of his body. It pressed its fingers into the sockets, squishing both eyes to jelly before sinking further into the brain.

The others failed to gain much distance.

One trooper found himself completely surrounded. He squeezed the trigger, showering the horde with energy as they closed in. Every which way he turned, he was looking into the glowing green eyes of a hungry fiend. They closed in on him and punched their rigid fingers through his neck and ribcage. Bones dislodged and blood spilled. The trooper let out a scream, which immediately became a high-pitched shriek as one of the undead coiled its fingers around his spine as though holding a baseball bat. Another attacked from the front and ended his scream by biting out his throat.

His companion ran to the south. For a moment, he had believed the horde was completely fixated on his ill-fated friend. The sight of several stumbling corpses in front of him ended that notion. The trooper stared wide-eyed at the things approaching him. They weren't human. They were Rippers, seven-foot tall aliens that had crocodilian jaws containing two-inch needle-like teeth. Their jaws were like chippers, able to bite with rapid precision that would strip a Vickel to the bone in minutes.

He let out a scream as they descended on him. His blaster bolts zipped wide, only to fizzle out uselessly in the distance. They wrestled him to the ground and brought their jaws down, starting with his arms. The meat came off the bone as though it had already been slow-roasted. The trooper writhed in agony, then slowed as shock overtook him. The last thing he saw was the naked skeleton of both arms, with only a few strands of meat dangling free, before the Rippers proceeded to gorge on the rest of his body.

Livingston grabbed Park by the hand and pulled him to his feet. The Sergeant's head throbbed, his senses slowly returning to him. When they did, his memory flashed the horrific events that led to his injuries. He looked to the rock and saw Jackman and Soviar kneeling where Ramos had fallen. He pushed the Captain aside and ran as fast as he could.

Ramos was still alive. She was on her back, her eyes nearly bulging from the sockets. She was in excruciating pain. Park shoved the medic aside and knelt by her.

"Come on, babe! We gotta go!" he said.

"Sergeant," the medic said. Park looked at her and she shook her head. *She's not gonna make it. She won't even survive the trip.*

"NO! You bitch! Patch her up so we can carry her out of here!" In Jackman's eyes, he looked as demonic as the undead as he screamed.

"Sergeant, I can't," she answered.

"She's right," Soviar whispered. The rest of the team gathered. Luke hung his head low in sorrow, seeing his teammate's mutilated midsection. The blast had opened a gaping hole, exposing charred intestines and stomach tissue. The human phrase was *she's lucky to be alive.* But there was nothing lucky about this. She would've been better off to have been killed instantly in the blast.

Park tried to scoop her off the ground. In shifting her body, she yelped loudly, then flailed her arms.

"Sergeant, STOP!" Livingston shouted, pushing him away. The Sergeant turned and pointed his weapon at his helmet, spurring everyone else to aim at him.

"You're only making it worse!" Jackman said.

"Sergeant..." Livingston kept his voice cool and collected. "Stand. Down." Park looked him in the eye, then at everyone else. All weapons were pointed at him, including Neill's minigun.

"Sorry, Sarge," the big man said. *I know you're in despair. But make a move, and I'll make you disappear.*

Park lowered his weapon and knelt again by Ramos. He held her head gently in his hands.

"Babe, I'm so sorry," he whispered.

Livingston glanced back. The horde was approaching. At the moment, they were obscured by the fog, but that would only last for another minute at best.

"We have to go," Livingston said. He leaned in toward Ramos. "I'm sorry to ask this, but it's up to you. I can…end it, if you wish."

She shook her head, trickling blood from the corners of her mouth.

"N-no," she said. "I'm not going out like a whiny bitch. Those things will be on top of you…unless I draw them away." She reached over for her rifle, but couldn't find it. Jackman found it for her and placed it in her arms. "Give me a double-dose of that painkiller…and help me up."

"Ramos, I…"

She interrupted the Captain. "Cap! Get your ugly face out of here! Blow up that damn lab!" She spat blood as she spoke. Livingston stepped back. She had chosen her fate.

"Yes, Private," he said. Jackman sank two needles into her arm, then allowed Neill and Luke to gently lean her up against what remained of the boulder. Ramos moaned, though the pain wasn't as horrible as before. She sat upright, grunting as she positioned her rifle.

"Go." Her voice was shallow.

"Let's go," Livingston ordered. Luke and Neill gave their farewell, then followed the Captain. Jackman suppressed a tear as she put her hand on Ramos' shoulder, wordlessly saying goodbye. She left, with Soviar running beside her. Last was Park, who appeared to be in shock as he stared at her and her injury.

I won't let them get away with this.

"Zach…GO!" she said. Full of rage and sorrow, the Sergeant ran after the others.

There was a slight sense of relief when he left. The last thing she wanted to see in her dying moments was that angry expression that had driven a wedge between them. She'd rather see the ghouls—at least they were mindless. Plus, she'd get to feel like a badass one last time.

And that feeling came as the horde emerged out from the fog. Several came at her, while others proceeded north after the sound of running feet. She armed an impact grenade and tossed it, blowing a few of them to pieces. The sound drew the rest of the horde toward her. She threw her last grenade and watched as the bodies flew in long arches, breaking into pieces on the way down. She propped her gun over her stomach, what was left of it, and blasted away.

Heads popped, shooting black paste. Bodies spun and fell, only to be trampled on by the next wave. Finally, they closed in on her. Not ready to be finished, she drew her knife and sidearm, then blasted and slashed with every ounce of strength in her, until finally, the claws and teeth broke through.

The one mercy she did have was not living long enough to feel the sensation of being pulled apart. The undead congregated around her body, clawing at each other in an effort to get a mouthful of flesh.

CHAPTER 19

Drops of rain splattered over Livingston's mask. The sky flashed with neon-blue lightning. The sky rolled, shooting bolts of electricity to each corner of the horizon. The deep thunderous booms were like the roars of an angry leviathan, determined to crush the tiny creatures below it.

The Captain could see the wall of rocks up ahead. They had been stacked fairly high by cranes and exo-suits. Behind those rocks was the hangar bay. They were close. They were SO close. But before getting behind that ring of rock, they had to worry about what was in front of it.

Livingston drew his knife and threw himself over the first of a dozen zombies that stood between them and their destination. It snarled, black veins swelling from its neck and face. His blade entered its eye socket, producing a wet, sticky sound. No sooner had the creature gone limp did Livingston grab one of his throwing knives. Another turned, drawn by the sounds of struggle. It saw him and began to sprint, but it only made a single step before the blade penetrated its eye and entered its brain.

Another one stepped over its body and started for the Captain. A flash of lightning glistened over the silver blade of another knife that soared through the air. Jackman's aim was perfect. The blade splattered black secretion as it entered the skull. The undead staggered, its brain shooting off signals for a few seconds before shutting down.

Luke went next. Using his gun as a hammer, he bashed one's skull, then moved on to the next. He swung the weapon as though it were a tennis racket, knocking the zombie's head clean off its shoulders. Beside him, Neill took the next one. His target saw him and began its approach, dripping slime with each step. He waited until it closed in, then stepped to the side while simultaneously sweeping his minigun downward like a golf club. The barrels caught the creature at the knees, sending it faceplanting into the rocks. Neill stomped his foot down on the back of its head, driving it further into the rock until hearing that sickening *crunch*.

Soviar waited behind, not feeling up for dealing with these creatures in close combat. She knelt down in the fog and watched as the team approached the rock wall, engaging each corpse along the way. They could not risk firing and drawing the attention of the horde that claimed two of their teammates. They had to keep it as quiet as possible. Besides, they were running low on ammo.

The soldiers waded through the small pack of undead, until finally there was only one left. A red-faced Sergeant approached the creature with a knife in his hand. His face was wet from a combination of rain, sweat, and tears. He wanted to scream but had to hold it in for the same reason he couldn't fire his weapon. All he could get out was a sneer. His voice cracked behind his teeth, all that could escape of his pent-up howl. He rammed the zombie and knocked it backwards, then brought the knife down into its eye. He twisted the blade and drove it further down until it finally quit squirming.

His breathing was rapid, his hand shaking against the knife hilt. He looked at the blackened, slimy face of the thing he had just killed, then at the infantry uniform it wore. His hatred for the Tarkadon had increased to levels even he couldn't imagine. Not only had they claimed his father, but now the woman he loved. The image of the dropship gunning Ramos down replayed in his mind, despite his efforts to keep it out. It was mental torture. It was as though some evil mastermind was deliberately forcing him to see it over and over again. His imagination took over, flashing images of these foul things tearing her apart. A horrible, slow death. His breathing quickened, his rage billowing like magma rising from the Earth's core.

Park grabbed a rock and smashed it over the dead thing's face repeatedly until its head was flattened against the ground.

"Sergeant? You okay?" Livingston whispered. Park stood up. Lightning flashed overhead, illuminating his vindictive gaze.

"I'm fine," he said.

No, you're not. Livingston was in a bind. The Sergeant was collapsing under pressure. But what could he do about it at the moment? They were minutes away from escape. He approached the rock wall, passing Jackman along the way.

"Sir?" she said. She had been watching Park's odd behavior.

"I know," Livingston whispered. "Let's get on a ship and get out of here first. Once we're past the satellites, we'll give him a sedative. I'll help to make sure he doesn't resist. Hopefully they'll have a hyper-sleep chamber we can put him in."

"Good idea," she whispered.

The Captain felt along the rocks, then found a place for him to climb. He hauled himself twelve-feet up until his head and shoulders were over the top. From there, he used his scope to study the facility it guarded.

The hanger bay was a large, cylinder-shaped facility. It was over a thousand feet wide and double that in length. Within the perimeter of rocks, there was a barracks area as well as additional holding cells for storing prisoners. On the south side was a maintenance shed, with some repair walkers sprawled out on the ground. Like the facility on Boracan, there were several guard towers along the perimeter, though each of them appeared to be vacant. There was no perimeter barrier, which made access easy. In fact, the whole station appeared to be powered down.

Livingston studied the area from several hundred yards out. There were a few corpses walking about, nothing they wouldn't be able to handle. Then again, he couldn't see the entire facility. There could be more on the other side, or inside, and he wouldn't know it. That is, until they showed up.

"Any Tarkadons?" Jackman asked.

"Not that I can see," Livingston said.

"They keep showing up wherever we go," Neill whispered.

"It's possible they're tracking us," Soviar said. "Hell, they might even be waiting in there for us."

"And they'll regret it," Park sneered. Nobody said anything for a minute. Livingston put the scope away and checked his ammo. He had half a battery loaded and one on his belt. He then pulled his knife half-way out of the sheath.

"I don't know about going hand-to-hand," Neill said. He was still breathing heavily from the previous encounters. "Those things are strong. They don't feel pain, so their bodies don't have any restrictions on how hard they can fight. As opposed to us, who…well…" His heavy breathing conveyed the rest of his point.

"And remember, you get a scratch from these things, you're doomed to become one," Soviar reminded them. Neill swallowed nervously and proceeded to check himself. Jackman found herself doing the same. Even Luke tried to look inconspicuous as he glanced at his arms and claws. Luckily, his rigid skin kept any of the gunk from getting into his bloodstream. He would soak his claws…hell, his whole body… in a bath of disinfectant before eating again, however.

"There are only a few," Livingston said. "Luke, you and I will flank them. We have to keep it quiet. There's still a large portion of the herd on the road. If they know we're here, and we can't get inside for whatever reason, then we're toast."

"Aye-aye," Luke growled. He bent his neck, appearing like a sea serpent, then clicked his mandibles. He was ready to add to his body count and tell his brethren of the demons he had slain. It was an enemy that none of them would ever face…hopefully. He couldn't imagine the ferocity of an undead Vickel.

"The rest of you follow us. Keep low and quiet, like we've been doing. If there are more coming, let us know through the commlink. And keep an eye on what's behind you. A swarm of these things can show up at any time."

"Yes, Captain," Jackman said. Livingston nodded to Luke, then the two of them quietly descended down the other side. Keeping low, they moved over a hundred yards, where they ambushed a few wandering corpses. Blades and claws penetrated their brains and splashed them to the ground.

The second unit followed up and branched out. Though the attack was silent, it still attracted the attention of a few wandering zombies. Jackman found one stumbling from a fallen exo-suit. Its attention was on the Captain, which prevented it from seeing her as she stabbed her knife through the back of its head.

Park threw the rock in his hand, pancaking the face of another. He closed in on it and stabbed it repeatedly. Jackman grimaced in disgust. It wasn't clear if he was making sure it was dead, or just raging out again.

She heard Soviar shriek. Jackman turned to the right and saw her. She stood over a freshly killed corpse, with her pistol drawn at another that was bearing down on her. Jackman threw her knife. The blade struck its temple, burying the tip in its brain. Soviar trembled, then looked back at her.

She had almost doomed the group right there. Jackman tapped her shoulder. *Don't worry about it.*

Only three hundred feet until they reached the hangar. There were other bodies on the ground, torn up by blaster-fire and decay. Some wore jumpsuits, others wore combat gear. Jackman passed an exo-suit and stopped. Inside of it was a corpse, his stomach and throat torn open. His arms and legs were still harnessed into the controls. Around his body were smashed corpses. By the looks of it, he had died while using the maintenance suit as a weapon. It appeared they were truly dead. Most of them, at least.

A few rose up from the ground, alerted by the fresh meat that disturbed their 'slumber'.

"Good Christ," Neill muttered. They were like praying mantises, patiently waiting for their victims to foolishly wander by. Luke was quick to smash their heads. Infected blood splotched the ground. The Vickel had to subdue a victorious roar.

"Well done," Livingston said.

"Hold on," Jackman said. She listened carefully. She could hear a corpse snarling somewhere behind them. Neill could hear it too. They both looked, but couldn't see any of them walking about.

"Where the hell is it?" Neill whispered.

"I don't see anything, but it sounds like it's nearby," Jackman said.

"It sounds like it's only one," Soviar pointed out. Jackman waited another moment, then followed the others to the hangar.

The steady drizzle escalated into a heavy shower as they reached the maintenance shed. The door had been caved inward by some tremendous force. Livingston shone his light inside. There were two other exo-suits along with a few other maintenance vehicles. Wandering between them were a couple of the undead. Livingston used his flashlight to draw them outside, only for Luke to behead them as they came through the doorway.

With no others in sight, the team converged upon the hangar entrance. The south module was locked from the inside.

"Damn it," Livingston cursed. He pulled Webb's terminal from the pack and started to run a bypass. He wasn't as quick as the late tech expert, and performing this function himself made him realize how small his team had become.

Jackman heard the snarl again. She watched the area carefully. There were no corpses walking nearby. The wind had blown away any fog. With each flash of lightning, she had a clear view of her surroundings. It felt as though an invisible corpse was stalking them.

Next came a mechanical squeal. This time, everyone was looking back. The initial concern was that an enemy vehicle was in the area. Whatever it was, the gears sounded as though they needed oiling.

"Jesus! Boss!" Neill said. He pointed to one of the mech-suits. The zombie harnessed inside was baring teeth, looking directly at them. Still strapped in, the mechanical arms and legs moved with its own. It stood up, now towering three feet over Luke. Biting the air, it came at them. It arms outstretched, subsequently reaching out with the clamps.

"What's the luck on that door, Captain?" Jackman asked.

"It's not responding," Livingston said.

"What do you mean it's not responding?" Neill said.

"There's a countermeasure in place. It's as though… they're expecting us," he muttered. The mechanized zombie quickened its pace. He tossed the terminal aside and moved from the door. "Disperse!"

The team disbanded, moving in separate directions. The zombie turned back and forth, deciding on a target, then settled on Neill. He backed away, gazing high at the rotting pilot. It reached, unconsciously swaying the arms. Its metal feet crunched the ground into pebbles as it chased him. Fighting this thing in close quarters was impossible. A swing of those arms would instantly break many bones, if not crush a man his size entirely.

Beyond the mechanical groaning was another noise. Moans. There were more zombies somewhere. The sounds were distant, though steadily growing more intense. Wherever they were, they were coming.

Neill kept his eyes fixed on the fiend. It moved slower than the others, not having mastered the exo-suit's movements. He raised his weapon to shoot it, then listened to the moans again. Finally, he glanced back. The storm's lightning brought the perimeter entrance into view. Beyond it was an ocean of zombies, drawn by the sounds of the exo-suit.

"Ohhhh... FUCK!" he said. There was no point in keeping his voice down now. They were a few hundred meters off. But that would change in a few seconds.

The pilot reached for him. Neill dove out of the way. The clamps buried themselves into the ground where he stood, then created a small fissure as the pilot swung itself to the right to pursue him.

He took a firing stance and began rotating the barrel. Before the weapon could fire, the creature lunged again. Muttering one expletive after another, the gunner dove out of the way, losing the rotation in the process.

Blaster bolts struck the right arm.

"Come on, turn this way!" Jackman shouted. As though on command, the pilot did. It growled and approached the medic, arms outstretched. Jackman aimed for its head but could not get a shot. The undead pilot had, without knowledge of doing so, created a defense by having its arms reaching out for her. She fired a few bolts, which exploded uselessly over the clamps. It quickened its pace into an unbalanced sprint. "Shit," she muttered. Her plan had backfired.

It lunged with both arms. The Corporal let out a scream as she fell backward. The clamps snapped shut twelve inches above her face. She saw the arms coming straight down like an executioner's axe. She rolled to the left. The blades punched through the layer of rock, then yanked back. The pilot growled, then rotated to follow her. Once again, its arms were outstretched, deflecting blaster bolts fired from Livingston and Park.

"Hey, prick!" Neill said. He was finally ready and in firing position. Jackman turned to the right and ran, tricking her pursuer to facing the gunner. She ran as fast as she could until she was past him. Neill blasted the minigun. His stream of energy punched through the pilot's body, mincing it into crisp pieces. The suit shook, cavities burning into the arms and legs. The gunner was not looking for a headshot, however. All he needed to do was ravage the body enough and destroy the bones and muscles below the neck. The torso exploded into chunks and hung loose from the harness. The dead dangled loose, its spinal column broken. The jaw still snapped, until the machine fell forward, crushing the skull.

Now, the horde was truly aware of the squad's presence. They came through the perimeter like a raging river and branched out in search of prey. There was little time before they would swarm the team.

"Neill!" Livingston called out. He pointed at the minigun then at the door, "Would you do the honors?" Neill quickly lined himself up with the target. The metal on the doors would not withstand a steady bombardment from the Viper.

"Knock-knock," he said, then unleashed his fury on the entrance. The bolts sliced through the metal, carving an opening for them. Immediately, the group entered the building and proceeded down a small corridor, which led into a large open lobby. They assembled at the next doorway. Luckily, this one was unlocked. They proceeded into the next corridor, where a small group of undead awaited. Livingston blasted all three, then made way for the others. Looking back, he could see all the way down to the exterior entrance. The undead were pouring inside and darting for the lobby. He shut the door, which shook a few moments after as the swarm converged on the other side.

"You think that'll hold them?" Soviar asked. The words had no sooner come out when the door began to succumb to the combined force behind it. The center of it began to swell, the edges peeling off the frame.

"No," Livingston said. They hustled down the corridor and stopped at the first juncture.

It was as though a rhinoceros had stampeded through the facility. The floor tiling had numerous cavities caused by something with immense weight. Pieces of ceiling and wiring hung in strands. Lights were out, though the power system was still online.

Mutilated bodies lined the corridor. They lay on the floor in twisted postures, their bodies pulverized. But not eaten. Again, it was as though they were caught in the path of something large rampaging its way through the corridor.

"Here," Park announced. He shined a light on a directory map on the wall. "Hangar One is to the west. Hangar Two is further north. Straight ahead, but a little bit further."

"West," Livingston ordered. They moved right away, leaping over the bloody corpses that lined the floor. They followed the signs, which took them to a right-hand turn. Livingston turned the corner and held up a fist, halting the team.

In the next corridor was an assembly line of undead. Several of them stood up from the body they feasted on and turned their bloodstained faces on the new meat that stood at the juncture.

"Back," Livingston ordered. He let off a flurry of blaster bolts, dropping the nearest two, then followed his team back down the corridor. The horde turned the corner, filling the air with hellish screeches. Blaster bolts flashed the corridor a bright red, sparking as it struck the brow. Livingston let off another few shots, then turned to run at full speed.

Park was at the front of the group now. After two hundred feet, they reached the intersection where they had found the directory. To the right was the corridor where they had come from. The automatic doors crumpled one last time before breaking completely off. A flight of zombies poured into the corridor, shrieking with no rhyme or reason.

The group took the left turn, heading north to Hangar Two. The further they moved, the worse the damage was. Debris was everywhere. Soldiers had been torn apart, but not as though they were eaten, rather as though they were pulled apart by a giant beast. Some had reanimated, their broken bodies attempting to grab the soldiers as they ran by.

The corridor ended at another juncture. They took the left turn toward the hangar. Two automatic doors were stuck half open, the edges of each one appearing to have been crushed. They passed through the entrance and formed a firing line. Neill fired first, laughing with joy as he watched the first wave of undead disintegrate from the condensed wave of blaster-fire. That joy came to a sudden end when the warning LED flashed. The battery pack was running low.

Park and Jackman provided additional support while Livingston ran to the door's control panel. He pressed the *close* button repeatedly, but with no response from the door.

"Manual control!" Soviar shouted frantically. "Below it! All these facilities have a manual control lever in case of a power issue! Right there!" Livingston saw the metal panel beneath the controls.

Go figure, it's bolted shut. His blaster solved that issue. He shot each of the bolts securing the panel then tore it free, exposing the lever. He cranked it, and with a dull groan, the doors gradually shut. They met in the middle, leaving only a tiny opening at the middle where the edges had been folded inward. The horde crashed into it from the other side. The doors shook but held.

"Hot damn," Neill said. The group backed away from the door, then observed the hangar. It was a large chamber, two hundred feet from front to back, with a thirty-foot ceiling. To their surprise, there were three ships lined in a row. The first one's cockpit had been smashed inward, the pilot and crew torn apart inside it. Among the dead were soldiers and scientists, lying between weapons, cargo boxes made from reinforced steel, and a medical stretcher.

Livingston approached the stretcher. It was high-tech, resembling the slabs he had seen in the lab. Every restraint holding the patient was broken, popped free as easily as toothpicks. His gaze returned to the cockpit. It had been smashed in like a matchbox. The control console was tattered. No way did the ship land like this, and there were no towing vehicles to suggest it was brought in. Something INSIDE the facility came in, killed the troopers, and had the strength to crumple a six-inch hull.

His eyes went back to the doors and focused on the slit where they came together. He could see the horde through the hole where the edges had been peeled apart. It was the exact same spot on both doors...as though an insanely strong person had pried his fingers through the slit and pulled them apart with his bare hands.

"What was that?" Neill said. He moved around the ship and approached the next one. It was empty...and intact. The third one, however, was in a similar state as the first. The sounds were coming from within its fuselage. Things were falling all over the place, giving the appearance that someone, or something, was ransacking the ship. "Got ourselves a live one."

"Careful, Neill," Livingston said.

"No worries, Cap. It's clearly just one," Neill said. He grabbed his pistol and approached the open fuselage. "I think I can manage..."

A deafening roar rang his ears. Out of the fuselage came a hulking humanoid beast with glowing green eyes. Its skin looked as though it were made of gravel. Beneath its sand-colored skin was an embellished musculature that would put Greek gods to shame. White bones popped out of the knuckles like spikes. There was some hair left on its head, though not much, and what remained had thinned.

It looked down at the gunner, who stood two feet shorter than itself. It roared again, baring spiked teeth, then lashed out with lightning speed. It lifted Neill off the ground and squeezed with both hands, crushing his ribcage. A bloody gurgle escaped his throat.

"Christ!" Park shouted. He let off several shots, hitting the thing in the shoulder. The bolts burnt small flakes from the skin, hardly fazing the beast. It raised Neill high then threw him hard into the floor, smashing his spine, neck, and the back of his skull. It thrust its body weight forward and brought its foot on his head, exploding it like a grape. A few more blasts seared its flesh. It turned and started for the Sergeant, who immediately started backtracking.

A volley of bolts hit the creature from various angles as the team spread out. It continued chasing the Sergeant, who found himself backed up to the door. Behind it, the horde pressed themselves to the gap. A hand reached through and nearly brushed his face. With the horde behind him and a hulking mutation approaching, he was trapped!

A yellow bolt struck the creature's shoulder. This time, it actually lurched backward, displaying pain with a deep howl. It turned again and saw the Vickel. Luke fired another shot, hitting it in the midsection. The creature staggered back. It was bleeding now. With the pain came increased ferocity. It charged the Vickel, taking a third hit to the chest. Despite the dark green blood that spilled from its wounds, it didn't slow.

Luke backtracked but realized there was no escape. He swung his blaster, striking the mutant across the face.

The creature landed a blow to his stomach, the spiked knuckles crunching the Vickel's ribs. The two of them wrestled briefly, the mutant easily outmuscling the reptilian. It rammed him against the wall, then slammed him to the ground face-first. Blood trickled from all three sections of his jaw. Teeth hit the floor. The creature stood over him, ready to pull him apart.

"Stay down!" Livingston yelled to him. He stepped out from between the ships, carrying Neill's minigun. The beast saw him, and with a deafening roar, began to charge. He blasted the gun, shredding its torso with an intense volley of lasers. The force of the hits drove the thing backward, the hot energy searing away its flesh. Blood was now pouring out in green waterfalls.

And right as it seemed the creature would succumb to the attack, the battery died out. Livingston looked down at the slowing barrels, then back at the creature. It had fallen to its knees, its breathing labored. It looked back at him, then bared its teeth.

Luke sprang into action, letting out a triumphant roar as he tackled the creature onto its back. He drove his claws into the wounds, shredding the soft flesh below. The beast screamed with each twist. After flailing its arms, it grabbed Luke's ankle and squeezed. Luke's roar turned into an ear-piercing screech as the hand crunched the bone.

He drew his arm back, straightened his fingers, then speared them through the chest cavity. The tips found the beating heart and ravaged it. The beast let out one final roar, then stiffened. Luke, exhausted, fell off his dead enemy and crawled away. His foot flopped behind his ankle. It was attached to his body by nothing but skin. It didn't bother Luke, however. He had defeated an enemy no Vickel had ever faced. Not only that, but by defeating this enemy, he had spat into the face of Tarkadon.

The victory was his, though it came at a cost. He leaned up and looked to the sounds of crying. At first, he thought it was Soviar, which made sense. She wasn't a combat soldier and wasn't used to such horror. He was wrong; it was Jackman, kneeling at Neill's battered corpse.

CHAPTER 20

Livingston set foot in the shuttle in Dock Two. It was a small ship, not much bigger than a typical Stinger. There wasn't much to its design. Cockpit, main fuselage, sleeping area, and bathroom, and that was about it. There was an engine room, down below, which was a compact space. Hopefully, he would not have to go down there during the trip. Hence, he wanted the ship fully inspected beforehand.

The engines came to life, much to his relief. He wasn't used to Tarkadon controls, but they seemed simple enough. Still, he wished Soto had lived. He was a good pilot and would have no problem figuring this system out. It was an inverted design, which would take him a little getting used to. The worst part would be taking off. Once in space, he'd be able to experiment a little more without the worry of crashing into anything. But before starting, he needed to familiarize himself with the radio controls. If he didn't get a signal out to allied forces, they would blow their ship away without hesitation.

Being in here without Soto made the cockpit feel empty, despite it being smaller than that of the Recon-Valley. Having lost so many team members, his mind started pondering some thought which he had tucked away. He felt he had seen enough people die, and way too many of them from the muzzle of his own blaster. He wondered how much longer he was willing to do it. He was nearing forty, his body feeling like that of someone ten years older. Half of those years were spent in the service. He had refused rank several times, not being the type to work at a desk. If he was going to lead men, he wanted to be in the trenches with them, which was something he was feeling less and less fit to do. In addition to his chemical burns, he was developing arthritis in his hands and lower back, which didn't present much of a problem now, but would in the coming years. For the first time in what felt like forever, he was thinking about life outside of the military.

He heard someone stepping up the ramp. It was Jackman. In her arms were some rations and water pouches, found in the battered ship in Dock One. Her face was still moist, though she had regained her composure. She saw the Captain looking back at her.

"I'm sorry, sir," she said. She turned to step out.

"Corporal," he said. She stopped. He stepped back from the cockpit. She stood in position of attention. "At ease." She did so and leaned against the wall. She was so tired, it was a struggle even to stand. Livingston searched for something to say. "Uh, how's Luke?"

"He's good. I set his leg and wrapped the ankle as best I could," she answered. "He's gonna need surgery. That thing completely crushed the bone. He's got some broken ribs as well. Probably has some damage to his spine. But he's in good spirits."

"He's a good soldier," Livingston said. "You all are."

"Thank you, Captain."

"Listen, uh…" Livingston looked away, still in search of words. "How long were you planning to remain in the service?"

Jackman chuckled. "I love the U.G.S. That said, I don't think I can handle any more of this mentally. I just can't. I think, after my contract expires at the end of this standard year, I'll head off to the Lake Rim where I grew up. Hopefully I'll land a job in a hospital." The Captain was glad to hear it.

"You'd be perfect for it," he said. Silence followed the statement. It was as though he wanted to say something but lost his nerve. It was the only time she ever sensed nervousness from the tough-as-nails officer.

Livingston was aware of how he looked. He had specifically stopped her to talk, then asked her about her intentions of staying in the service, which was clearly leading. And he knew that *she* knew it was a leading question. But his personal doubts resurfaced. The first being the uncertainty that he could ever return to a normal life after spending so much of it at war. Then came his inner voice, whispering to him that she deserves better. He thought of his deformities, which reminded him that he was in no way an attractive man. Physically fit, maybe, but definitely not easy on the eyes. Thanks to that damn chemical burn.

"Is that all, Captain?" Jackman's voice broke his thoughts. Then he did something she never heard him do; he stuttered.

"Excuse me," he cleared his throat. "Yes, that's all. We'll be heading back soon." She nodded then walked down the ramp. Those inner demons had beaten him, a feat not many could claim. Livingston was lost in his thoughts. How could he muster up the mental stamina to endure long missions far from home like this, yet, not manage to ask a girl out?

Against regulation, he justified it. Of course, he knew that didn't mean anything.

Park entered the shuttle in Dock One and kneeled by one of the dead scientists. He had been ransacking their clothes in search of any data pertaining to the location of the Tarkadon's High Command. There was a window on the other side of the ship, giving him a view of the shuttle that they would use to depart. His eyes narrowed, catching a glimpse of his

Captain standing in the fuselage. In his possession was the portable terminal taken from the facility. Park was sure that somewhere in those files were clues to the location of his target.

The ones who killed dad...who killed Dawn, will suffer the same fate.

He continued checking the dead scientists. He pried their lab coats from the dried corpses and checked the pockets. Most were empty. Frustrated, he checked the last one, who had been crushed near the backseats.

There was something at the dead man's feet. Something that had fallen from his grasp. The Sergeant knelt down to pick it up. At first glance, it looked like a miniature flashlight. He picked it up then saw the LED. It was a scanner. No, a key! A key to what?

Park looked back at the steel boxes. They were somewhat large, three-by-three feet. On the top right corner was an inch-long screen for the key. He pressed the key to it and squeezed the button, lighting the LED. He heard a couple of *clicks* and the lid slid back, revealing the contents inside. Park gazed down at the vials of serum the scientists had stashed away. There were several of them resting in protective casing attached to the sides. In the center were injection needles and digitized note cards. The crew was attempting an escape, and would've succeeded if—he looked back at the stretcher—if their patient hadn't broken loose.

He picked up one of the vials and gazed at the serum inside.

"Interesting stuff," Soviar said. She expected him to jump but he didn't. Park didn't even glance back at her as she stepped up the ramp.

"This isn't the toxin," Park said. "We saw the samples in the lab. The green stuff causes the reanimation. But this here does something else."

"They were trying to make super-soldiers," Soviar said. She took another vial from the box. "We saw the experiment. It gives enhanced strength and durability. It's a mutagen that hardens the skin and increases muscle and bone mass. They can be killed, but it takes a hell of a lot to do it. If your Captain didn't have that minigun, we'd all be dead right now."

"We could use this," Park said. Soviar chuckled. "I'm serious," he continued. "We can use both this and the Star Virus."

"You want to inject yourself with that stuff?" Soviar said.

"You don't think it'll work?"

Soviar looked over at the dead mutant. "I think it's a work in progress," she said. "If you were to be in command of an army of super soldiers, you'd probably want them to keep their human brain function. You think that thing had any intelligence? No, it was just a rampaging animal seeking revenge on its creators. You take that stuff, the same thing would happen to you."

"What if the patient was given a limited dose?" Park said. He pointed at the empty vials. "Look at that. There's at least eight of them. If they gave them all to that freak, no wonder he turned into a giant ogre. One would probably do the trick."

"It's a reasonable assumption, but there's something you're not considering," Soviar said.

"And that is--?"

"That these might not be containing the same type of serum," Soviar said. "They could cause different types of mutations. Some might enhance bone structure and muscle mass. Others might have more hideous effects. Take this one for example…" she picked up one of the vials. On the label were the words *Provectus Regeneratione*. "This one was clearly intended for advanced healing."

"Good," Park said. "We'll take that one for ourselves."

"You want to try it? Be my guest," she laughed.

"You think it causes something like cancer?" Park said.

"No, but it might cause other mutations, like make you grow extra limbs or something like that."

Park thought of the survivor that Livingston and Weatherford were forced to gun down in the holding cells. Whatever its effect was, it wasn't the same as the thing they just killed in this hangar. But he was experiencing some kind of mutation, similar to the Star Virus but different. The Sergeant looked over the labels again. Each one contained some kind of scientific name, the language being something similar to Latin. There was no way he'd know that they were, or what they did, without extensive research.

I wonder what would happen if someone took more than one of these things. He realized he was starting to think just like the scientists who conducted these experiments. That bothered him at first, but the feeling fleeted away. *Sometimes to beat an enemy, you have to become like them.*

Suddenly, the fluid began to splash in the vials. The glass clattered in their slots. Park and Soviar could feel the vibration beneath their feet. The others could hear it too. Luke sprang up and balanced on his good leg, while Livingston and Jackman grabbed their weapons and hurried to the west wall.

They could hear the sound of ion engines circling above. Then came blaster-fire, followed by popping sounds of impact. Livingston peeked through one of the viewing windows.

There were two Tarkadon dropships circling the west side of the perimeter, their gunners blasting away at the undead below. Their bodies exploded into black splotches as the energy tore through them.

"Just lovely," Jackman said.

"Nothing we can't handle," Livingston said.

"Do they know we're here?" Jackman asked.

"They'll find out soon enough," Park bellowed.

"Let's see what they do," Livingston said. "Come on crew, let's set the table for our guests."

"Excuse me, Captain?" Soviar nervously said. She was behind him.

"Just get in the shuttle, Doctor. You'll be safe there," Livingston said.

"Okay, but sir, I don't have a gun," she said. Livingston looked back at her. It made sense to give her something to defend herself with. He unholstered his pistol and handed it to her. "Be careful, that one has a little bit more kick than the usual blaster." He turned his eyes back to the battle outside. The ships nearly had the landing zone completely clear of zombies.

"Oh, I believe you," she said. Livingston noticed her reflection in the glass. The gun was pointing right at him. He saw the flash, heard the crack, and felt the impact on the back of his helmet. Everything else was a blur. He spun and fell, his helmet trailing smoke where the high-powered bolt struck it on the side.

"What the—" Park raised his rifle, but Soviar already had him in her sights. She fired twice. The first shot nicked him in the shoulder, throwing his aim off. The next hit him in the right breast, throwing him backward.

Soviar turned and dashed behind one of the ships, evading blaster bolts from Jackman. Luke limped his way around Dock One, only catching a glimpse of what just occurred. Jackman ran to the Captain's side. The helmet had been split open down its left side, exposing Livingston's charred face. He was alive and conscious, though still in a daze.

"Sir, you've been hit," she said.

"Yeah...with my own gun," Livingston said. It was the worst kind of humiliation. He looked back. "Where is she?"

"I don't know. She went that way and—oh no," Jackman muttered. She was looking out at the ships, which were now turning toward the hangar. Their ventral guns were glowing green. Livingston grabbed her by the arm and threw her back as far as he could.

The wall exploded behind them. A shockwave shook the entire complex, deactivating the overhead lights. Red flashers twirled from each corner of the room while wailing sirens echoed through the complex.

Livingston was on his stomach. He squinted, feeling a rush of heat against his face that he wasn't used to. It was at that moment he realized his helmet had come off entirely. Already, he was finding it difficult to breathe. He resorted to his therapy, taking deep slow breaths through the nose, then exhaling through the mouth.

His vision cleared and he looked around for his team. Burning debris had been launched all over the compartment, filling the air with smoke. The blast had thrown Luke and Park backwards as well. He couldn't see them, nor could he see Jackman.

From around the back of the hangar stepped Dr. Soviar, holding his pistol at her side. Livingston didn't bother saying a word. It was obvious; she had tricked them. Played him a fool, and did it well. And she knew it. She smiled as she stared at the helpless Captain. His armor was damaged, his weapon lost in the blast, and most important of all, his mask was gone. She had actually envisioned him to look worse than he did. His whole left side was marred by skin grafts, but it wasn't anything completely odd looking. She had expected him to look as hideous as the undead corpses they were fighting. Hell, his hair was surprisingly well-kept. There were some bad burns on his throat, which had turned black by now, but the effects were still obvious. No wonder the need for his mask.

She watched through the ravaged wall behind her as the dropships started to touch down. She had a few moments to waste. With one hand keeping the gun on Livingston, she reached into her pocket and pulled out a metal square. Livingston knew what it was; a tracker.

All at once, it explained everything. Who she was, how the Tarkadons found the Recon-Valley while cloaked, how they'd managed to intercept them so many times.

"Well, thanks to you..." she said, "I don't have to worry about performing an investigation of what went wrong at my research facility."

"*Your* research facility?" Livingston said. The doctor smiled. "Your name isn't Soviar, is it? Yet, you *are* a doctor. You know all this stuff too well not to be." All of a sudden, it came to him. "It's you. You're Major Liskai."

"You're smart," she said. "But I'm smarter, as I've just proven to you. I should thank you; you've helped us secure this hangar. It would've been difficult had you not taken care of the rogue mutant for us."

"You must be dedicated if you were willing to have those fighters blow you up along with the rest of us," Livingston said.

"All hail Tarkadon," the Major said proudly.

"Is that what your fellow trooper said when you killed him in the holding cells back on Boracan? After slaughtering all those prisoners, and switching clothes with one of them? Had to leave no loose ends in order to infiltrate us, didn't you?"

"And now that we know what the Star Virus is capable of, we will launch capsules deep into U.G.S. space. Salvage teams will find them and expose themselves, and be the first to spread the virus. Soon, it will spread through the entire Republic, and by the time they realize what's happening, it'll be too late."

Livingston knew she was flaunting her victory in his face. She wanted him to wallow in the gut-punching effect of knowing he failed. Unfortunately, it was working. Once that virus left this planet, there'd be no stopping it, and he would not be able to get a warning out.

The dropship landed and unloaded a dozen troops that hustled toward the hangar.

"Well Captain, it was nice knowing you," Soviar said. She extended the gun and pressed her finger to the trigger.

From out of the flames, Corporal Jackman sprang into action. She threw a kick, striking Liskai in the ribs, throwing her aim to the side. A blaster bolt bounced off the hull of the shuttle. She turned to fire at Jackman, who landed another kick, doubling the Major over. A blow to her wrist knocked the gun away, and the Corporal raised a knee, smashing Liskai in the face, then landing a left hook to the jaw. The Major staggered backwards and raised her hands to guard against a flurry of punches that pursued her face.

The troopers entered the breach.

Livingston dove for the pistol. Gripping it with both hands, he rolled to his back and fired down between his knees. His bolts caught the first trooper in the face, dropping him instantly. The next one let off a shot, but aimed high. Livingston's shot, however, was on point, hitting him in the left collar bone. The rest came pouring in, sending blaster-fire his way. The Captain sprinted back, disappearing behind a wall of flame.

"Move in toward Dock One!" one of the officers yelled out. They moved to the right and converged on the decimated shuttle. There, they saw Sergeant Park lying face down. Blood poured from his chest wound. His hands were tucked under his chest. They stepped over his body and grabbed the boxes of serum and toxins.

"Heads up!" one yelled.

From around the front of the ship came Luke. He raised a blaster and sent a bolt through one of the troopers. A volley of return fire drove him back. Several of the troopers proceeded to carry the boxes back through the breach, while others provided cover.

Luke was crouched around the bow of the ship. He reached around and blindly fired a shot, only for his weapon to spark near the frame. It had been damaged in the fight with the mutant, and in the worst of moments, it was failing on him. Despite his physical superiority, he would not survive a barrage of enemy fire.

Luckily, the Tarkadons were unaware of his damaged weapon, and had no desire to face off against a Vickel. The gunners remained in place while the crates were taken outside.

"Sir!" one called out. "We've got infected crawling all around. We need to move!"

"Major Liskai, you copy?"

"Just a minute," the Tarkadon Major growled. She had taken another blow to the face, which nearly flattened her nose. She stepped back, slapping away a jab. Jackman sprang forward and lashed her arms out to get them around Liskai's neck. The Major lunged at the same time, landing an elbow to Jackman's face. Grabbing her by the collar, Liskai landed a knee to her stomach, then spun to the left, crashing her against the hull of a shuttle. Jackman hit the ground, dazed but ready to continue the fight. But the Major had already started running for the ship. Its rail gun was pointed at the breach. If she went out, she'd be torn to pieces.

She felt a pair of hands lift her to her feet.

"On your feet, Corporal," Livingston said. It was the first time she'd seen his face. The pain he was feeling was obvious. The contact with the air was causing his nerves to go haywire.

The Captain was getting lightheaded.

"Get...get out..." he said. It hurt to even speak. He fell to his knees. Now, it was Jackman who was trying to help him up.

"Captain, come on," she said.

"Just...go," Livingston demanded, his voice weak. He started to fall over. Jackman caught him and eased him to the floor, not before stomping out the nearest flame. She opened the shuttle's portside ramp and entered, then found her medical bag intact. She loaded a syringe with painkiller then returned to the Captain's side.

"This'll hurt," she said.

"I told you to—AGH!" Livingston screamed as she jabbed the needle into his neck. He tensed, clawing the floor around him. He gasped for breath, then relaxed himself. The painkiller was starting to take effect. He opened his eyes and looked up. "You disobeyed a direct order, Corporal."

"Yeah?" Jackman helped him up. "Go ahead and court-martial me."

The last of the troopers filed out through the breach, leaving Park lying on the floor, presumably dead. Luke limped around the ship and rushed to the Sergeant's side. He rolled Park to his back to check his vitals. Two empty vials rolled from underneath him. In his hand was an injection gun taken from one of the crates.

You fool, you injected yourself. One of the vials had the regenerative capabilities. The other, nobody knew. Not even Park.

His eyes shot open, shocking the battle-hardened Vickel into staggering backward. His chest wound had completely healed. But healthy was the last word Luke would choose to describe what he was seeing. Park convulsed, arching back so far, he was practically balancing on his head and heels. He was screaming now. His hands clawed at his chest, ripping his uniform off, exposing the rippling skin underneath it.

It had turned into a dark shade of grey. Park yelled as several parts of his body shifted. It was as though his torso was comprised of a hundred movable pieces. His skin hardened, appearing as though made of granite. His hands, legs, and head grew before Luke's very eyes. Bones protruded through his neck, back, and knuckles. His skeleton was growing, inducing a level of pain that no medication would alleviate.

More clothing tore away as Park grew another twenty inches in height. His shirt was gone entirely now, his pant-legs shredded. Finally, the waistline tore, popping the belt buckle. Park was naked, though there was nothing there to identify him as a man. The serum continued to misshape his body. There were no genitals left. His toes were curved and razor-sharp like a reptilians'. His head and face were elongated like a goblin. All his hair had fallen out. Had Luke not witnessed the transformation, he would have simply assumed that Park was still missing, and that this was the beast that killed him.

In an abrupt motion, the brute that was Park was on its feet. He bared shark-like teeth, his cheeks peeling back like a canine. Luke wasn't sure if it was a snarl or a smile. Or both.

Livingston and Jackman came around the corner. Luke held up one of his claws, warning them to proceed with caution. They moved around the front of the dock and saw the thing. Livingston's first instinct was to shoot before he saw the clothes under the mutation's clawed feet.

"Park?!"

Now, the thing really was smiling.

They could hear blaster-fire outside and the buzzing of ion engines. Park turned around and sprinted for the breach.

Liskai strapped herself into the center seat, followed by her troops. Several zombies wandered from around the north and south ends of the perimeter. The gunners blasted away, shredding the ones that drew near. She watched the breach. Any moment, one of those pathetic U.G.S. soldiers might attempt to stop them.

"Let's go!" the Major said.

"Ma'am," one of the pilots said. "We still have men…"

"Lift off or I'll throw you out there myself," she snapped. The pilot knew she was serious. He pulled up on the joystick and ascended. The remaining troopers jumped for the fuselage, only to fall short. Liskai smiled. Soon, more corpses would converge on the hangar and tear apart Livingston and what remained of his team. So, she didn't get to kill him herself. She could live with that. Besides, the death that awaited him was far worse than a blaster bolt to the forehead.

"What the hell?" one of the pilots said. Liskai looked out the window at the hangar. Something enormous burst through the breach and was racing toward them. It was an abomination. A mutation.

"PARK!"

The Sergeant leapt over the ground troops and reached high, grabbing the starboard engine and hauling himself onto the ship. Like an insect on a branch, he climbed his way onto the cockpit, then pressed his brow to the glass. He smiled grotesquely at the terrified pilots inside, then smashed the reinforced glass. The ship spun as though caught in a tornado.

The ship crashed down, throwing Park off the nose. There was a sizzling sound, like a fuse sparking. A moment later, the port engine erupted, rolling the ship to starboard. Liskai thrashed in her seat, the harness digging into her shoulders and waist. Soldiers fell around her, bouncing off the walls and ceiling. The ship rolled over four times before coming to a stop.

The Major sucked a deep breath in and forced herself to focus. She was hanging to her right, meaning the ship had settled on its starboard side. Three other troopers were standing on the wall below, while four others were dead or unconscious. She unclipped her harness and lowered herself down.

There was no escape through the fuselage. She'd have to leave out the cockpit. She went through the passageway and found the two pilots, who were pancaked into their seats. Not bothering to wait, she climbed over the console and through the panel...

...just in time for Park to step into view. Liskai tensed as the monstrosity approached. She was frozen stiff. Her scientific mind descended into childish imagination, hoping that she was somehow invisible to the razor tooth brute.

She wasn't.

Park snatched her from the ship and held her high with one hand. His revenge on the Tarkadons would begin here. Liskai struggled, only for Park to tighten his grasp. His fingers crunched her ribcage and arms. Blood trickled from her gums.

"Thanks for providing those capsules!" Park roared. His voice was demonic, his eyes glowing dark green. He extended his jaws and bit down on her skull, crushing it.

The troopers panicked and tried to retreat back into the ship. Park tossed Liskai's body aside and continued to bash the remains of the ship. He rolled it over and ripped open the fuselage, then reached inside like a child in a cookie jar. He pulled one of the troopers out and ripped him in half. The next one he threw to the ground and stomped, turning him into a red splotch in the rock. The last two made an escape through the cockpit. They fired their rifles, only for the bolts to spark against his hardened skin.

He charged the two troopers, smashing his spiked fist into one of them. The impact caved the trooper's whole body inward and sent him several yards back. Park backhanded the other, knocking him to the ground. He raised his foot and stomped down twice, crushing each of the trooper's legs.

Groaning in pain and unable to move his legs, the trooper tried crawling away. A shark-like grin creased the Sergeant's face and he looked at a small gathering of the undead that approached.

"They look hungry!" he roared.

"No! NOOO!" The trooper screamed. Park grabbed him by the shoulder and tossed him to the zombies, who proceeded to gather around him and eat him alive.

Park savored each scream, each drop of blood, every sound of flesh ripping. He looked at his hands and his arms, then down at his body. With the battle won, he started to think of what he had done to himself. What would Dawn Ramos think? He knew the answer; she'd be mortified.

She's dead. The words blasted in his mind as though through a bullhorn. He wouldn't have done this to himself if she was alive.

Park looked to the sky and roared.

"The Tarkadons wanted to make monsters? Now they have one!"

CHAPTER 21

"Come on, come on! Let's get on board," Livingston said. He extended his blaster and blew a hole through another ghoul that arrived through the breach. Luke engaged another with his battered rifle, which still functioned well as a club. A single swipe took the corpse's head clean off. He smashed another, momentarily clearing the hangar of the undead. Following the Captain's orders, he and Jackman stepped onto the ramp.

Heavy steps shook the ground outside. Behind the rupture in the wall stood the thing that was Park. Livingston readied his gun, unsure what state of mind the Sergeant was in. Was he still in there? Or had he truly become a bloodthirsty beast with no remnants of his personality?

"I'm gonna need that ride," Park growled. Jackman shook as he spoke. His voice, much like his appearance, was truly demonic.

Livingston didn't budge. The fact that he spoke and still recognized him gave some clues of his mental state; he wasn't *quite* as mindless as the mutant that killed Neill. Not yet, anyway.

"What's the idea, Park?" he asked. The Sergeant stepped into the hangar, deliberately swinging his elbow into the edge, breaking off a section of rubble to demonstrate his strength.

"I'm gonna take myself a little ride. Oh, and I'll need that terminal," he growled. Livingston didn't back down. The mutant was big, but still small enough to fit in the pilot's seat, and he did have a little flying experience. Assuming his memories were intact, he would have no problem getting off the planet.

"And do what with it? Cause an undead uprising in over a hundred different systems? And what if that spreads into ours? What then?"

Park stepped forward until his chest was inches from Livingston's face. Still, the Captain didn't back down.

"Captain, you're ugly enough as it is…" he threatened.

"Almost as ugly as you," Livingston retorted. *Inside and out.* The answer to whether Park was human or a mindless beast was worse than he feared. He was a beast with malice!

Park made a razor smile. He wasn't going to waste any more time talking to them. Anyone who got in the way of his revenge was the enemy, plain and simple.

"Well, let me change that!" Park raised a fist, but was suddenly knocked back by a tremendous force. A broken heel did not hinder the Vickel's spring-like legs from launching him to the defense of his Captain.

He drove the mutant backward, then proceeded to thrash his rifle across his face.

Park and Jackman aimed their pistols and fired at the Sergeant. Their blaster bolts exploded uselessly against his skin, doing little more than to burn away a few thin scrapes. What was worse, those scrapes heeled almost instantly.

Luke lashed out again, raking Park across the face. The mutant absorbed each blow, then sprang forward. Luke let out a high-pitched roar as the spiked knuckles crunched his remaining ribs. He continued to lash out, but could not outmuscle the brute as it grabbed him by the shoulders and threw him face-first into the floor.

Park pressed his knee to Luke's back, pinning him to the ground, then wrapped both hands behind his jaw and pulled up. Luke spasmed then went limp. There was the simultaneous sound of ripping and crunching as Park pulled his head clean off his body.

He turned and held it high, taunting Livingston and Jackman.

Your turn!

He stopped, realizing the Captain had opened an exterior panel in the ion engine. He started forward to grab him, then stopped again. Livingston jumped back and raised his hand. In his grasp was a detonation device, linked to an explosive device placed inside the engine.

"You make a move, and I'll blow that engine, and you'll never get out of here," Livingston warned. Park held still. He was trembling with anger.

"You blow that up, and you're stuck here too!"

"I can live with it," Livingston said.

"You'd maroon yourself to save an enemy you've been fighting for years to defeat! That makes you a traitor!"

"You're willing to kill billions of innocents to fulfill your bloodlust. That makes you a murderer and a terrorist!" Livingston retorted.

"There is no innocent Tarkadon," Park growled. He took a step forward.

"Ah-ah!" Livingston said, moving his thumb over the button. They stood in a standoff, nobody moving except Jackman, who gradually stepped back behind the Captain with her rifle pointed at Park. Her stomach stiffened as Park smiled again, taking another step toward them.

"Three other hangars," he said. "I don't think I'll have much of a problem finding a new ship. Go ahead and blow up that little cherry bomb."

"Suit yourself," Livingston said. He pressed the button. Park expected to hear a small explosion. Instead, it was electrical sparking, resulting from an activated ion-overcharge.

Right then did he recognize the white labels on the detonator. His memory flashed to Boracan, where the Captain had seized the device from the enemy hangar.

"Zach, you've allowed yourself to become so jaded, you don't even have good judgement anymore." He heard Ramos as though she were standing next to him.

The engine exploded as though full of TNT, throwing Park across the hangar. He hit the south wall and fell, his body covered in burns and shrapnel. He groaned like a lion that had been shot by a poacher. There was a creaking noise coming from the wall behind him. Park, lying on his right elbow, looked over his shoulder. The doors were slowly opening, the undead on the other side reaching through the crack. He looked across the room and saw his former comrades at the secondary console.

Livingston and Jackman had run to the wall to evade the blast, which had nearly consumed them as well. The Captain hit the button for the door. Luckily, this panel was functioning properly.

The undead poured onto Park and sank their claws into his wounds, ripping them wider before they could heal. The mutant roared and ripped the zombies off of him, smashed them to black mush, then tossed them away…only for more to take their place. They had no regard for his mutation. Anything that didn't already contain their strain of virus was food to them.

The two soldiers ran out the breach. The wind nearly lifted them off their feet, and if it had, the torrential rain would've slammed them back down. The storm swirled overhead with a rage that rivaled Park's. It threw its lightning bolts across the sky like a god, lighting the path ahead of them.

"This way!" Livingston said. They ran south, shooting a few lumbering zombies in their path. There were a few up ahead but no sign of the main horde. From the looks of it, they had been eliminated by the dropships, and what remained were inside the facility.

"We can't outrun him," Jackman said.

"I know," Livingston said. It was true; retreat would only get them killed. The only way to survive was to kill Park. "Go there! Climb that guard tower."

"What about you?" Jackman asked.

"I'm going for the maintenance shed," he answered. "Go! Before he comes out!" Jackman darted for the guard tower as fast as she could. These posts carried the same design as they had for many centuries. She climbed the ladder all the way up. The guardhouse was vacant, though the weapons were left intact. There were sniper rifles, machine guns…even a couple of bazookas.

"These might come in handy," she said to herself. She grabbed one of the sniper rifles, loaded a full battery, then set up a firing position. She watched Livingston through the thermal scope as he made his way to the maintenance shed.

Livingston's face throbbed as he neared the entrance. From around the corner came a drooling corpse. It bared teeth and sprinted for him. The Captain fired his pistol. The zombie spun as the bolt splattered the entire left side of its head off. He dashed through the entrance and checked for other zombies. A few blaster bolts took care of those that had wandered inside. With the shed cleared, he moved to the row of slots on the back where the exo-suits were kept. At the end of its arms were two large clamps. He got on the computer and powered up the assembly units. Several droids on wheels rolled to the exo-suit, each containing two mechanical arms like cranes. With the computer, he instructed him to remove the clamp on the right side. The machines removed the bolt and lifted the heavy clamp from the suit. A selection of replacements flashed on the screen. Livingston selected the drill bit.

The droids rolled to the far side of the room, then returned with a three-foot long drill bit, attached to a cylinder base. They attached it to the arm then rolled away. The computer screen flashed, *Upgrade complete.*

Livingston climbed aboard and harnessed himself in. He inserted his arms and legs into the joint slots and powered the machine on. He raised the arms and took a step forward, reminding himself of how the machine felt before heading out to greet the Sergeant. He spun the drill, testing it on the steel wall. Ribbons of metal twisted and fell to the floor. He retracted the bit and examined it. There was hardly a scratch on it.

"This oughta do the trick," he said.

Park roared in agony as he battled the horde around him. He lashed his fists out, bashing skulls and knocking their corpses away. He felt as though he was battling a colony of ants. No matter which direction he faced, there was always one that managed to leap on to his back and bite into his wounds before his mutation would heal them.

He lurched back as a couple sunk their claws in and tore some tissue free. He threw himself backward against one of the ships, smashing the two creatures. The horde followed him. Claws struck against his skin, while teeth clamped down. Park swung his arms as though splashing water, knocking heads off their shoulders.

Gradually, their numbers decreased. He grabbed one by the legs and swung it like a baseball bat, splattering its head against the wall. His knuckles found another, and another, and another. One-by-one, the horde disappeared into a pile of rotten flesh. Until one remained.

Park grabbed the zombie and twisted its head completely around, then yanked it clean off. Blood trickled from the neck stump, the jaw still opening and closing, still intent on biting the target.

Park smiled, staring at the head.

"Captain, this is for you," he said, as if Livingston was right there in front of him. Not only would he kill Livingston, he would see to it the Captain became a reanimated corpse, serving his cause to spread infection across the Tarkadon territories.

With his wounds fully healed, Park started for the exit. He slowed to a stop. Something was happening. It felt like a storm was taking place inside of him. He fell to his knees then vomited. A maniacal roar followed. His insides twisted, his bone structure shifting back and forth. He rolled to his side and screamed.

The saliva from the undead surged through his system and clashed with the mutagen. The regeneration did its work, but the toxin was overwhelming his cellular system. It did what it had to do to protect its host; it bound with the foreign cells. The process ignited a new mutation.

Black fluid secreted from Park's skin. Bones protruded from his wrists, extending two feet out like swords. Veins popped from the skin and burst, spraying fountains of murky fluid onto the floor. He gagged again, vomiting secretion. His teeth extended another inch, his gums dripping toxic saliva. He was a living carrier.

He stood up, spitting more residue from his mouth. He looked at his hands and the bone-swords that protruded over them. His fingers were elongated, their tips as sharp as his bone-spears. His skin had a leathery texture to it now, though still durable.

Park stood back up, his insides still feeling as though in a blender. He stumbled until he was leaning against the wall. More fluid shot from his mouth like snake venom. His cries turned into satanic laughter. He wouldn't have to use carriers to deliver the toxin...he could spread it *himself* now.

There was only one obstacle in his way. He charged out through the wall, embracing the torrential downpour that engulfed him. He started for the south side of the perimeter.

Standing over a hundred feet ahead of him was Captain Livingston, wearing a robotic exo-suit that equaled his own size.

Even after everything he had seen on this planet, Livingston was still stunned to see the advance in Park's mutation. At first, he wasn't even sure if it was him, or some other mutation that may have been lurking in the facility. That wide smile eliminated any doubt.

"Sergeant, you look like you could use a shower," he said.

"You sound awfully funny for a man who's about to die," Park snarled.

"Then that makes two of us," Livingston said.

Park waved his bone-spears. "You're a fool if you think you can kill me." He brushed one of the spears against his stomach, slicing the skin several inches. Livingston watched the bizarre rippling effect as the wound healed itself. Park brought the spear to his mouth and licked his own blood from it, then pointed it at Livingston. "Now I'll have yours."

Livingston shook his head. "God...if Ramos saw you now..."

The mutation cocked his head back. That glow in his eyes brightened, the blood soaring through his veins as rage overtook him. Park threw his arms back and roared.

Titan and machine charged each other and met in a colossal display of thrashing arms and biting teeth. Livingston threw his arms up, blocking against a series of thrashes. The bone-spears chipped against the metal, creating small grooves with each strike. Park struck with a side swing, knocking the guard to the side. Livingston spun, struggling to balance the machine. With no other way to recover, he accelerated the spin, bringing himself around a full three-hundred-sixty degrees. As he did, he thrust his right arm out. The drill bit sliced through the air, catching Park across the face.

Livingston moved in, catching him with a swing of the left arm, then cut him across the chest with the bit, slashing as though it was a sword. Park stumbled back, then sprang again, thrusting one of his spears to the face. Livingston, predicting this attack, thrust the suit's left arm upward and caught Park's wrist in the grip. The clamps tightened, crunching the bone underneath. Park roared and tried to stab with his other hand. Livingston, predicting this as well, beat him to the punch by thrusting the drill bit into Park's left shoulder. The cylinder spun, driving the bit through flesh and bone. He drove it in further. With a grinding sound, it tore through the shoulder joint, jamming Park's left arm.

The mutant reared his head high and screamed. He looked Livingston in the face and extended his jaws. Livingston leaned back, keeping his face out of reach from those snapping teeth. Park leaned in again and bit, but his teeth hit nothing but air. He straightened his stance, then gulped. Livingston noticed a slight bobbing in his head and a hunching of the shoulders, like someone on the verge of vomiting. He saw the drops of black forming at the gums.

Livingston rotated to the right and swung the left arm across, redirecting Park. A river of black residue spat from his mouth and sprayed the rock ground.

"Fuck me," Livingston muttered in disgust. Park turned his head and smiled. Grunting in pain, he pulled his locked arm back. The machine groaned, its joints rotating against its will. Park twisted his arm back and forth, slicing his skin against the grips. Then with a final yank, he ripped his arm free entirely, severing his broken hand. He jumped backwards, freeing himself from the bolt. Then, he charged like a bull, tucking his head down and raising his right shoulder. Livingston raised both arms to absorb the blow. The mutant collided with the force of an S-5 Mattin Tank at full speed. The blow threw Livingston several yards backwards. His head snapped back as he fell. Had there not been a neck support, he might've ruptured a vertebra.

Livingston found himself staring skyward, physically stunned from the impact. His vision started to cloud, the blurry curtains of unconsciousness attempting to take hold of him. He snapped back into reality and looked downward.

Park stepped toward him, his right arm held close. He could hear the wet sticky sounds of regeneration. The stub took new form, the flesh and bone extending further and further out. This time, there were no fingers. There wasn't even a hand. It evolved into one long spear. Meanwhile, his shoulder healed, allowing him use of his other arm again.

Livingston held the drill bit up, warning him away. Park let out a horrid laugh.

"What? You gonna drill me again?"

"I oughta put it up your ass," Livingston said. "That's where you deserve it." He leaned up and thrust the bit out, only for Park to knock it away. A kick to the shoulder flattened Livingston back against the ground. Park drew the spear back and moved in for the kill.

A flash of red streaked down and exploded against his face. Park shrieked and stumbled away from his opponent. Another large blaster bolt streaked down and struck him in the forehead, blowing away portions of flesh and bone. He staggered back and looked up to the guard tower.

JACKMAN!

Another sniper bolt struck, their power over three times as powerful as that of a standard blaster. It struck just above his right eye. His thick skull withstood the blast, but enough of these shots would eventually break through.

He sidestepped to throw her aim off. It didn't work. Her next shot hit him right in the left eye, exploding it into a shower of soggy green strands. He spun in pain and fell against the side of the building. With his remaining eye, he looked at the wall he was against. It was the personnel entrance for Hangar One. He recalled the horde they ran into when the team attempted to find a ship there. Where there were some, there were likely others.

He thrust his spear into the rim of the door and pried it open, using his other hand to tear it away entirely. He roared and stepped back, drawing the attention of the undead that lurked inside.

Like bees swarming to protect their queen, they rushed out into the storm. They snarled and sniffed, inspecting the mutant. With the scent of the Star Virus, they backed off in search of more prey.

From the guard tower, Jackman watched as ten or more of the undead stepped out and started for Livingston. The Captain was still on the ground, struggling to right the machine. Jackman pressed her eye to the scope and focused in on the one nearest to him and fired.

Its head exploded, the residue caught by the wind and thrown across the compound. Another bolt struck the next one, producing a similar result. Jackman panned slightly left and centered another in her crosshairs. As she fired, she heard heavy footsteps drawing near. She looked down in time to see the mutant body slam the support beams beneath her. The guard tower rocked heavily, causing her to fall to the floor.

Park struck again, then grabbed hold of the legs. He rocked side to side like a sea monster sinking a ship.

"Rock-a-bye baby!" he roared. He lifted up on the cross beams, tilting the guard tower backward. Jackman felt the floor starting to incline. She started to slide back. Realizing she was moments away from smashing against the ground, she pushed to her feet and ran up for the loophole. She jumped and grabbed the ledges. The tower fell back. For a split second she dangled from the loophole. The back wall smashed inward as it hit the ground, shaking her like a ragdoll. Her grip slipped away and she fell, landing in a pile of debris and supplies.

Livingston heard the crash and looked over. The sight of the ravaged guard tower sent his mind in a frenzy. Yelling, he shifted his weight to the left. The machine rolled. He thrust his arms out, pushing up until the feet were once again planted on the ground.

Hungry zombies clawed at the metal, their fingertips grazing his clothing. With a swing of his arm, he sliced one of their heads clean off with the drill bit. It fell to the side, still biting at nothing. Livingston swung again, decapitating another. He swung a left hook, smashing two skulls at once with the grip. He thrust the arm out and squeezed the grips on the head of another, exploding it.

A slash of his drill bit decapitated another. After smashing two more skulls with the grip, he came upon the last zombie. He spun the drill bit and stabbed it through its face, grinding the skull into nothing.

Running feet drew his attention to Park, who was charging from his left. Livingston spun to face him and lashed the still-spinning drill out, slashing him across the face. He then struck with the blades of the grip, lacerating Park's neck, then punctured his windpipe with the drill. He retracted both arms, blocking a slash of Park's spear. The bone caught the left elbow joint, denting the gears. Livingston stumbled back, briefly inspecting the damage. He had only partial range of motion with the arm, as it would not extend beyond a forty-five degree angle.

Park sucked in several deep breaths, then stood straight to look directly at Livingston, deliberately showing off his healing capabilities. He bared a drooling smile.

"Face it, Captain, you have no way of killing me," he said. Despite how he felt inwardly, Livingston displayed no fear. He held the drill bit out threateningly.

"Why don't I put this through your skull and see if you can regenerate your brain?" he said. Park's smile shifted into a sneer. Roaring, he came at the Captain. He struck violently, attacking Livingston's guard. Bone struck metal, chipping its tip, only to regenerate. The metal, however, was gradually wearing down.

Livingston jolted left and right from each impact. It took all his strength to keep the arms up to protect his vulnerable center. Park swung downward, sweeping Livingston's legs out from under him. He fell hard on his back. A streak of lightning flashed overhead, illuminating Park's ugly face looking down at him. He rolled to the right as the spear came down. The tip smashed into the shoulder joint, shredding bolts and wires. The ripping and tearing of metal rang in his ears. Park grabbed the suit's left arm and pulled up. Metal whined and groaned as though the machine was crying out in pain. Realizing the arm was coming off, Livingston pulled his hand free. With a loud crack, the grip detached from the exo-suit, then bounced against the rock after being tossed aside.

Park laughed, then roared, ready to impale the soft meat now exposed.

With over a hundred pounds of weight gone, Livingston spun with increased agility. He rolled over his right arm, dodging the spear, which splintered against the rock. Livingston, now on his feet, charged. He thrust the drill bit at Park's forehead. The mutant shifted, throwing his aim off slightly. The drill caught him in the jaws, splitting it right down the middle. Park shrieked and thrashed his arms back, driving his attacker away. For a moment, his jaw was similar to that of a Vickel. The mutation started its work with the healing process, which in itself generated pain.

Livingston watched in horrified fascination as the jaw healed oddly. The two sections did not mend, rather, they became two separate joints containing spiked teeth. A human tongue flapped between them, flinging saliva everywhere. The spear-hand regenerated, also taking new form. Instead of a single pointed spear, it was a two-pronged bident.

The beast closed his fist, waving the bone-spear that protruded over it. With the exo-suit down to one arm, Livingston would not be able to defend against an impaling, and Park knew it.

Jackman groaned as she rolled to her hands and knees. She pushed chunks of debris off of her and stood up. A flash of lightning illuminated the wreckage, bringing her attention to a rupture in the wall. It was wide enough for her to escape through.

The wind whipped her hair over her face as she stepped outside. Another bolt of lightning traveled the skies, its light shining over a rampaging mutant and a one-armed maintenance exo-suit. She screamed as Park slashed with his bident arm. Livingston pivoted to his left and deflected the attack with his remaining arm, exposing his back. Park drove his fist into one of the power cables and sliced it with his bone spear. With its source of power gone, the right leg gave out. Livingston tried shifting his weight, but still fell to one knee. A blow to the back knocked him forward.

Park roared triumphantly, ready to strike the killing blow.

Jackman dove back into the guard tower and rummaged through the wreckage for weapons. She tossed a piece of siding away and found what she was looking for. The bazooka was undamaged aside from a few small grooves. She loaded a round and carried the heavy weapon outside. She engaged the targeting sequencer and focused on the mutant.

"Hey, Sergeant!" she yelled. Park stopped and turned, surprised to see her alive, and was even more surprised to see the bazooka pointed at him. "Let's see you heal from *this*."

The explosive shell soared from the weapon, striking Park square in the chest. A red explosion knocked the mutant on his back. His chest was wide open, his internal organs ravaged, the skeleton splintered. Park gasped for breath but was unable to take in any air, not until his lungs patched themselves back together.

Livingston balanced the suit on its functioning leg and arm. He could see Park lying several yards from him. The healing process had already begun. He had seconds before Park would be ready to fight again, his mutative properties distorting him into an even worse fiend.

He clawed the ground with the drill bit and pushed with his leg, closing the distance. Park lifted his head, his lower jaws hanging slack. As the bones healed in his left shoulder, he tried raising his arm. Livingston propped his leg under him, then sprung with all the power he could muster, throwing himself onto the mutant. He slammed the drill into the freshly healed shoulder, breaking the bone yet again. With both arms unable to function, Park had no defense. His toxin vomit had spilled into his body, the sack containing it not yet healed. He bit and screamed, unable to fight the Captain off of him. Livingston pinned him down with the suit's knee, then positioned the drill bit between his eyes.

Park growled. "You're protecting the enemy. You're a fool. You're—" Livingston rammed the drill through his skull, shredding ribbons of bone and turning the brain to mush.

"Shut the fuck up."

Park spasmed, his head splitting in two. Finally, his body stiffened, shaking slightly from the drill's vibrations.

Livingston locked the suit in position, allowing the drill to continue running as he unharnessed himself. Careful not to set foot in Park's chest cavity, he jumped off and walked away.

"Captain!"

Jackman ran to him and they embraced. She hugged him so tight she nearly choked him. To his slight relief, she loosened up.

"Thanks for your help," he said.

"You better be! You were getting your ass handed to you," she chuckled. Finally, they let each other go. Through the wind and rain were the faint sounds of moaning. The undead were out of sight for the moment.

"Well, what's the plan now?" Jackman asked.

"First, let's salvage what equipment we can. There are other hangar bays in this facility. I'm sure at least one of them has a functioning ship."

CHAPTER 22

Glorric's dark blue clouds amassed over the mountain fortress, the storm's lightning strikes flashing over the undead that crawled on it. The undead paid no attention to it as they wandered around in search of new prey to spread their deadly virus. Nor did they notice the deep booming crack that resembled thunder. It was so loud, it seemed the sky was being torn apart.

The clouds split open and the atmosphere turned red. The energy beam came down like a flaming tornado. Its tail cut deep into the mountain, shredding the rock and metal inside of it. The laser cut like a drill, going deeper and deeper, until it finally reached its target.

From afar, the mountain looked like a dormant volcano come to life as it exploded from within, sending flaming debris traveling the sky for miles. Miles to the north, another red twister struck down, producing a smaller, but still devastating effect on the hangar, eliminating it and the virus samples it contained. The air was thick with smoke and dust, which was spread far and wide by the storm's fury.

The flashes of energy faded into nothingness, their objectives complete. And disappearing with them were any traces of the horrible bio-weapon that was produced there.

Livingston watched the glow on the planet's surface through a viewing panel in the Tarkadon defense satellite. From their perspective, they were like two tiny red dots, each the size of the head of a pin. But they were more significant than just specks. They were a sign of victory, and the cost that came with it.

"Here," Jackman said. Livingston turned and saw her holding his helmet. She had found it when they returned to Hangar Two to salvage the portable terminal and its data. "I fixed it the best I could. Hopefully it'll last until we get back."

Livingston took the helmet and placed it back on. Immediately, it was much easier to breathe.

"Thank you," he said. He noticed a hint of sadness in her face as his disappeared.

"Perhaps it's time I look into alternative treatment," he said.

Jackman's eyes lit up. "Really?"

Livingston looked away, then back at her. "Yes. I think it's time."

"It'll take a while, especially the recovery time. You might not be able to return to active duty."

"I think I've done enough," he said. "I think I'm ready to live my life."

"Yeah?" Jackman smiled. "Where do you think you'll go?"

"I'm trying to decide. I heard that Lake Rim's nice," he replied. Jackman's smile widened and she threw her arms around him. Military regulation be damned.

They entered the shuttle, found intact in Hangar One. They set the coordinates for their home base in the Molani System and engaged thrusters. The battle was over and the mission was complete. With a little luck, they would slip through Tarkadon space and arrive home.

The End

CHECK OUT OTHER GREAT SCIENCE FICTION BOOKS

PAUL E. COOLEY

DERELICT
MARINES

DERELICT: MARINES
by Paul E. Cooley

Fifty years ago, Mira, humanity's last hope to find new resources, exited the solar system bound for Proxima Centauri b. Seven years into her mission, all transmissions ceased without warning. Mira and her crew were presumed lost. Humanity, unified during her construction, splintered into insurgency and rebellion.

Now, an outpost orbiting Pluto has detected a distress call from an unpowered object entering Sol space: Mira has returned. When all attempts at communications fail, S&R Black, a Sol Federation Marine Corps search and rescue vessel, is dispatched from Trident Station to intercept, investigate, and tow the beleaguered Mira to Neptune.

As the marines prepare for the journey, uncertainty and conspiracy fomented by Trident Station's governing AIs, begin to take their toll. Upon reaching Mira, they discover they've been sent on a mission that will almost certainly end in catastrophe.

ALLIANCE
THE ROAD TO WAR

MARINES

JOHN MIERAU

ALLIANCE MARINES
by John Mierau

One by one, all of Earth's colonies have gone dark and silent. Reach, the last colony, teeters on the verge of civil war against its Earth-loyal overlords...and Reach-born rebel Lee Zhang has sworn to push the planet over the edge.

As the colony descends into total war, a convoy from Earth races across the galaxy, carrying news of a threat unlike anything mankind has faced before. The colonies have all been destroyed by a vast alien horde, and now Earth has fallen, too. Time is running out for sworn enemies to learn to trust and unite, or the human race is extinct. The Takers are coming to destroy mankind. If we don't do the job for them first.

 SEVERED**PRESS**

facebook.com/severedpress
twitter.com/severedpress

CHECK OUT OTHER GREAT SCIENCE FICTION BOOKS

SPACE MARINE AJAX
by Sean-Michael Argo

Ajax answers the call of duty and becomes an Einherjar space marine, charged with defending humanity against hideous alien monsters in furious combat across the galaxy.

The Garm, as they came to be called, emerged from the deepest parts of uncharted space, devouring all that lay before them, a great swarm that scoured entire star systems of all organic life. This space borne hive, this extinction fleet, made no attempts to communicate and offered no mercy.

Humanity has always been a deadly organism, and we would not so easily be made the prey. Unified against a common enemy, we fought back, meeting the swarm with soldiers upon every front.

PLANET LEVIATHAN
by D.J. Goodman

The cyborg commandos of the Galactic Marines are the greatest warriors in the galaxy, but sometimes one will go bad. Too unstable to be let back into the general population and too powerful for a normal prison to hold them, there is only one place they can be sent: Planet Leviathan.

www.ingramcontent.com/pod-product-compliance
Lightning Source LLC
Chambersburg PA
CBHW061236170626
46809CB00007B/2699